COWBOY BEBOP

A SYNDICATE STORY

— RED PLANET REQUIEM —

COWBOY BEBOP

A SYNDICATE STORY

— RED PLANET REQUIEM —

A Novel By

SEAN CUMMINGS

TITAN BOOKS

Cowboy Bebop: A Syndicate Story: Red Planet Requiem
Print edition ISBN: 9781789097757
E-book edition ISBN: 9781789099836

Published by Titan Books
A division of Titan Publishing Group Ltd.
144 Southwark Street, London SE1 0UP
www.titanbooks.com

First Titan edition: November 2021
10 9 8 7 6 5 4 3 2 1

A CIP catalogue record for this title is available from
the British Library.

Printed and bound in the United States

"Never rat on your friends and always keep your mouth shut."

– *Jimmy Conway,* Goodfellas

The year is 2161.

The solar system is overrun with criminals.

Pirates. Thieves. Outlaws.

But even in this new Wild West, any scoundrel worth his salt knows one thing to be true:

THE RED DRAGON CRIME SYNDICATE is king.

After all, the Red Dragon controls everything.

Gambling. Drugs. Women.

In this outfit, life is *damn* good.

The champagne? *Cold.*

The suits? *Loud.*

The guns? *Louder.*

It's the golden era of the gangster.

Well… maybe not for *everyone.*

-ONE-

"JANITORS"

"I never understood why they called it blood *splatter*."

This wasn't the first time Fearless had thought about this. To be honest, he'd probably thought about it more than any normal person should. *Spray*, maybe. Or *mist*, even. Because when you spent your days disposing of dead bodies, and with that, a myriad of body fluids (but mostly blood, given the human body's propensity to carry quite a bit of it at a given time) you began to crave a word for the whole experience that was a bit more dignified.

One that didn't sound like a toddler got into a box of crayons and later upchucked them onto the wall. *Splatter.*

"What about blood *squirt*?" offered Vicious. He was crouched opposite Fearless, his snow-white hair glistening with sweat. They were positioned on either side of a man freshly deceased from a single bullet to the dead-center of his forehead. It was eerily precise. The work of a professional. But not just anyone.

This was the work of the Red Dragon. And when it came to the business of murder, they were the best.

The aforementioned *splatter* decorated the living room wall of a four-bedroom, high-rise condo with vaulted ceilings, imported marble floors and other high-end finishes including, coincidentally, a Pollock that the owner had stolen from Earth during the chaos of the Gate Disaster. And now, ironically, the splatter seemed to hang next to it, like some kind of morbid, abstract piece of modern art.

"Of all the words you want to go with *squirt*?" Fearless's lips curled to a grin. *Disarming, irresistible.* He knew the effect it had on people. And later in life, women. As a young boy he had learned to weaponize it. When you grew up on the streets, facial expressions were more than emotions. They were a physical currency. A way to lure in the unsuspecting and pluck their wallet from their back pocket when they were most vulnerable. It wasn't just a grin. It was a survival tactic.

Vicious sighed and shook his head. "Get your mind out of the gutter and keep rolling. I wanna get out of here at a decent hour. *Unlike* last night. When you forgot to duct tape your end of the rug. And the body slipped out right onto 12th Avenue in front of a bunch of cops. Or did you forget about that?"

Fearless scoffed. As if to say, *Who, me?* Then grinned. "You're an asshole."

The thing was, Fearless was right. Vicious *was* an asshole. But not in the derogatory sense. He was an asshole in the hereditary sense, a rich asshole descended from a long line of rich assholes from various parts of the rich asshole tree. So, yes, he was an asshole. But he was not an *asshole*. There was a difference.

"3... 2... 1... !"

They team-lifted the body into position atop a nearby

burgundy and gold flecked oriental rug that the poor bastard would be rolled into, duct-taped and disposed of. In the Red Dragon, they were known as "janitors" for a reason. The clean-up crew a veteran assassin called in after a hit so they didn't have to get their hands dirty. It was part of the organization's hierarchy.

And Fearless and Vicious were planted firmly at the bottom.

"Let's get this over with," Fearless replied with about as much enthusiasm as you'd expect from a guy who spent the better part of his day disposing of dead bodies.

They rolled the dead man, careful to do it slowly, until they ran out of rug and the poor sap was snug in its center, like the soft, fleshy, ooey-gooey filling of a Swiss cake roll.

And as they secured both ends with the duct tape, Fearless's eyes ticked to the still-smoldering bullet hole in the drywall. He studied it closely with an educated glare, like an archaeologist carefully examining the contents of a dig, careful not to disturb what priceless treasure lies underneath.

"A thousand woos says it was a .32."

This was another game they played. Albeit a higher stakes one. Vicious raised an eyebrow to the wager and turned his attention to the bullet hole. He studied it closely. Not convinced. And proclaimed, with the utmost certainty: "It's a .380. Fired from a Sig Sauer. Double or nothing."

Fearless took in the bullet hole again. As close as his eye allowed. He turned back to Vicious. Incredulous.

"Bull-*fucking*-shit. Do you even *see* the condo we're in? A .380 is going to wake up half the building. Before you know it, you'll have a housewife wearing a silk robe with a Bichon tucked under her arm banging down the door and half the ISSP in the lobby. You'd need a suppressor." Fearless smirked. Then delivered the punch line, "And what kind of dumb fuck mounts a suppressor on a Sig-*fucking*-Sauer?"

When, as if on cue from the other side of a nearby bathroom door, *a toilet flushed*. The color drained from Fearless's face. *Shit*. He was still here. The door opened. And a voice boomed: "This kind of dumb fuck."

The voice belonged to Spider, a veteran Red Dragon assassin. He was also an asshole. Not the rich kind of asshole. The other kind. An *asshole-asshole*. The kind that wore a tie with a matching pocket square and sunglasses indoors. At his side was his partner, Karma. He too, was dressed like an asshole. But he wasn't much for words. He preferred that Spider did the shit-talking. And so did Spider.

They were made men. *Red Dragon royalty*. The kind of guys that had a table at Ana's Bar where the upper echelon of the organization wined and dined with a monthly tab that would rival most people's mortgages. The extracurricular activities that they enjoyed as part of the Red Dragon was the reason that Vicious and Fearless signed up to be a part of the organization in the first place. Their personalities? Not so much.

"Every assassin worth his paycheck knows that you can mount 9mm suppressor onto a .380, if you know what you're doing. Which I do. Which also explains why after two years you two career underachievers are still janitors."

Spider pulled a pack of cigarettes from the inside of his jacket and plucked one out. It dangled from his mouth as he lit it with a gold-plated lighter. It was one of those vintage ones with a flip lid that made a metallic grinding sound when lit. *Flick. Flick. Flick.* After a few tries, the cigarette finally took. Spider took a long drag and looked over their handiwork with a skeptical eye—

"Hurry up and get rid of that rug. I don't want to have to come back and put a bullet in the building's super because you two took too long debating the word *splatter* and he walked in on you two rolling up his tenant."

Fearless turned to Spider, facetious. "The term is blood *squirt.*"

Spider headed for the door to leave, but not before he turned back to them. A grin on his face. Far different than the one Fearless wore. This was your regular old douchebag shit-eater.

"Oh, and Vicious. A penthouse, huh?"

Vicious clamped his jaw down. If you listened closely, you could hear his teeth slowly grinding away. It was all he could do to keep it bottled up. The darkness. The part of him, if Vicious allowed it, that would shatter the vintage Bordeaux that sat mere feet away on the floor-to-ceiling, temperature-controlled wine rack and use the tinted French glass to dig Spider's eyes out from their sockets.

"Pretty nice digs for a fucking *janitor.*"

Fearless locked eyes with Vicious and slowly shook his head with an almost imperceptible subtlety. He knew this part of Vicious well. He'd had a violent streak inside him since they were teenagers. Fearless called it *the darkness.* It was the only thing about Vicious that scared him. It wasn't the fact that he'd murder someone without warning that frightened him—it was how far he took it. It was never enough for him to just kill a man. He had to render them unrecognizable. *Destroyed.* It was more than a temper. It was something else entirely. It was *vicious.* And it had gotten them in enough trouble over the years that Fearless had learned to see the darkness lurking below the surface—like a shark's fin that ever so poked above the water—even before Vicious did. Most of the time.

Fearless faced down the assassin. "Don't worry, Spider. One day you'll make enough cash so you can stop jerking off in your mom's basement and get a place of your own."

Spider took a drag on the cigarette. He shook his head with a chuckle, then exhaled a plume of smoke. "That's the difference between you and I, Fearless. One day, the Red Dragon is going to place a bloodstone ring on my finger and make me an elder— and you'll still be rolling bodies in rugs and making jokes."

Fearless considered this for a moment. He scrunched his face in thought, then turned back to Spider. "But if the Elders give you a bloodstone ring... then how will you fit your finger up your asshole?"

"Fuck you, Fearless," Spider snapped back. He flipped a middle finger in Fearless's direction as he stomped off toward the door. Karma followed close behind, as Karma did.

Fearless exhaled. His eyes ticked to Vicious. The blood drained from his cheeks. The darkness had retreated back to its quiet little cave.

For now.

The Tharsis skyline shined down on the Tharsis City crush yard, the place where old cars and the bodies of the Red Dragon's handiwork went to disappear. The lights of the city's many unoccupied luxury apartments and fluorescent floating billboards advertising the latest advancements in genetically engineered bio-meat illuminated the discarded bits of automotive chrome and glass scattered about.

Mars's biggest city was to be the first step towards colonizing the entire solar system. It was the brainchild of the most accomplished architects and builders from across Earth with grand buildings of glass and steel that were reminiscent of Dubai and with the footprint of two Manhattans. Those who visited it in the early days hailed it as the next great metropolis. But to live there felt like living inside a decorative snow globe, the kind you bought for your grandmothers at a Christmas shop. The city was filled with the constant hum of street sweepers buffing and polishing the asphalt. The skyscrapers were architectural marvels, but on the inside they remained unfinished and likely to stay that way. The rain was scheduled. All that was missing was a steam engine with a delightful conductor that circled the city every few minutes. It felt about as real as a movie set.

"How the hell do they know where I live?"

Fearless and Vicious slowly swayed back and forth, each clutching one end of the now 180-pound oriental rug. It was quiet at this time of night, albeit for the sound of the industrial compactor grinding away just inches from their feet. The one that by day could devour an entire car in mere seconds, and by night destroy any trace of a dead body. They built up enough momentum and each let go of their end of the rug, watching in morbid fascination as it hit the compactor's rotating, interlocking steel teeth with a tremendous *thud*.

And within seconds, it was gone. The rug—and, with it, the body—was ground into an unrecognizable paste. Some bits of skin and hairy flesh would remain, but it was enough to conceal what had taken place in the vaulted-ceiling condo with the stolen Pollock. Not that anybody would care enough to go looking for the poor bastard.

Fearless dusted his hands off, then shrugged. "Of course, they know where we live. They know our blood type, how much cash we have in our bank account—hell, they probably know what color our piss is in the morning. But it just so happens that my shithole apartment with the roaches as big as rats and the toilet you have to sit side saddle on if you want to take a freaking dump with the door closed isn't as of much interest to assholes like Spider as your *penthouse*."

Vicious quickly corrected him. "It's not *my* penthouse."

Fearless sighed. *Goddamnit*. Vicious always did this. Every couple months, he needed an *it's-OK-to-be-born-into-generational-wealth* pep talk. After all, it was Fearless who was the one who was born on the streets of East Tharsis. The one who was left alone as an infant, in a second-hand bassinet, in front of a nightclub. The one that no one wanted. The one who was made to scrap for a bowl of cold noodle broth and an awning to sleep under that would protect him from the artificial rain that coated the city once a week.

But sure, Vicious wanted to talk about *his* problems.

"Look. You were born a rich kid. And that's OK. It's not your fault that you grew up eating lobster at Francona's on Saturday nights and spent your summers gravity sailing in Europa with an instructor named Claude. But it *is* your fault that you let mediocre dicks like Spider get under your skin. And the sooner you accept what you came from, the sooner you'll grow into the man you were always destined to become."

Vicious chewed on his semi-inspirational words for a moment. Yes, Fearless had given him this exact speech—many times—before. The truth was, as Spider had reminded them, they had been stuck at the bottom rung of the Red Dragon ladder for almost two years now. They had never been promoted, but a few weeks before, their role had been "adjusted." Meaning, in addition to spending their nights cleaning up after career-dicks like Spider, during the day they now had to drive around a sweaty, swollen-fingered capo named Dodd.

Fearless sighed. *Again*. Hoping his friend would pick up on it. He could only play to Vicious's insecurities for so long.

"Look, we can either stand here and you can continue to contemplate hanging yourself in a motel bathroom where you have to swipe a credit card to flush the toilet or whatever it is you fantasize about when you stare into the abyss like this *or* we can go get *drunk* and try to convince women we're much more important than we actually are so they'll sleep with us. It's your call."

Vicious continued to stare. Into the abyss. Then said, "It was Monroe."

Fearless scrunched his brows Vicious turned to him. With a slight grin.

"My gravity sailing instructor. His name was Monroe."

Fearless laughed. Maybe he'd got him wrong. Maybe he really was the other kind of asshole.

Three tumblers were lined up on the bar as a shimmering gold liquid splashed into the bottom of each. A tattooed hand poured a few fingers in each. A more than generous pour, given who it was for.

Fearless grinned as he took all three glasses. "I'll get you next time, Felix."

The bartender, the one with the aforementioned tattooed hands, rolled his eyes. "I won't count on it."

He held the bottle high. The bright yellow label was emblazoned with a red, fire-breathing dragon. Above it was the word KUDO. One part tequila, one part absinthe and three parts bad idea. He gave the golden liquid a careful swirl. "Lucky for me you're the only one that drinks this pirate piss."

Fearless winked. Given his paltry entry-level Red Dragon salary, it was lucky for them both indeed.

He returned to the high-top next to the street-side window where Vicious stood with a raven-haired, take-no-shit Red Dragon sophomore by the name of Goldie. A former jewel thief, the organization recruited Goldie to join their ranks after she knocked off a string of diamond dealers with ties to the organization. They were impressed by her work.

Vicious and Goldie winced at the sight of the glasses. *Kudo. Great.*

The three of them tapped the table with the bottom of their glasses and then gulped the liquor down their gullets in unison. Goldie recoiled from the aftertaste. Kudo tended to linger on the palette like burnt gasoline, even to the previously initiated. It wasn't the kind of thing you got used to.

She shook her head. "Last time I drank Kudo I woke up naked in the bathroom of an orbital casino outside of Io."

Fearless raised an eyebrow. Goldie put that to bed. Quickly. "You even *think* about me naked and I'll slit your throat and dump your body in the acid reservoir outside of East Tharsis."

"Fair enough," Fearless replied with a chuckle. Goldie was their best friend within the organization. Fearless had secretly pined for her for some time, but he kept that secret buried deep inside him. There was an unspoken rule among them that they wouldn't dip their pen in the company ink, so to speak, in order to maintain the status quo and not let things get messy. Well, at least that's what Fearless told himself. The truth was, he'd never had a meaningful relationship with a woman and the idea of baring his soul to Goldie—or any woman, for that matter— scared the shit out of him. In Fearless's mind, it was better to have lost than to have never loved at all.

Across the street, a white-hot sign flickered to life. The sight of it through the bar window immediately caught Fearless's attention. The lettering was styled in simple cursive neon reminiscent of the one that hung above Rick's Café Américain. The exterior of the joint didn't need to be particularly eye-catching. Every pirate, scoundrel, and outlaw worth their salt knew what was inside. It was called *ANA'S BAR*. Named after the prickly owner who oversaw the joint— and the exclusive list of its members. And then, as if drawn up by the universe just to torture Fearless, at that exact moment Spider and Karma strolled by and glad-handed the doorman as they disappeared inside.

Fearless gritted his teeth. "You've *got* to be shitting me."

Goldie laughed. Clearly she enjoyed watching Fearless wallow in his misery. "I never understood your fascination with that place. It's just another bar."

Fearless scoffed. He turned to the bartender, "Felix, what's the name of this place?"

Felix stared back, quizzically. It felt like a trick question. "This place? The Bar."

Fearless turned back to the two of them. His point already made for him. Because they were *literally* standing in just another bar. But, as they explained to Goldie, Ana's wasn't *just* a bar. To drink at Ana's meant that you had made it. That in the Red Dragon's eyes, not only were you somebody—but you were damn good at it, too.

Goldie rolled her eyes. "Only men would care about what bar they're *supposed to be* drinking at. That your worth is somehow determined by whether or not you are allowed to pay two thousand woos for the same hooch you'd drink in a bar called The Bar. I, of course, being a *woman*, don't have that kind of insecurity."

Then, suddenly Vicious perked up. Something had caught his eye. He motioned across the bar with a less-than-subtle glance.

"*Maybe* being relegated to The Bar isn't so bad after all…"

Seated at the far end of the counter were two women, both in their early-twenties. One, a close-cropped, punk rock blonde. The other had auburn hair with a matching shade of gloss on her lip. They ordered two soda waters with lime, and when Felix wasn't looking, had reached into their bras to procure their own pre-purchased airplane bottles of cheap, Russian-sounding vodka and emptied them into their glasses.

And now, Fearless and Vicious were looking to Goldie to help broker the deal. Sure, they were nobodies. But in their experience, at the very least Goldie was able to convince girls like them to let the pair buy them a drink. She was what they lovingly referred to her as their *wing-woman.* Goldie preferred *one-night-stand liaison.*

"Oh, come *on*," Goldie demurred. "When was the last time you offered to help *me* get laid?"

Fearless motioned to himself and Vicious. "The two of us *are* single, you know."

"I'm not that desperate and I *never* will be," Goldie snapped back. Fearless and Vicious grinned as she turned and reluctantly made her way from their table through the crowd of sweaty, half-drunken patrons and towards the two women idling at the bar. It wasn't lost on them what kind of friend she was. The best kind.

"You girls always bring your own liquor when you go out on the town? Or did Felix not tell me they started selling those little airplane bottles you two have stuffed in your bras?"

The two women grew stiff. Their eyes searched feverishly for the nearest exit; they could only assume that Goldie was an undercover employee of sorts and that the jig was up. She was quick to reassure them that she was anything but.

"Relax. I'm not here to bust you. I actually thought that the airplane bottle move was pretty ingenious."

The women loosened up. The blonde was named Fiona, her auburn-haired friend Penny. They were fresh out of Tharsis University and were broke like people tended to be at that age.

Goldie motioned to the other side of the room, where Fearless and Vicious stood by the high-top and were now engaging in an overly enthusiastic conversation in a piss-poor attempt to hide the fact that they had been watching the entire time as Goldie talked to the two women.

"See those two guys?" The women nodded. Intrigued, but not entirely impressed.

Goldie clocked their lack of enthusiasm. And grinned. Now *this* was going to be fun.

"They're *rich*. Like, stupid rich. They both own *huge* houses. And ships. *Big* ships. The one with the white hair actually uses his ship as a floating storage unit in orbit. He doesn't even fly it. That's how rich they are. And they'd like to buy you a drink. And honestly? I'd let them buy you a lot more than that. Hell, buy the most expensive thing on the menu. Money is no object. Trust me."

The women exchanged a glance. *Why not.*

Goldie smirked. She turned back towards the boys—and held a resounding thumbs up in the air.

———•———

A champagne cork popped. The intoxicating bubbles turned white as they flowed from the open mouth, down the bottle's curvature and past the decadent French label, before spilling onto the faux-wood table and coming to rest right at Fearless's fingertips. He stared at the bubbles, wide-eyed, as if calculating in his head how much each bubble was worth.

"Woo!" Fiona laughed as she poured the champagne into four flutes, the liquid gold spilling and overflowing about.

Fearless looked to Vicious with a subtle glance, as if to say, *you were born rich and for that reason, you're paying for this.* Vicious matched his glance with the slight raise of an eyebrow as if to reply, *I'm always the one who pays.*

"So—" Fiona smirked as she sat back on her stool. "What kind of business did you two luck into in order to be able to drink champagne that's older than all of us?"

Fearless carefully considered his response. This question had gotten them in trouble before. In the past he had told women that they were Red Dragon capos, promising to stake them at the orbital casino the organization controlled that spun outside of Saturn or a VIP table at the hottest new club opening in Tharsis that weekend.

This, as one could imagine, almost always backfired. Especially when they stopped telling women they were in the Red Dragon and pivoted to more lucrative fake professions. For instance, there was the time at a Tharsis steakhouse when Fearless had told a pair of women they were doctors, which went surprisingly well until at the next table over a guy went into anaphylactic shock and the waitress did the old, *Is there a doctor in the house?* routine, to which Fearless answered *yes*, because he was a) in too deep at that point and b) still trying to get laid. It didn't go well. Especially for the guy who had unknowingly consumed a pine-nut pesto. And so Vicious took the lead this time:

"We're in the import-export business."

It was important-sounding enough to justify the price of the champagne, but vague enough that they could make up the details as they went along. They regaled the women with their trips to Venus and Europa, recounting the fabulous hotels in which they stayed and the many exotic delicacies that were consumed, all without ever touching on what the day-to-day of that business would actually entail.

Fiona looked to Penny. They traded a coded glance of their own. And then a smirk, as if both of them coming to the same conclusion without saying a word. Penny, the more soft-spoken of the two, spoke up:

"What if we took this party somewhere a little more... *private?*"

Fearless was quick to jump in before Vicious could change his mind. "Unfortunately, my place is actually being renovated." He motioned to Vicious. "But my friend here has a penthouse that is just *divine.*"

Vicious gritted his teeth. The darkness wasn't there yet, but by the look on his face Fearless could tell that part of him felt like waking it up.

"If you'll excuse us, for a moment, ladies—"

Vicious grabbed Fearless by the arm and forcefully ushered him towards the men's room where he quickly locked the door behind them. With a single toilet in the corner, it was a bathroom that was clearly meant for one. He turned to Fearless. *Seething.*

"Divine? *Divine?*"

Fearless shrugged. And began to take a leak. "What's the big deal?"

"I told you. It's my father's penthouse. Not mine."

"So?"

"So, we're not taking those women back to my father's penthouse."

Fearless shook. Then flushed. "*Yes*. We are."

He zipped up and opened the door, but Vicious quickly slammed it shut again.

"No. We are *not*."

"Well Mr. Imports and Exports, we can't take them back to my place where you have to sit sideways on the toilet, now can we? That was *your* cover, not mine."

Vicious fired back, "My father *loves* that penthouse. And if so much as a carpet fiber is out of place, he'll have my ass."

Fearless smirked. "Then we'll make sure the girls take off their shoes, won't we?"

He mulled this for a moment as Fearless continued: "Come on. What's the point of having all this *stuff* if you can't get a little *joy* from it every once in a while?"

Vicious sighed. He's right. "Fine. Tonight. *One night.* That's it. You're my best friend, Fearless—but sometimes I cannot fucking stand you."

Fearless grinned. That *grin*. "I know."

The private elevator door opened with a delightful digital melody. The sound was perfect. It was as if it had been developed in a lab by scientists who had figured out what digital notes would be most pleasing to the human ear—mostly because it had been.

Fiona and Penny stepped into the penthouse apprehensively. The beauty of it—the white oak floors, the custom marble countertops, the floor-to-ceiling windows that offered 360-degree views of Tharsis City—was unbelievable, if not incomprehensible.

Vicious smiled, "Beautiful, isn't it?"

Fiona choked back her wonder. But managed: "I thought you guys were full of shit."

615 Park was the most exclusive address in all of Tharsis City. The majority of the rich folks who owned the sprawling, 3,000-square foot apartments didn't even live there. It became the ultimate status symbol purchase. Like owning a racehorse. Or a baseball team. There was never going to be a return on investment because no one else could afford to live there. You owned an apartment in the building just so you could tell your fellow rich assholes that you did.

Vicious and the two women stepped into the living room as Fearless appeared with four glasses of scotch and handed them out to each of them. Whatever brand and vintage it was, it smelled *expensive*.

Vicious quietly turned to Fearless. He angry-whispered, "Where did you get that?"

Fearless shrugged. "Where do you *think*? Just shut up and drink it."

A silence fell between the four of them. They all knew where this was heading and now they were at the will-they or won't-they portion of the evening. They were just waiting for someone to make the first move. And that person, as was his custom, was Fearless.

"Say, Fiona… how would you like a… private tour of the penthouse?"

She smiled. And played along. "That sounds… *great*. Let's do… *that*." Together, Fearless and Fiona disappeared into the seemingly endless penthouse.

Vicious and Penny remained in the living room. There was an awkward silence. And then an awkward chuckle. He motioned for her to sit on a nearby white leather U-shaped couch with him. Penny did a happy little bounce on the cushion.

"This feels like no one has ever sat in it before."

Vicious smirked. "To be honest, we may be the first."

She took this in, confused. "What do you mean? How is it possible that you never sat on your own couch?"

"Well, to be honest, my father never let anyone sit on it. To him, it was a piece of art. And over time, sitting in it would cause the leather to crease and crack, thus diminishing its value."

Penny chuckled as she sipped her scotch. "But… it's just a *couch*."

Vicious explained. "To you, yes. But to him, this penthouse and the things inside of it are part of his collection. A collection of things. Many of these things are very, very expensive. And you're right, they just sit in this beautiful penthouse, without anyone to appreciate them. To see them. Touch them. Enjoy them. But that's just the way it's always been."

Vicious took a long sip of the expensive scotch. It was a 45-year. From Earth. He instantly recognized the slightly smokey yet sweet taste on his tongue. It was the same bottle that he had stolen a pour from as a teenager when his father was away on business. He remembered it clearly. It was a small, subtle act of revenge. His father had called home to say goodnight and ended

20

up chastising him for receiving a 99/100 on his math exam that day. But Vicious knew that even if he scored a perfect 100, his father would have asked why he didn't receive a 101. The best was never good enough. *Not for the king.*

Penny mulled this over for a moment. "But what kind of life is that? What kind of person amasses a collection of expensive things that they don't even see?"

Vicious admired the scotch in his hand for a moment before he answered, all of the evening's swirling liquors inside him, enticing him, begging him to reveal more than he should to this stranger. "The life of someone who values things more than people. Possessions more than feelings. Like that couch you're sitting on. You see, that couch is a perfect design. Every stitch. Every seam. But people, people aren't perfect. They make mistakes. They don't live up to expectations. Quite often, they let you down."

Penny interjected, "But that's human nature."

Vicious took another sip. Weathered the bite. "The thing is, you can fix furniture. But you can't fix people. No matter how hard you try. Or where you send them…"

Penny realized this conversation, and the evening was taking a turn. A dark one. But she was transfixed by him. This intoxicated, sad stranger.

"Send them where?"

Vicious looked to his glass. It was empty. But his eyes, they began to fill. He looked to her. Glassy.

"The worst place you can imagine."

-TWO-

"The Pits"

The truck stank of blood. The smell was both strange yet unmistakable. Blood had a distinctly metallic scent. Like water that flowed from an old pipe.

A few feathers danced about inside the truck's covered bed as it rumbled along the uneven pavement. The sight of them, pure white and soft, gave him hope that the blood belonged to animals. Chickens, maybe. But he couldn't be for certain.

He had heard rumors about this place for years now. That kids had died there. The cousin of a friend of a friend. Those kinds of rumors. But he never believed them. It sounded like stupid stories that kids made up to scare each other at sleepovers.

He didn't believe a place like this could be real. No one did.

"Ay, rich boy."

The White-Haired Boy looked up from his corner. The truck was packed tight with boys. They sat shoulder-to-shoulder. All of them teenagers, give or take. Most of them were dirty. Their clothes tattered. Their hair unkempt. Their nails caked with mud. They had come from different corners of the solar system. From

23

dark sides of planets and rundown pockets where they would be easily forgotten. No one would be looking for these boys.

He was easily the smallest. He stood average height, but was painfully thin. His mother told him not to worry, that he was born lanky. But he knew he looked frail. His hair was stark white. Like he had been struck by lightning. He had buzzed it down to the scalp the night before. But it was already growing back. And seemed somehow whiter than before.

The voice belonged to an older boy. He had a homemade tattoo on his arm. The product of a sewing needle and the ink from a ball-point pen. It was a skull. The design was poor. The edges jagged. But the manner in which it was applied made the design, and its owner, all the more menacing.

The White-Haired Boy cowered in the corner. No one was supposed to know who he was.

The older boy motioned to his sneakers.

The White-Haired Boy looked down. The shoes, too, were white. And without a scuff. He had told himself he had thought of every-thing. His hair. His clothes. He even stopped brushing his teeth.

But he never thought anyone would even care to look at his shoes.

He pulled his knees close to his chest. Trying to hide them from view.

The older boy snickered. It was too late. He was marked.

The truck came to a jarring stop. The driver didn't even bother to turn around. He didn't want to. If you do this job long enough, you become haunted by their faces. So, he just shouted over his shoulder instead:

"GET OUT. ALL OF YOU."

The White-Haired Boy reluctantly followed the others out of the truck. He hopped down to the road. The asphalt crumbled under his feet. The roads were turning to dust. Just like the decrepit buildings that lined them. It was the middle of the day, but it was dark here. The city was located underneath the giant, humming pipes of the planet's atmosphere generators. A few burning trashcans illuminated the street, but it was like trying to light a candle at the bottom of the ocean. People were never intended to live here. The wealthy elite of Tharsis City, and with them the government, shunned the needy from their glistening streets. And so, East Tharsis was born. A town no one wanted to live in, full of people who no one wanted.

The White-Haired Boy took a deep breath. The air singed the back of his throat, like the smoke of an unfiltered cigarette. The air quality was poor here. It always had been. The oxygen vents opened up in downtown Tharsis City and flowed outward. By the time the air made it here, it had been stripped of its life-giving elements. The air people breathed here wasn't air at all. It was human exhaust.

But that's how everything was in East Tharsis. Forgotten.

An older Korean man approached the group of boys. He walked with a cane. He looked over them as if they were livestock. He motioned to a couple of the boys and dismissed them with a flick of the cane. The White-Haired Boy hoped that he would be next. He figured he could make his way back home. And even if he didn't, he thought it would be better than whatever was waiting for them.

"Nal ttalawa."

The Korean Man pointed his cane toward a small store front. "Follow me." The box-light sign that was hung above it flickered. Flies frantically danced about inside. The White-Haired Boy felt like them. Trapped. It read:

드라이 클리닝

A small English translation was inscribed below it. DRY CLEANER.

The boys walked single file through the interior of the dry cleaner where elderly Korean women used industrial rotary irons to press shirts and replaced buttons by hand. None of them looked at the passing boys. They didn't seem to notice. Or maybe they were just used to it.

Or worse—maybe they didn't care.

The Korean man approached the back door. It was made of heavy gauge steel. Like the kind used to secure a bank vault. He entered a pin into a keypad, making sure to cover the numeric sequence with his free hand.

KA-CHUNK!

The heavy locks clanged and the door slowly swung open. A concrete staircase led down into a dark basement. The boys began to slowly file down the stairs.

The White-Haired Boy reached the threshold and hesitated there for a moment. Unsure of what horrors awaited him in the darkness below. And then, he heard it. His eyelids peeled back. An involuntary reaction to the sound.

The sound ran up the staircase like the swell of a wave, then back down again, as it receded back to the ocean.

It was people.

They were cheering.

The work lights swayed as the White-Haired Boy made his way through the tunnel. The sound of the crowd grew louder with every step, as the earth began to vibrate all around him and

26

flecked his skin with dirt. And as the tunnel opened up and they stepped into an impossibly cavernous room, he saw them.

The boys.

They were shirtless. They glistened with sweat and blood. Some of the blood was their own, some of it was the blood of others. Some of it had dried hours ago. Some of it was still tinted ruby, freshly oxygenated.

They fought in pits. Hollowed out from the earth. They were surrounded by risers, where businessmen in tailored suits and women in couture cheered on the child fighters. Bookies roamed like coyotes, snatching woos from the manicured hands as bets were placed.

The fights were quick, dirty and at times downright ruthless. Was this Hell? No.

But it felt like the closest thing to it.

It seemed impossible that the sleeping quarters held twelve beds. Six bunk beds, most of them broken and some without a mattress, were packed into a room no bigger than a studio apartment.

There were mice everywhere. But they no longer scurried across the room, they just sat. They had grown used to the company.

A bald, short man waddled into the quarters. He was shaped like an egg. He seemed to be sweating uncontrollably and constantly dabbed his wet forehead with a dirty rag. He was the manager and fight promoter of this establishment. His name was Lucky but the boys nicknamed him Humpty long ago, like the children's rhyme.

"Welcome to the Pits. We have one rule here. No weapons. Just fists and feet and whatever else you need to win. Fights are

three rounds of two minutes each. Fighters will be paired up at random. There are no weight classes. Each of you will fight once a week. Win, you eat. Lose, you don't. Lose three times and you're back on the streets."

He assigned them numbers at random, thirteen through twenty-four. Humpty didn't care what their names were or where they were from. None of that mattered anymore. The only thing that mattered was their number, used to identify who would be fighting who that night. That was because the Pits had a revolving door of two dozen fighters. Boys one through twelve were relegated to the sleeping quarters across the hall. The White-Haired Boy had arrived with nine others, which meant only three fighters from the drop-off before theirs were still here. He wondered whether they had lost or just run away.

Humpty turned and scribbled the fight schedule on a nearby chalkboard.

The White-Haired Boy was number thirteen. His opponent was number twenty-one. He nervously scanned the room, hoping he'd draw one of the smaller kids, until his eyes landed upon: the older kid from the truck. The one with the homemade tattoo. He smirked. And gave a nod. The White-Haired Boy's lip began to quiver.

Humpty motioned back to the chalkboard. "There is one more rule. No one fights on the first night. I suggest you get some sleep."

Humpty waddled back through the door. The boys began to unpack their things, which were limited to whatever they could fit in their pockets. Some had brought candy. Others photos of family members they no longer knew.

The White-Haired Boy reached into his pocket and pulled

out a chess piece. It was carved from ivory by hand. Part of a custom-made, luxury set.

He'd taken it before he left.

To remind himself why he was there.

The King.

When, he heard a whisper. An Irish accent.

"Hey, you."

He turned and met the voice's gaze. A smiling, blue-eyed, red haired Irish teenager who introduced himself. His eye was swollen shut and was the color of a ripened plum. "Name's Twenty-Two."

The White-Haired Boy smiled. It felt good to smile. "I'm Thirteen. I guess."

"It's just a number. You'll get used to it."

The White-Haired Boy motioned to his swollen eye. "Take it you've been here awhile."

"Well, I've won three fights in a row. So that's three weeks. And from what I've seen around here so far, that's three weeks longer than the new boys usually make it."

The White-Haired Boy laughed. "Any advice?"

"Yeah. Run." The Irish teen smirked then motioned toward the door. "Hey, we're going to watch him fight. You in?"

He thought about this for a moment. "Watch who fight?"

The Irish kid shook his head, as if to say: you've got a lot to learn.

"Him."

They say he moves like water. He was only about twelve years old, no one knew for sure, but he fought like someone twice his age. There were rumors about where he had trained. Some had heard he was a descendent of the legendary Jeet Kune Do master Bruce Lee. Others heard he was a special forces recruit, some kind of government asset. But the only thing they knew for sure was he was good.

Really good.

The White-Haired Boy stood with the other boys beneath the risers, their faces pressed between the gaps in the benches trying to get a glimpse of him. He had a quaff of jet-black hair that jutted out from above his forehead like a cartoon character. It softly bounced as he jumped in place, a half-hearted warm up.

The Irish Boy nudged him. "That's number six. Rumor is he's been here for years, now. He's never lost. Not once."

The White-Haired Boy motioned towards Six's opponent. He was twice the size of him. The veins in his arms bulging blue. His legs were thick like tree trunks.

"That hulking fella is number nineteen. But they call him the Roach."

The White-Haired Boy furrowed his brow. He didn't get the nickname. And asked why.

"Been here for three months now. That's the longest of anyone besides Six. And no matter how hard anyone knocks him down... he always seems to get right back up."

DING!

The fight began. Six slid around the ring in a fluid dance. The soles of his bare feet seemed to hover about the surface.

Nineteen cracked his knuckles as he lumbered toward Six. There was nothing technical about his fighting style. He was hunched over and heavy footed, with the discipline of someone who had gotten into too many drunken bar fights—even though he was too young to drink.

WHOOSH! *Nineteen threw a hard right. A near miss!*

Six kept dancing. And although he usually fought without emotion, there was a glint of happiness in his eye. He seemed to be enjoying this.

This appeared to only infuriate Nineteen more.

He threw a left! WHOOSH! *Then a right!* WHOOSH! *Then another!* WHOOSH!

But all three failed to land.

The crowd began to stir. They could feel something coming. The anticipation was palpable. The bookies collected more bets. All for Six.

Nineteen clapped his knuckles together, like a boxer without gloves. "Come on! Let's go!"

And then, Six did it. And everything seemed to change.

It was a small. Subtle. Blink and you would've missed it.

A grin.

He moved towards Nineteen with alarming speed, like an alligator emerging from the water.

CRACK!

Six delivered a kick just below the right knee, causing Nineteen to buckle.

He followed with a left to the rib cage, then a right to the opposite side.

And then, he waited. For Nineteen to strike.

The White-Haired Boy watched, mouth agape. It felt like they were moving in slow motion.

WHOOSH!

Nineteen threw an absolute haymaker, the force of the punch frightening. The drag it created was immense, the air fluttering Six's hair as it whizzed by his face...

And then, there it was before him. A window. Six brought his fists to his chin—then planted his back foot. His front foot lifting and wrapping around his body as he spun, like a serpent coiling around its prey.

And then, he connected.

Flat foot to chin.

Nineteen's jaw broke almost instantaneously.

Nineteen fell to the dirt with an audible thud. The blood slowly beginning to trickle from the corner of his mouth.

The crowd erupts. It was bedlam. But other than the slight grin, Six showed no emotion.

He just returned to his corner. And sat.

The White-Haired Boy turned to the Irish Boy.

"If they call Nineteen 'the Roach'... then what do they call him?"

The Irish Boy turned to him. Then smiled.

"Fearless."

-THREE-

"DODD"

Drool dribbled from the corner of his mouth like an infant. He also slept like one. After all, who wouldn't in a double king-sized bed with vintage, one-thousand thread count sheets imported from Earth? To be honest, it was the best sleep he'd had in years.

Until the door was kicked open.

"Fearless! Wake up! Wake up, you absolute fucking moron!" Vicious shouted. He was a ball of pure, uncut anxiety. Fearless shielded his eyes from the morning sun that flowed from the floor-to-ceiling windows and softly fell across the bed.

Fearless yawned, "What is the matter with you? I was *finally* having a good dream. I was on the beach of Callisto, swinging in a hammock with a dark and stormy in my hand. There was also this giant crab running around, but that's besides the point—"

Vicious whipped Fearless's clothes from the night before at him; they hit him in the chest with a resounding *whack.*

"Get dressed. We overslept. We're supposed to be outside Dodd's place in ten minutes."

33

Fearless considered the clothes from the night before. Then looked to Vicious.

"Where's the girls?"

"Not here. They must have snuck out early this morning."

Fearless's eyes narrowed. He grinned. "How much sleep did you get?"

"Too much."

Fearless sighed. "You went emo, didn't you?"

"I didn't go *emo*. We had a lovely, intellectual conversation about furniture." Vicious remembered the night before, the drunken fog beginning to lift. "… and also about my father. *Shit*. I did go emo. I went *way* emo."

Fearless shook his head as he buttoned-up his wrinkled, champagne-stained shirt. "Can't imagine why she didn't want to sleep with you. After all, it's every girl's dream to be taken back to an immaculate penthouse only to have the guy that lives there go all Jungian on her ass."

"Freud."

"What was?"

"The Oedipus Complex. It was Freud."

Fearless scoffed. "Whatever, dude, I don't care if it was fuckin' Socrates. You need to get laid. You're starting to crack."

"Would you… Would you just put on your pants, please? We needed to leave ten minutes ago. Dodd is going to demote our ass if we're late. If that's even possible at this point."

Fearless shimmied his black suit pants up his legs. And then he froze. He furiously patted his back pockets, but he already knew it was gone.

"Son of a—*bitch*." Fearless looked to Vicious. "She stole my wallet!"

"Who did?"

"Miss Jupiter." He growled, "*Who do you think?*"

The edges of Vicious's lips begin to curl. He tried to fight it, in a futile attempt at showing some compassion for his friend, his entire life pilfered away in an instant by a one night stand, but before long, Vicious couldn't resist and doubled over.

And he wasn't just laughing. He was positively *cackling*. Wheezing, struggling to breathe in between fits. Fearless remained stone-faced. Waiting for Vicious to finish. Part of him knew he deserved this, as the irony was not lost on him. But still he was annoyed.

Vicious stood up straight, finally coming to. "Christ. I needed that. I *really* did."

Fearless's eyes narrowed. "I'm glad that the violation of my personal belongings was able to aid in your momentary catharsis." He threw his suit jacket over his shoulder as he made for the bedroom door. "Let's go. We're going to be late."

Vicious followed, emitting a tiny cackle in his wake.

Fearless snapped back over his shoulder.

"I heard that."

The air conditioner had been broken for weeks. The temperature on Tharsis City was usually regulated to a perfect 72 degrees Fahrenheit. It was one of the benefits of living downtown. But a meteor had passed by Mars earlier that day and the atmosphere generators weren't particularly adept at dealing with screaming blazes of space radiation. Vicious and Fearless sat in a town car, parked outside of a luxury high-rise. Fearless grumbled as he pounded the bottom of his fist on the passenger-side vent.

"I thought he was going to get this piece of shit fixed."

Seated behind the wheel, Vicious shrugged. "Dodd likes the interior warm. Why would he bother fixing it? He doesn't care if you and I sweat."

The town car was an older Earth model and it showed its age. The leather seats wore deep wrinkles and the passenger air bag had been hastily stuffed back inside after the previous driver had fallen asleep one night and clipped a streetlight. The Red Dragon had offered Dodd a new car. Multiple times. But he preferred this one. Neither of them knew why.

Fearless sneered. "Doesn't mean we should have to watch him soak through his clothes."

Outside, Dodd emerges from the front door of the luxury apartment building. He was old school, like a small-time gangster out of a movie. His hair slicked back with Vaseline and a gold chain that dangled from his neck. His mistress lived on the fifth floor and it was their job to drive him to and from his daily tryst.

Dodd slipped the doorman a few hundred woos as he left in order to keep their arrangement secret from the mistress's husband who worked the night shift at the synthetic beef factory on the other side of town. Fearless marveled at the transaction.

"In the Red Dragon, even the doormen are on the payroll."

"You're late," Dodd gruffed, as he climbed into the backseat. "When I say I want you outside fifteen minutes early, I want you outside fifteen minutes early. Got it?"

Vicious put the car in gear. He looked to the rearview mirror; Dodd was already starting to sweat through his white linen shirt.

"How's the temperature for ya, boss?"

Dodd didn't look up, he just muttered something that sounded like *fine.*

Vicious looked to Fearless, as if to say, told you so. Fearless mouthed back to him, *Fuck you.*

Today, like most days, they drove in silence. They had heard that the other capos liked talking to their drivers, bragging about their trysts and regaling them with tales of the bygone era of the Red Dragon, "when gangsters ruled the galaxy." It was how relationships were formed. And eventually, how jobs were given once their trust was earned.

But not Dodd. He didn't offer them a goddamned thing. Except the stink of sweat and cigarettes on a Tuesday morning.

The town car came to a stop in front of an old, dilapidated warehouse. A small, unremarkable sign hung next to the main door that read THE THARSIS CONCRETE COMPANY. But, Fearless and Vicious knew it as the headquarters of the Red Dragon— the business was a cover. No concrete was ever poured, unless they needed to conceal a body or two of course. Dodd shimmied to unstick himself from the worn leather seat and grumbled as he slowly reached for the door handle. Vicious glanced into the rearview mirror:

"See you tomorrow morning, boss. Fifteen minutes early."

Dodd stopped, as if remembering something. He smirked.

"Hey, Vicious. What's this I hear you live in *Buckingham-fucking-Palace*?"

Vicious's eyelids flared. In an instant, his ears went from white to blood red. The darkness had awoken. And if they weren't parked in front of the concrete company with half the Red Dragon inside, he'd have climbed into the backseat and choked Dodd out with his own gold chain.

The comment caught Fearless off guard. *For two fucking months, the guy hadn't said more than three words to them and now he's throwing real estate jabs?* He side-eyed Vicious. And gave him a subtle shake of the head.

Vicious cleared his throat. "Not quite, sir."

"What building?"

He tried to buy himself some time to make up an excuse.

"Say again, sir?"

"Are you hard-of-*fucking*-hearing? I said what building?"

Vicious took a beat, and against his better judgement, told the truth.

"615 Park."

Dodd had a dead-eyed look in his eyes, as if he had had a stroke. For a minute there they thought he might have. And then, after a brief moment of paralysis, he uttered, at an almost imperceptible volume:

"Then what in the *world* are you doing here?"

Vicious began to explain, "Well, I'm very driven and I don't think my upbringing is a reflection on my work eth—"

But Dodd didn't even let him finish. He slowly shook his head. His mood oddly dark. He looked out the window, and then, he said:

"Every couple years… one of you shows up. The story's always the same. You have a complex about the way you were brought up. You're ashamed of it. And you need to prove to yourself— and, most likely, someone else—that you're not just some white-sneakered rich kid from Tharsis. So what do you do? You climb down from your ivory tower and you join the Red Dragon. And you let some low-class, former East Tharsis prick like me shit on you, day after day because it makes you feel better. It gives bruises to your apple that you can show to that special someone, to prove that you're different now. But guess what, buttercup—you're not

38

any different. You're still that white-sneakered kid from Tharsis. And you always will be."

Dodd popped the door handle. And just before he slid out of the back, he made eye contact with Vicious in the rearview mirror. Then said:

"Next time get a fucking therapist."

The door slammed shut. As Fearless tried to think of something—*anything*.

But Vicious didn't want to talk about it. Dodd's words had seared through and cut him in half.

He just wanted to drive.

Big Jae's Noodle Bar was the worst ramen joint in town. The restaurant was understaffed. The noodles were chewy. The chopsticks left little splinters in your mouth. But the chef always saved a seat for Fearless at the bar. It was the only place in town that felt like home. Maybe that's why he kept coming back.

"These noodles taste like cardboard," Vicious muttered. He was in a dark mood. Dodd had done a number on him. Over the years, Fearless had learned it was better to not try and cheer him up when he was like this. He just had to wait for the storm to pass and hope that his boat didn't capsize in the darkness' wake.

Fearless slurped his noodles. "That's why I like this place. The noodles always taste like cardboard. It keeps your expectations low. So when the day comes that the noodles are actually good? Well, now *that* will be a good day."

Vicious fumed. "What kind of business model is that?"

"A bad one." Fearless shrugged. "But Big Jae saves me a seat at the bar."

"See, this is the problem with having low expectations. People feed you dog shit and you just eat it. After a while, you don't need to even know it's dog shit anymore."

When, a few stools down, a glass shattered loudly on the bar. Fearless and Vicious turned toward the sound to find a pair of heavily tattooed men in their mid-twenties sitting a few stools down. They were both properly shit-faced, shouting obscenities at the waitstaff and spilling beer all over the counter.

Vicious shook his head. "And look at these two. Not only is the food dog shit, but the customers are dog shit, too."

Fearless shrugged and turned back to his bowl of noodles. "Looks like they're having a good time if you ask me."

"Fuck this place," Vicious growled. He stood up from his seat at the counter.

Fearless turned to him. His eyes narrowed. Concerned. "Where you going?"

"Bathroom."

Vicious marched off toward the back of the restaurant. Fearless called after him as he motioned to his bowl of noodles. "You gonna finish that?"

But Vicious just kept on walking. Fearless gleefully slid Vicious's bowl of ramen over. He stuffed the noodles in his mouth. Gave them a slurp. And shrugged. "This dog shit tastes pretty good to me."

Fearless heard a surprising sound come from the far side of the restaurant. *Laughter.* It wasn't that no one ever laughed at Big Jae's, it was just no one ever seemed to enjoy themselves there. His eyes ticked to the sound. There were four of them. They were having a conversation. He couldn't hear them, nor could he tell what it was about. But they all wore the same expression on their face. Fearless had never felt it. Whatever it was. It transcended happiness. It was warm. And it was eternal.

They were a family.

And *it*... was love.

Two parents. Two children. A boy. A girl. He marveled at the way they all listened to each other, the way they took turns speaking, even when they didn't. The way how the dad softly rubbed the mom's back every so often, not even realizing he was doing it.

True love is muscle memory. An emotion that is repeated, over and over, but never goes away, even after they're gone. It remains. Hovering in the ether. Forever.

Fearless's lips slowly began to curl. Not to a grin. But something else. For a brief moment, he did something that even surprised him.

He smiled.

In the bathroom, Vicious shook and zipped his pants back up. He walked over to the sink. The once white porcelain was now stained a ghastly yellow. The rusted-over faucet squeaked and sputtered as he turned the water on. He rinsed his hands and pumped the soap dispenser—but it only gave off a stale pump of air. *Empty.* Vicious grumbled. He turned to the paper towel holder and turned the wheel. *Nothing.* It too was empty.

Then, without warning, Vicious struck the paper towel dispenser with his fist. The plastic orb that normally encased the paper towels shattered. The shards clinked along the surface of the cracked linoleum floor. Vicious exited the bathroom. He didn't bother to look at himself in the mirror. He didn't need to. He knew what was coming.

Vicious stepped into the dimly lit hallway that connected the bathroom to the restaurant. At that moment, one of the drunken men from the counter stumbled into the hallway. He was skinny and boyish, his neck tattooed with an alpha and omega, the first and last letters of the Greek alphabet. He wobbled with his eyes half open as he approached Vicious, who was standing in front of the bathroom door.

"Fuck outta my way, man," the drunk croaked.

But Vicious didn't move. He just stared down the man with a condescending glare for a moment, then responded, "Maybe you should learn some manners."

Without hesitation, the drunk unzipped his pants, pulled out his member, and began pissing on Vicious's foot. Vicious looked to his boot. The glistening yellow liquid slowly absorbed into the custom-cut leather. His eyes ticked to the door that led back to the restaurant. For a moment, he wondered if a waiter, or, worse yet, the other tattooed drunk would walk through the door and see what he was about to do. But he didn't care. The darkness had already made up its mind.

The drunk gave his member a shake. Then looked Vicious dead in the eye. "Fuck you."

CRACK!

Vicious palmed the drunk's head and slammed it into the wall! The drunk screamed as he stumbled about the hallway. Vicious grabbed him by the back of the shirt, then proceeded to throw him through a nearby door that led to the alley behind the restaurant.

The drunk stumbled in the dark alley that was enclosed by nine-foot fencing on both sides. There was nowhere to run. The drunk's lip quivered. He slowly backed away from Vicious.

"Look, I'm sorry, man! I drank too much, alright. I shouldn't have done that."

Vicious grinned. "Too late."

CRACK!

Vicious kicked the drunk in the chest with his dripping boot, splintering his sternum. The force of the blow momentarily lifted him into the air, until he came to an abrupt stop as his head struck the heavy steel dumpster. He slumped against it. Blood began to trickle down the back of his neck.

Vicious stepped into the light. He stood over the drunk.

The drunk gurgled. He locked eyes with Vicious. "Who the hell are you?"

Vicious knelt down next to him. "I am Vicious."

"What kind of name is that?"

"A name that, unfortunately, you will not remember after I'm done with you."

Something caught his eye. A tattoo on the drunk's forearm. On it was an intricate tattoo of a Grecian woman in a flowing white toga riding a bull. The artistry was high-end. It looked expensive. Vicious considered it for a moment. Then looked him in the eye. Curious.

"What is that tattoo?"

The drunk struggled to stay conscious. His eyes fluttered. But managed to say, "Europa. The Queen of Crete."

"It's beautiful." Vicious slowly nodded as he took it in.

"Mister..." the drunk begged in a whisper. "Please..."

Vicious leaned in close to the drunk. He placed a comforting hand on his shoulder. And then, he whispered back.

"*No.*"

Crack!

Vicious wound up and struck the drunk across the face so hard the man's orbital bone caved in. And then, he struck him again. And again. And again. There was no one to pull Vicious off. No Fearless to tell him the drunk had had enough. He was alone with the darkness. And they both planned to leave the boy unrecognizable.

Crack.

Inside the noodle bar, Fearless was still sitting at the counter. Both bowls of ramen sat in front of him, now empty. Vicious approached and stood next to him. He didn't say a word. Fearless scrunched his eyebrows at the sight of him.

"What took you so long?"

Vicious motioned to the bathroom. "There was a line."

Fearless looked him up and down with a suspicious glare. "You feel OK? You look like you just saw a ghost."

"Let's just get out of here," Vicious replied with an unusual urgency.

"We still have to pay."

Fearless dug into his pocket for some cash. He slowly counted the bills out in his hand as he glanced at the bill that sat on the counter. Vicious glanced at the other drunk who was still seated at the counter. It wouldn't be long before he went looking for his friend. And so, Vicious pulled a credit card from his pocket. He quickly ran it through the magnetic reader that was built in the counter.

Fearless clocked the credit card, surprised. "Damn, thanks man. I owe you one."

"Let's go," Vicious said as he headed for the door.

Beep! The credit card reader's digital display prompted him to tip 10%, 15% or 25%. Fearless motioned toward it, but Vicious kept walking.

"I said, let's go."

"No tip?" Fearless cringed. "Damn. You *are* a psychopath."

The next morning they were parked outside the mistress's luxury apartment building thirty minutes early. Vicious hadn't slept much the night before. But it wasn't the drunk that had kept him awake. It was Dodd. He was determined to prove him wrong. So much so that Vicious made a list of things that they would improve upon. Starting with showing up early.

Fearless yawned. "This better be worth it. That extra fifteen minutes ruined my morning."

Vicious sipped his coffee. "That extra fifteen minutes is going to make us made men. You'll see."

"I'm not gonna lie, after what Dodd said to you yesterday, I thought I was going to wake up to find out that you went on a five-planet killing spree." Fearless thinks about this for a moment. Then. "You didn't kill anybody, *right?*"

Vicious's eyes widened ever so slightly. He wasn't expecting the question. And was desperate to change the subject.

"Of course not."

Vicious's eyes ticked to the car's digital clock. It had been thirty-three minutes. His eyes narrowed. Huh.

Vicious rolled down the window and shouted to the doorman. "He get in late last night?"

The doorman shrugged. "Never showed up."

Vicious turned ghost white. *Shit.*

Fearless slowly turned to him. Concerned. "OK. I'm gonna ask you again. And I need you to be honest with me here. Did you *kill* anyone last night?"

Vicious brushed him off. "No, I didn't kill anyone last night."

"Are you *sure*?"

"Yes, I'm sure I didn't kill Dodd. Where the hell is he?"

Fearless shrugged. "Who cares. Let's go get some breakfast. I'm starving."

Vicious began to spiral. "Who cares? *I care!* We're here to prove Dodd wrong! And if he didn't come sleep here last night, then we should be wherever he's waking up, OK? We need to be anticipating his needs."

"I'm sorry—did you just say I need to be *anticipating Dodd's needs?* I'm not the woman who lives on the fifth floor of that building, OK? I don't need to anticipate *shit*."

Vicious snapped back. "You know what? Maybe that's why we've been stuck at the fucking bottom of the ladder for almost two years now. *You.*"

"*Me?*"

"Yeah, *you.* Because *you* don't want to put in the extra effort to take us to the next level. You just want to *fuck* around, do the bare minimum, then *fuck off* to the next bar!"

Fearless snapped back. Harder. "Because I like having *fun!* I'm sorry I don't want to be a sad bastard with you all the time! You... *sad bastard!*

Buzz-buzz. Buzz-buzz. Buzz-buzz.

They traded a nervous glance. Where was that buzzing coming from?

Vicious reached into his pocket. Pulled out his phone. The caller ID read "HOME".

When you start off in the Red Dragon, you're required to keep three specific identifiers in your cell phone's contact list. "CLEAN UP" was a call coming from an assassin in need of a janitor. "PICK UP" was a call coming from your capo when they needed a ride. And "HOME" was a direct call from Red Dragon headquarters.

You never wanted a call from Home.

He gulped. "It's them."

Fearless gulped, too. "Answer it."

Vicious's thumb hovered over the Accept icon for a moment, then pressed it.

"Yeah."

The voice on the other end sounded oddly official. Like they worked as small-time salesmen and the call was coming from corporate.

"We need you to come in. Now."

Click. The voice on the other end hung up.

Fearless and Vicious traded a look. *Shit.*

You never wanted to be invited to the Tharsis City Concrete Company before sundown. It could only mean one of two things: Either they were going to kill you, or you were in so much trouble that they might kill you anyway. Fearless and Vicious knew that in either scenario, they were completely screwed.

As they approached the door to the concrete company, Fearless grabbed Vicious by the arm.

"We can still run."

Vicious shook his head. "No, we can't. They'll find us. We both know that."

Fearless sighed. "I can't believe that we're finally going to make it inside headquarters and then I'm probably going to die."

In the daylight, the interior of the infamous Red Dragon's headquarters wasn't the evil super villain lair that they had built it up to be in their minds. It was a dark, dusty cavernous shell of a warehouse with a few scattered offices and skeletons of hulking concrete mixing machinery that were too heavy to dispose of. Not only did the concrete company make for a convincing cover for their enemies, but the Elders wanted to make sure their underlings didn't get too comfortable.

Fearless shook his head. Then whispered to Vicious. "This place is a *dump*."

A whistle came from a corner office. Dodd was standing in the doorway. He waved them over.

Fearless and Vicious approached the office. Vicious cleared his throat, nervous. Then said: "Listen, Dodd. Mr. Dodd. I just want to say, I, *we,* rather, are determined to—"

"Shut up. Sit," Dodd said, cutting him off. He motioned to a pair of folding chairs on the opposite side of a glass desk that was smudged with finger prints and streaked with dry condiments. Fearless and Vicious traded a glance. Then followed orders.

Dodd reached under the desk and pulled out a titanium briefcase. He placed it on the table in front of them.

"Do you know what this is?"

Fearless slowly side-eyed Vicious. It was obviously a *fucking briefcase*. But neither of them wanted to say it. But what else were they supposed to say? So neither of them said anything. They just let Dodd talk. And it worked. Thank God.

"It's an opportunity."

Vicious perked up. This was the last thing that either of them expected. "Sorry a… what?"

"A project. An assignment. An errand. *A fucking job.* Do you need me to get a thesaurus or do you two special kind of dicks understand now?"

They turned to each other, a slight grin between them. Then back to Dodd. They nodded.

"The briefcase is to be delivered tonight to the financial district. There's a small Italian restaurant called Angeli. It is owned by a woman named Slade. She is also in charge of the most expansive and important drug distribution network in the solar system. I think it goes without saying that she is an *extremely* important asset to the Red Dragon. Without her, our drug business falls apart. When you arrive, do not make small talk. Do not sit down. Do not stay for a drink, even if she offers you one. Do not do anything but give her that briefcase and leave. Got it?"

Fearless and Vicious nodded. Dodd dismissed them, as they tried to contain their excitement. They headed for the door, briefcase in hand— when:

"And fellas," Dodd called after them. They turned back around.

"Do not, under any circumstances, try to open it."

-FOUR-

"THE JOB"

The bathroom mirror was fogged over with a thick layer of condensation. The building was old. The realtor referred to it as "vintage" with "character", which Fearless knew was just a fancy way of saying "old" and "a total piece of shit." He, like the rest of the residents that had the misfortune of signing a lease, quickly realized that there was never enough hot water for the entire building. In fact, the only way to guarantee a hot shower was to rip the knob off and rejig the temperature regulator the landlord installed with a pair of pliers. The result was a scalding stream that left Fearless's fair skin flamingo pink for hours after the fact, but it was better than the alternative. As a child, he had spent too many nights on the streets of East Tharsis, just trying to stay warm. And just the thought of shivering in his own apartment was enough to make his skin crawl.

Fearless wiped away the condensation with one hand. His body was lean, but the muscles were dense. It was a fighter's body. The kind of body that was earned over time, as the fast-twitch muscle fibers slowly hardened with every blow. It was a form of environmental adaptation. The body was always preparing for the next punch.

He took his body in, his eyes finding the dark pink scar on the right side of his torso, just below the rib cage. It had faded a little more since the last time he noticed it. But not much. It would never go away completely. The knife had plunged too deep below the surface. The scar tissue had grown thick.

Not that he wanted it to go away. Hardly. Fearless liked to be aware of his mortality. Most people looked at it as a finish line. But the scar reminded him that it was right there with us, running by our side all along.

Kn-knock. Kn-knock. Kn-knock.

"Alright already. I'm coming. Christ." Fearless made his way from the bathroom through the almost comically narrow one bedroom apartment. He whipped open the front door. There stood Vicious in a tailored three-piece suit, mid-knock.

Fearless took in his outfit. It wasn't the kind of thing you could just buy off the rack. It was made for Vicious. And it looked damn good. Not that Fearless would ever admit that.

"You're wearing a suit."

Vicious's eyes ticked below Fearless's waist, then back to his eye-line.

"You're naked."

Fearless shrugged. "And *you're* early. That's a you-problem."

He motioned for Vicious to follow him into the cramped apartment. Outside of the second-hand mattress that lay on the bedroom floor, there was no furniture to speak of. No houseplants. Not one personal effect. Not even a dirty coffee mug in the sink. You couldn't even make the joke that it looked like Fearless just moved in, because then there would at least be a cardboard box or two in the corner. This place was empty.

Fearless disappeared into the bedroom and returned with a black vinyl suit bag in tow to find Vicious slowly strolling about the living room.

"Love what you've done with the place," Vicious joked, as he gestured to, well, nothing.

Fearless ignored him. He griped, "I can't believe you're wearing a suit. The only time anyone should wear a suit is a wedding or a funeral. And even then, it seems a little excessive."

He unzipped the vinyl bag to reveal a wrinkled, two-button thrift store suit with a slim black tie that was three sizes too small.

Across the room, Vicious raised an eyebrow at the sight of it. "I take it you don't have another suit that doesn't look like it was stolen from a man who sells counterfeit astral gate tokens in the bathroom of a casino?"

Fearless smirked as he pulled the suit on. He quickly knotted the tie and pulled it loose at the neck, then rolled the jacket's sleeves above the wrist to conceal their lack of length. Somehow, he had made this dime-store suit look as good, or even better, than the one that was meticulously created for Vicious down to the last stitch.

He turned back to Vicious. Then smirked. "Who says I stole it?"

Vicious drove the town car with his hands at ten-and-two. He slowly eased the gas pedal down, careful not to exceed the speed limit. He didn't turn the radio on. He barely said a word. Fearless had never seen him more nervous. He knew how much this job meant to Vicious. It was their first opportunity in two years to prove to Dodd and the rest of the Red Dragon that they could be more than the guys who scraped dead bodies off the marble floors of luxury high-rises.

But Fearless knew there was something else to it. Or rather, someone else that Vicious was desperate to impress. His father. *Caliban*. A businessman renowned across the solar system for his deep pockets and even deeper connections. What that business was, though, no one could really say. Some said he was an arms dealer. Others said he was a real estate magnate that specialized in acquiring unlisted, off-the-grid housing for the kinds of criminal enterprises that needed that level of protection. But what struck Fearless as the saddest part of all was that even Vicious was in the dark. He couldn't tell you if his dad was an apple salesman from Earth or the prima ballerina in the Tharsis City ballet. Over the years, Vicious had tried to inquire about his father's business in hopes that one day he'd be able to join him—but Caliban always turned him away. His father seemed to enjoy belittling Vicious, constantly reminding him that he'd never be smart or talented enough to run the family business. *After all, what boy doesn't dream of adding "and son" to the name above their father's business?*

"You're driving like my grandmother," Fearless quipped.

Vicious tightened his grip on the steering wheel. And checked his rear view. Then retorted, "You don't have a grandmother."

"I don't know my grandmother. There's a difference. I'm an orphan. Not an alien."

Fearless reached down to the floor of the passenger seat, pulled out the titanium briefcase Dodd had entrusted them with and set it in his lap. He carefully examined the locking mechanisms on either side of the handle. They were digital, each requiring a separate three-digit combination to unlock the case. Fearless clocked a flat keypad. It was built directly, if almost imperceptibly into the surface. He pressed a few numbers. The case beeped loudly.

Vicious did a quick double take in Fearless's direction. "Hey! What are you doing?!"

Fearless ignored him. "What do you think's in here? Cash? Diamonds? Gold bricks?" He tried another three-digit code on each side. The case beeped loudly again. *Incorrect.*

"Well, it's not 1-2-3 or 0-0-0. But I think I'm getting close."

Vicious quickly grabbed the case from Fearless and placed it on the backseat. His eyes narrowed as he glared at Fearless. Fuming.

"I need you to tighten it up, Fearless."

Fearless grinned. "I love it when you say my name. It makes you sound so... *serious.*"

"I *am* being serious."

Fearless snipped back, "No shit—*Dad.* Look, I'll pull it together if you relax a little bit. Alright? You can't walk into Slade's place with a goddamn flag pole up your ass. Yeah, it's our first job. But *she* doesn't know that. And if we want to start building a relationship with the biggest drug dealer this side of Jupiter, then we have to act like we've done this a million times over."

Vicious took that in. Chewed on it for a moment. Then relented. "Fine."

Fearless exhaled. "Thank you."

It was silent for a moment. The decaying town car vibrated as it motored through the skyscrapers of downtown Tharsis, past the labyrinth of polished glass and shimmering steel that extended as far—and as high—as the eye could see.

Until Fearless grinned. *That* grin. "You think Slade's single?"

Vicious's head whipped so hard in Fearless's decision it made an audible *crack*.

"Fearless, I swear to *God*—"

The financial district had seen its fair share of eateries. Most of them high-end, gastronomic-focused places where minimalistic cuts of bio-beef were served on top of a bed of billowing smoke from dry ice. But with its domed red-awning with the name *Angeli* written in simple script font, the restaurant looked like a relic from Earth. The place was underlit. The silverware was dull. The drinks were watered down. But still, people came from across the solar system to dine here. Some of them to pay their respects to Slade, but most of them to order the one delicacy that her restaurant had access to that even the most celebrated eateries couldn't find: beef. *Real beef.* Not the kind that was grown in a lab. And if you served beef, it didn't matter that your restaurant had an old awning in a town where it didn't rain.

The door creaked loudly as it shut behind them. The restaurant was quiet. It was early in the night, before the dinner rush. Fearless and Vicious stood in the doorway, without a clue of where to go. Or how to find Slade.

Vicious whispered to Fearless. "How am I supposed to act like I've done this before if I don't know what the hell I'm doing in the first place?"

Fearless brushed him off. "Just follow my lead."

He approached the bar where an old bartender wearing suspenders and a bowtie stood, methodically wiping down the counter. He didn't bother to stop, or even look up from the task, as Fearless and Vicious stood in front of him.

Fearless cleared his throat. The bartender continued to wipe. "I'm... sorry, *we*... are looking for Slade."

The bartender looked up to Fearless. Then to Vicious. His eyes slowly scanned their pristine suits. He didn't utter a word. He didn't have to. The eyes said it all: *These guys are fucking amateurs.* He shook his head and motioned to the back of the restaurant where a corner booth was illuminated by a small lamp that sat on the table.

Fearless nodded to him. "Thank you."

Vicious and Fearless made their way toward the booth, past a couple occupied tables where elderly, well-to-do regulars sat quietly and ate their beef. Fearless turned to Vicious and whispered.

"Talk about the graveyard shift."

Vicious elbowed him. A sharp jab into the ribs, as if to say, *what did I say about taking this seriously?* Fearless rolled his eyes.

Slade was waiting at the table for them. She wore her hair down to the scalp, a faint yet elegant bleach blonde mohawk. Her fingers were full of exotic jewelry that looked as if it was poached from kings and emperors from across time. A mix of rubies and emeralds that sat atop thick, meticulously polished settings. But the *pièce de résistance* was the solid gold skull she wore on her middle finger. It was scuffed. A bit worn around the edges. And if you looked closely, you could see that it was flecked with blood. She never cared or cleaned for it. Slade wanted anyone sat across from her at this table to know how far she was willing to go.

Slade's lips curled to a smile as she gave them both a long once over. She motioned to the other side of the booth.

"Sit."

Fearless and Vicious quickly followed her order, the old vinyl seating crackling beneath their asses as they slid into the booth. Once seated, they looked across to Slade, who simply raised a single eyebrow. Vicious nodded in her direction, then turn to Fearless. He cleared his throat.

Fearless looked at him quizzically. Whispered. As quietly as he could.

"What?"

Vicious again cleared his throat. This time with a deep, mucus-laden gusto. His eyelids and nostrils flared. *The case, you idiot.* Fearless's eyes went wide. Then narrowed. *Right.* He reached under the table and procured the titanium case at his side. But before he could place it on the surface, Slade raised five fingers to stop him. Not pleased.

"I don't do business until I've had a proper drink."

Vicious began, "With all due respect, Slade, we were told that—"

Slade cut him off. With vigor.

"If you're going to choose to begin a sentence with a phrase like 'with all due respect,' then what follows out of your mouth is most certainly going to lack any respect at all, now isn't it?"

Vicious swallowed back his nerves. Then continued. "It's just that, our boss—"

Slade groaned. "Yes, yes, I'm well aware that Dodd doesn't want his errand boys to stay for a drink. You're certainly not the first ones to tell me this. However, this is my restaurant. Therefore we play by *my* rules. Not Dodd's."

Fearless spoke up. "In that case I'll take a Kudo."

Slade's eyes ticked to Fearless. She held his gaze for a

moment. Her eyes narrowed as she took him in with a heavy dose of skepticism.

"You come to my restaurant… On a job… And you order… a… *kudo.*"

Vicious rubbed his eyes as he quietly muttered to himself, almost certain that their careers were over before they've even begun.

Fearless shrugged. "Is that a problem?"

Slade chuckled. She admired his confidence. "No. In fact, let's make it three."

BANG!

The muzzle of a MP5K submachine gun flashed, briefly illuminating the under-lit room. Slade's head whipped back unnaturally, a single bullet seeming to pass through her eye in slow motion as a dozen more pockmarked the peeling papered wall behind them. A light pink spray followed, a ghastly mix of retina and blood.

Out of instinct, Fearless flipped the table on its side to create a barrier between them and the shooter. He turned to Vicious, who sat frozen, and quickly pulled him to the floor just as a spray of bullets annihilated the booth, ripping through the vinyl and exploding its white filling into the air, right where they were just sitting.

Vicious looked to Fearless and gave him a single nod. "Thanks."

Fearless reached into his jacket and procured his Red Dragon issued 9mm handgun. Vicious did the same, and they both racked the slide and chambered a round. Fearless held a fist to Vicious, instructing him to wait. And after a moment, the gunfire stopped. An eerie silence filled the room. *The shooter was reloading!*

"Now!" Fearless shouted, and he and Vicious jumped to their feet, guns drawn. The shooter was standing in front of the restaurant's open-air kitchen. He was wearing a black jumpsuit and a ski mask. Whoever the hell this guy was, he didn't want to make himself known.

Pop-pop-poppopop!

Vicious unloaded his clip at the shooter. It was a chaotic spray of bullets that pinged every which way, ricocheting off the commercial ovens and copper cookware. The shooter dove behind a nearby booth, untouched. Vicious's 9mm emitted a hollow *click.* Empty.

Fearless side-eyed Vicious. "We need him *alive.*"

Suddenly, the shooter reappeared from behind the booth clutching his once-again fully loaded MP5K. His finger slowly squeezed the trigger. Fearless quickly lined up his shot, taking aim at the shooter's right arm clutching the submachine gun. And just as the shooter was about to open fire and lay waste to Fearless and Vicious—

Phhhhhp!

Fearless's single bullet struck the shooter's collar bone, shattering it to pieces. The shooter yelped in pain as the sub machine gun fell from his grip. It skittered across the floor as he retreated back behind the same booth. He was incapacitated—and now they had him cornered.

Vicious turned to Fearless. "Nice *fucking* shot."

Fearless shrugged. Smirked. "Thanks. Been working on that one. Call it *the neutralizer.*"

Vicious and Fearless approached the booth together, their guns down at their sides. They walked with a cocksure pep in their step, only to find—*the shooter was gone!*

"Shit!" Fearless yelled, his eyes quickly darting to the kitchen. The shooter was making a mad dash for the rear exit. Fearless turned back to Vicious, "Grab the case and meet me around back!"

The double doors that led into the kitchen swung violently on their hinges as Fearless ran through them, his 9mm leading the way. He carefully scanned the area for the shooter, but the only thing he found was smoke slowly billowing from the grill and steel pots bubbling over on their burners. It appeared the chefs—and his assailant—were long gone.

Fearless gave the air a hard sniff. The smell stopped him dead in his tracks. It tingled on his nose. It was a smell he remembered smelling once, as a boy, when he secretly lived in the basement of a black market butcher shop. *No*... he thought. *It couldn't be*...

He approached the flat top where a single eight ounce cut of real, genuine beef slowly seared. His mouth began to water. He knew they had a more pressing issue at hand, but he couldn't help himself. He grabbed a nearby butcher's knife and plunged it into the pink flesh. The grill simmered as the ruby red juices ran down onto the hot surface. Fearless brought the knife to his nose, then took a bite. He slowly moved the morsel around his mouth, making love to it with his tongue. When:

WHOOSH!

Fearless instinctively fell to one knee as the shooter reappeared, swinging a copper frying pan at his head. The pan ever so lightly grazed his scalp, mere millimeters away from bashing his skull in. Fearless took the opportunity to shove the remainder of the delicious, tender beef in his mouth and then flipped the butcher's knife in his hand so the butt of the weapon faced him. Then, he plunged the blade into the shooter's thigh, turning the handle like a door knob for good measure.

"*AHHHH!*" the shooter yelped in pain. He hobbled backwards a few steps on one leg and regained his footing. But even with a bullet hole in his collar bone and a butcher's knife still twisted in his leg, the shooter somehow managed to stay upright. Fearless clocked his resilience. He raised an eyebrow at his foe. *Impressed.*

The shooter looked down at his leg. Then shrugged. As if to say, *That all you got?*

Fearless scoffed, "*Dick.*" And quickly reached into his waistband and raised his 9mm at the shooter. But it wasn't quick enough.

Twang! The shooter swung the frying pan and knocked the 9mm to the floor underneath a utility sink. Fearless eyed it. *Shit.* Well, that didn't work. Then, suddenly—

WA-WHOOSH! WA-WHOOSH! WA-WHOOSH!

The shooter begun to advance on him, swinging the frying pan with the ferocity of a man who had been both shot *and* stabbed in the same damn day. Fearless dodged the frying pan as he backed away down the narrow, galley-style kitchen. There was nowhere to go from here. There was no side-door or table to crawl under. It was a dead end.

As he kept one eye on the frying pan that was hellbent on decapitating him, Fearless's hands feverishly swept the industrial stainless steel counters on either side for another weapon, but nothing seemed to be in reach, when he saw it.

A deep fryer. The oil inside bubbling with rage. The temperature surely somewhere between scalding and blistering hot.

And as the shooter realized he now had Fearless trapped, he grinned as he swung the pan at him without remorse. This would be the death blow. Or so he thought.

Fearless side-stepped him and contorted his body out of the frying pan's path. It was as if he was moving in slow motion, his muscle memory from the Pits was coming alive. But this time, it wasn't a fist or a foot he was dodging. It was high-end cookware. The pan passed by his face and continued its downward trajectory toward the hot oil. Fearless popped back up, and in one fluid move that would make Bruce Lee blush, grabbed the shooter by the forearm—causing him to drop the pan as Fearless forcefully plunged his assailant's hand into the screaming hot oil.

And scream, the shooter did.

Fearless ignored his wailing and began to interrogate him. "Who the fuck are you?! Who sent you to kill Slade?! Tell me!"

But the shooter wouldn't talk. He just screamed. And screamed. And screamed some more. All the while, the oil from the fryer popped and splashed onto Fearless's suit. He grunted at the sight. *Goddamnit.* That was going to be *impossible* to get out. He turned back to the shooter. The bad cop thing wasn't working. It was time to switch to *insane* cop.

"Listen asshole! I can do this all night! That's right! Welcome to Kentucky Fried Flesh, motherfucker! So either you tell me who ordered the hit, or I fry you from head to toe and serve you with gravy and a fuckin' biscuit—"

BANG!

A single gunshot rang out. The shooter slowly slumped to the ground. Blood poured from the hole in the side of his head where his ear used to be. His crispy, half-melted hand dangling besides him. Fearless slowly turned toward the direction of the gunfire.

It was Vicious. His 9mm still smoking in one hand. The titanium briefcase in the other. He smiled. "I know what you're going to say."

Fearless gritted his teeth. *Pissed.* "Oh, you do, do you? What was I going to say, Vicious? Tell me what I was going to say. Because I'd *love* to hear it!"

Vicious swallowed. This wasn't the reaction he was expecting. *Shit.*

"Well, I mean, I thought you were going to tell me that it was a pretty great fuckin' shot, because, I mean, well… *it was*—but now… I can see that you're upset."

Fearless's eyes bulged. "That's because *I am* upset! What did I *just say* about needing him alive?"

Vicious shrugged. "It looked like you were in danger!"

Fearless replied, "How?" Then motioned to the shooter slumped on the floor, "I was deep frying his hand!"

Vicious took a deep breath, tucked his gun in his waistband and placed the briefcase on the nearby industrial counter. "OK, *OK.* Fine. I'm sorry. But we both know we didn't *need* him alive. We wanted him *alive.*" He removed his tailored suit jacket and approached Fearless. "What's most important to Dodd is that the case is secure."

Fearless rolled his eyes. He was right. But that didn't make him any less annoyed. "I still can't believe you killed him."

Vicious knelt down next to the shooter and slowly pulled his ski mask off. The shooter looked to be in his mid-twenties. Other than a few scattered freckles, his face was fairly unremarkable. Vicious looked up to Fearless.

"You recognize him?"

Fearless smiled a big, toothy sarcastic grin. "Oh yeah, that's Bill! We grew up together in East Tharsis! Can't believe I didn't realize it was old Billy Boy. Guess we can go home now. We know who killed Slade. Case closed."

Vicious rolled his eyes, "Very funny." Then turned back to the body. "Maybe he's got an ID on him."

He searched the shooter's pants pockets. But there was nothing to be found. He didn't have any identification on him. Or, for that matter, a wallet. Not even a balled up receipt in his pocket. This guy was a ghost. Vicious scratched his head. Stumped.

Then, Fearless chimed in from above. "Roll up his sleeve."

Vicious hesitated. "Why?"

"Because he might have marks. Tattoos. Ink. A lot of the families are wearing them now as a sign of loyalty."

Vicious held his breath. He didn't want to know. But he had no choice. And so, he slowly rolled up the shooter's sleeve, to reveal—clean skin.

Vicious exhaled. "No marks."

Fearless shrugged. "Well, yeah, on one arm. I Kentucky fried the other one. Remember?"

Vicious clenched his jaw tight. *Shit.* "Oh. Right."

Fearless clocked Vicious's reaction. He could see it in his eyes. It wasn't a look of frustration. It was one he didn't see often. He was nervous.

They were interrupted by a voice shouting from inside the dining room. Fearless recognized the sound of it. Growing up on the streets, you get used to hearing *that* sound. The kind that came from the mouths of wannabe hyper authoritative assholes with a God complex. *Cops.*

"ISSP! Come out with your hands up!"

The ISSP stood for Inter-Solar System Police. They weren't particularly good at their jobs. Most of their cases went unsolved out of sheer laziness or because someone coughed up enough coin to make the trail go cold. But boy, did they have a hard on for putting the Red Dragon behind bars.

Fearless and Vicious traded a glance. Neither of them needed to say a word. But they both knew they needed to get out of there. *Right now.* Fearless grabbed the briefcase from the counter. They quickly hustled out the kitchen's back door, narrowly evading the ISSP by mere seconds as the cavalry burst through the door.

The pair spilled out into the dark alley and hustled to the sidewalk ahead. A raucous, drunken crowd from the nearby nightclubs had formed in front of the restaurant to rubberneck the crime scene. The ISSP had trouble keeping the onlookers at bay, which allowed Fearless and Vicious to blend in seamlessly with the revelers. They were home free. For now.

Fearless turned to Vicious. "Look. We need to call Dodd before he finds out that the Red Dragon's top drug distributor is dead and that we were there to see it."

But Vicious didn't react. He just shook his head. Then said, "We're not calling Dodd."

"What are you talking about?"

"We need to get the hell out of Tharsis. Tonight."

Fearless pulled Vicious into the nearby alcove of a drug store. He locked eyes with him.

"What's going on with you? You've had that same look in your eye since we left the restaurant. Like you saw a ghost."

Vicious took a nervous breath. Then spoke softly. "I don't think the shooter was trying to kill Slade. I think the shooter was trying to kill me."

Fearless stared at him sideways. "That's impossible—"

But Vicious just shook his head. Then came clean. "Last night. At the noodle bar. When I went to the bathroom. I walked out. Into the hallway. And I ran into that drunk with the tattoos. We had some words. He pissed on my boot. And then something happened."

"What do you mean, *something happened*?"

Vicious took a breath. Then.

"I hit him. I couldn't stop hitting him. I don't even remember when I stopped. Or if he's alive."

"*What?*"

Fearless looked over his shoulder, to make sure no one could overhear their conversation. Then turned back to Vicious.

"Fuck, Vicious! Are you fucking crazy?!" Fearless punched the nearby wall. He was angry. But it quickly passed as he began to mentally extinguish the flames. "No one saw you, right?"

"No. I don't think so."

"No? Or you don't think? Which is it?"

"No one saw me." Vicious swallowed nervously, then said, "There's something else."

"What is it?"

Fearless took him in. He expected the worst. He was always expecting the worst.

Vicious looked to his boots for a moment. Then looked up. "He had marks on his forearm. A Grecian woman riding a bull. I've never seen it before. But after what you said back in the restaurant—"

Fearless cut him off. "I've seen it before." He froze for a moment. It was as if all of the possible implications of Vicious's violent outburst flashed before his eyes at once. And then, he looked to Vicious and said:

"It's the Europa Crew."

–FIVE–

"The Call"

He always ate alone. It wasn't by choice. Nor had there been a prior incident that would warrant the space the other boys gave him inside the water-damaged, cockroach-infested excuse for a cafeteria. They just knew better than to take a seat next to him. It was just one of those things. An unwritten rule of sorts. In fact, it had been so long since someone had attempted to make conversation with him that some of the boys had never even heard his voice. His name was Fearless. But they were all afraid of him.

"I heard he murdered his parents with a hatchet," the Irish Boy speculated. Seated across from him was the White-Haired Boy and Number Fifteen, a boy the others lovingly referred to as Lefty—because of his missing right eye. No one said it was a good nickname, however. The three of them sat in the far corner of the cafeteria as they ate synthetic sardine sandwiches with a single squeeze of yellow mustard and chased them down with expired blue raspberry sodas that had lost their carbonation long ago.

Lefty rolled his eye, *as if to say*, here we go again. *"You don't know shit."*

"And what do you know about Fearless, smart ass?" the Irish Boy snapped back.

"I heard he was a pirate slave. Parents sold him to some raiders on Io when he was a kid. He learned how to fight on the ships and when he escaped he ended up here."

The Irish Boy stared at Lefty in disbelief. *"So you're telling me that a bunch of pirates taught Fearless karate?"*

"That's what I just said, didn't I?"

"Pirates don't do karate, shithead."

"You don't think pirates know karate?"

"Of course they don't! They're fuckin' pirates!"

"It's not karate," the White-Haired Boy interjected with a meek whisper. He was still trying to find his voice in this place, to say the least. *"It's Jeet Kun Do."*

The Irish Boy raised an eyebrow. *"And how do* you *know that?"*

The White-Haired Boy shrugged. *"I've seen* Enter The Dragon *like a hundred times. That's how Bruce Lee fights. Side kicks. Backfists. The way he dances around the ring and keeps his opponent just barely out of reach like he's made of liquid. Just like Bruce Lee."*

Lefty stared back at him. Slack-jawed. *"What do you mean you've seen it a hundred times?"*

The White-Haired Boy shrugged. *"I dunno, like that movie."*

"No, no—" Lefty clarified, *"You're telling me you own a copy of that movie? And a way to watch it a hundred times?"*

"Yeah. My parents have a holo-player. What do you guys have?" the White-Haired Boy replied with shocking earnestness.

The Irish Boy and Lefty stared back at him. If the three eyes between the two of them were any wider they'd fall out and bounce off the grease-stained table right there. The Irish Boy cleared his throat. He hesitated for a moment. Not quite sure how to put this. And then, he slowly uttered:

"You have… parents?"

But before the White-Haired Boy could answer, a meaty hand snatched his sardine sandwich from his tray. It was Number Twenty-One. He stood at the edge of the table and shoved it down his maw in what seemed like a single bite. Two other rough looking boys flanked him on either side. They had only been there for a couple days and allegiances were already forming.

"Delicious." Number Twenty-One licked his fingers one by one, taunting him. "You probably don't eat syn-sardines where you come from. No, you're too fancy for that. I can tell. You probably eat good. Like a king. What do you eat? Huh? Syn-salmon? Syn-lobster?"

The White-Haired Boy didn't make eye contact. He just stared at his now empty tray. Number Twenty-One's eyes narrowed. He took in the White-Haired Boy for a moment, then began to chuckle as it occurred to him.

"Hol-ly shit. You eat real beef, don't you? You probably never had a piece of syn-fish in your entire life. How fuckin' rich are you, kid?"

The White-Haired Boy didn't flinch. He hoped that if he played dead long enough, that the bully standing next to him would just go away.

"Give me your shoes." Number Twenty-One snickered.

The White-Haired Boy's eyes slowly ticked up to meet Number Twenty-One's. "What?"

"Don't act like you didn't hear me," Number Twenty-One snapped back. "Now give me your shoes."

"Don't do it, Thirteen," the Irish Boy interjected.

"Fuck you, leprechaun. Rich boy can speak for himself."

The White-Haired Boy looked to the Irish Boy, who softly shook his head, reiterating his plea not to give into Number Twenty-One. The White-Haired Boy considered him for a moment, then looked down to his feet. He sighed. Then slowly slipped off his sneakers and handed them over to the bully.

Number Twenty-One took the pristine white sneakers in his hands and cackled at the sight. "A brand new pair of shoes. And you just... gave them to me. Un-fucking-believable. I hope you have more fight in you tomorrow night than you do right now, Thirteen." He walked away from the table with a chuckle, motioning for his two lackeys to follow.

The Irish Boy waited until he was out of earshot, then turned to the White-Haired Boy with his teeth gritted. "Are you out of your mind, kid? You can't let a guy like that walk all over you! Especially before your first fight! If he's in your head now, what do you think he's going to do to you in the pit?"

"They're just shoes," the White-Haired Boy softly whispered.

"No—they're not," the Irish Boy snapped back as he stood up and stomped away from the table. Lefty followed suit. The White-Haired Boy was left alone at the table. He slowly took a sip of his blue raspberry soda, his eyes drifting across the cafeteria until they landed on the only other boy who was seated by himself—

Fearless.

They locked eyes. The White-Haired Boy wondered if he had been watching the entire time. If he had seen him give away his *only pair of shoes without even the slightest bit of fight. He felt ashamed. As if somehow, he'd let Fearless down. They had never even met, but for some reason, the White-Haired Boy felt drawn to him. Like they were kindred spirits. And so, he did what no one else had done before. He waved.*

But Fearless didn't reciprocate the friendly gesture. Instead, he just kept staring at the White-Haired Boy. And then, after a moment, he stood up and walked away.

Thud! Thud! Th-thud!

The sound of a fist striking a speed bag echoed throughout the empty training room. The punches were uncoordinated and errant. A far cry from the speed bag's signature rhythmic, repetitive hum when used in the manner in which it was intended. The White-Haired Boy stood before the piece of boxing equipment strung up by a rusty chain in the corner of the training room. He was drenched in sweat. When the boys weren't fighting, you could find them working on their bodies or sleeping. Equipment was sparse in the Pits. There were two punching bags, each of them hard as bricks. You'd sooner break your hand working out on one before you became a better fighter. The rest of the equipment didn't fare much better. Half the speed bags were deflated. The jump ropes cracked. The free weights were eroding away.

It was late. The White-Haired Boy was alone. He was too afraid to sleep in the same room as Number Twenty-One. And too ashamed to look the Irish Boy in the eye. So he began to wail on the speed bag again. Thud! Thud! Th-thud!

"What in the hell are you doing?" The voice boomed from the other side of the room. The White-Haired Boy startled.

As he quickly turned towards the direction of the voice to find—Fearless.

He was dressed in a tattered white T-shirt and gym shorts. Short black hairs speckled his cheeks, doing their best impression of a beard. Physically, he looked to be the same age as the other boys. But his eyes told a different story. They were dark. A deep brown. Almost black. The kind of eyes that babies are born with that gradually lighten up, day by day. But there was no childlike wonderment behind them. This was a kid that had seen his share of darkness in his short time alive. Maybe too much.

"S-Sorry—I didn't think anyone was up," the White-Haired Boy stuttered as his eyes searched for the nearest exit. "I was just leaving. Sorry again."

"What are you apologizing to me for?" Fearless snapped back as he approached.

The White-Haired Boy shrugged. "I don't know. It's just a thing I do. I apologize when something isn't my fault. Or if I didn't do anything wrong. I just say I'm sorry."

Fearless's eyes ticked to the White-Haired Boy's bare feet. "Is that why you gave that kid with the skull tattoo your shoes?"

The White-Haired Boy glanced at his feet. A wave of shame rolled through him. For a moment he had forgotten about his shoes. He looked back to Fearless. "Part of me hoped that everyone would've forgotten about that by now."

"Forgot?" Fearless chuckled as he shook his head. "No way, man. You just made things worse. A lot worse."

The White-Haired Boy swallowed. A knot began to form in his throat. He was afraid to talk. He felt like if he opened his mouth he might burst into tears right there. So he just kept quiet. And let Fearless speak.

"Guys like him? They're a dime a dozen around here. They've always been the big kid in school. The one everyone is afraid of. The ones that pick out the smallest kid in the class and whale on them just to get a laugh. And when they're not whaling on them, they're pulling shit like taking a guy's shoes. You know why? Because no one's ever made them feel small."

The White-Haired Boy motioned to the speed bag. *"Well, to be honest, that's why I was in here tonight. So when he pulls that shit again—I'll be ready."*

"Yeah, right." Fearless chuckled to himself, then shook his head. *"Every once in a while, we get one like you, too. A kid with a family. A kid with a roof over his head and clothes on his back. A kid who's never once had to rob some poor old woman for the couple bucks she has in her purse to buy her granddaughter a birthday card because he knows if he doesn't, he's gonna have to go dumpster diving again because the thought of getting food poisoning again from some half-eaten, three day old synthetic burger is enough to convince yourself to ruin some innocent lady's day. But that's who you are. A kid who's stupid enough to wear a brand new pair of sneakers to a place like this. The least you could do is scuff them up before you got here and pretend that you're not just another rich kid who thinks that coming here and catching a couple beat downs and maybe a black eye or two is going to turn you into something that you're not. You're not from the streets. You never will be. So stop acting like you belong here. You don't."*

The White-Haired Boy gritted his teeth. His fantasy of being Fearless's friend was just that—a fantasy. *"You don't know shit about me."*

"Sure I do," Fearless said with an air of arrogance as he turned to the speed bag. *"The moment I walked in here and saw*

you hitting that speed bag like it weighed seventy pounds I knew everything I needed to know about you. You don't know what the hell you're doing. And you sure as hell won't learn it here. So do yourself a favor and go home. Go back to your peanut butter and jelly sandwiches with the crust cut off and your bedtime stories and your mama kissing you on the forehead before she turns the light off."

Fearless turned and headed for the door. The White-Haired Boy stood there with his fists clenched. He was angry. And hungry to prove everyone—including his father—wrong. "And what if I stay?"

Fearless turned back. His lips curled to a dark grin. "Well, then the next time your mama sees you, you'll be in a casket. And if she's lucky, they'll be able to keep it open during the funeral."

And then, Fearless disappeared back into the dark hallway. The White-Haired Boy turned and struck the speed bag with his fist.

Ta-thunk!

The speed bag snapped off the chain and fell to the floor.

On Saturdays, the boys were allowed to use the holo-phone. It was an older model that displayed the person receiving the call in a translucent, pixelated blue hue. The newer models were able to replicate a person's skin tones so accurately that it was like being in the same room with them. Almost eerily so. But the boys took what they could get. It was nice to see a familiar face and momentarily forget the temporary hell they found themselves in. Most of them didn't have parents, so they'd usually call a relative or a friend. Some of the boys didn't even have that, so they'd call the 1-800 number from an infomercial and talk to a stranger about deep fryers or pool cleaners or whatever it was they were selling that day. Sometimes it was just nice to have an interaction with someone who wasn't trying to beat the piss out of you.

The boys sat on the floor in the hallway outside Humpty's office where the holo-phone was rigged up. The White-Haired Boy scanned the faces that waited in line for their five minutes of conversation. He wanted to see Fearless. To prove to him that he wasn't going anywhere. To prove it to everyone. But there was no Fearless to be found.

"Thirteen, you're up," Humpty called.

The White-Haired Boy scrambled to his feet and approached the office where Humpty stood outside the door with a stopwatch.

"You've got five minutes. For every minute you run over that you owe me a hundred woos. If you can't afford it, then don't go over. Got it?"

The White-Haired Boy entered the office and closed the door behind him. Humpty's office was an old converted bathroom with a sink in the corner of the room. The walls were lined with pictures of the ghosts of fighters past. Humpty always made sure to get a photo with the pit's top fighter every year. It was the only time anyone had ever seen him smile. A huge steel desk was in the middle of the room. The boys liked to joke that Humpty was secretly sitting on a toilet behind it so he would never have to get up to take a piss or shit.

A single folding chair sat in the middle of the office. In front of it was a round, disc-shaped projector with a keypad next to it. The White-Haired Boy punched in a twelve-digit number, then sat back in the chair. He smiled with a giddy, child-like anticipation as the holo-phone rang. He, more than anyone, was in desperate need of a familiar face. Suddenly, an image flickered to life. A pixelated figure began to emerge as the holo-phone slowly collected the necessary data. The White-Haired Boy smiled even wider. When, suddenly the image clarified. And the White-Haired Boy's face fell flat. Clearly, it wasn't who he was expecting.

"Hello, boy," the man said. He sat in an antique high-backed leather chair that looked like a throne. He was wearing a cashmere robe, his wet silver hair slicked back from a shower. He had a crystal tumbler of liquor in his hand. And by the detached look in his eye, it was clear it wasn't his first pour. His name was Caliban. And in this family, he was the king.

"Dad?" the White-Haired Boy asked with a surprised tone. "I thought you said you were going to be away on business for the next few months?"

Caliban grumbled. He had clearly not planned on being home. And was clearly displeased that he now was. "That was the plan, yes. In fact, I had a series of meetings that were to take place in the outer planets that would have likely been extremely lucrative for my business had I not had to cut my trip short."

"Really? What kind of meetings?" the White-Haired Boy asked, inquisitively.

Caliban's stare went cold. "Meetings that you are not to ask about. I only talk business with men. Not boys. This isn't some father and son store where they repair shoes and have a laugh after work. This is my *legacy. Not ours. Do you understand?"*

"Sorry, sir," the White-Haired Boy replied. Then, he realized something was entirely strange about this conversation. Something—someone, rather—was missing. "Where's Mom?"

Caliban took a sip from the tumbler. He locked eyes with his son for a moment, then spoke in a flat, emotionless tone. "Your mother tried to kill herself."

The words seared through the White-Haired Boy. He sat frozen. His chest slowly rising then falling with each careful breath. He wished that he was dreaming. Or that this was all some kind of practical joke. But he knew neither was true. He pursed his lips together. Careful not to show any emotion back to his father. Then, the word formed.

"How?"

Caliban took a deep, irritated breath. As if any further clarification was a nuisance. "She swallowed a bottle of pills. I found her on the bathroom floor. Half-alive. I told her next time throw herself off the roof and save me the inconvenience."

The White-Haired Boy's lip began to quiver. "Was it an accident?"

Caliban chuckled, as if even the idea of an accident was preposterous. "No. No it was not. Your mother was weak. And when weak people don't want to face their problems, they take the easy way out and leave a mess for the rest of us to clean up."

"When... did this happen?"

"The day you left," Caliban responded flatly.

The White-Haired Boy stood up from the chair. He could feel the blood vibrating through his veins. He began to pace. His father grinned. He seemed to take an enjoyment in making his son squirm. The White-Haired Boy leaned back against the steel desk and placed his hands on the surface. Unbeknownst to him, he was pressing down on the intercom button that Humpty used to make announcements.

"Mom tried to kill herself two days ago! Two!"

"I'm aware."

"You could've come here! To tell me in person! Or called! At the very least!"

Caliban scoffed. "What? So we could hug? So I could tell you everything is going to be alright? Is that what you want to hear? Or do you want to hear the truth? Because the truth is, you're just like her. You're weak, too. That's why I sent you to Lucky. To teach you how to stand up on your own two feet so you don't end up writhing on the floor in a puddle of your own vomit, begging for attention like she did. She will do it again. And when that time comes, I will not save her. Neither of us will."

The White-Haired Boy seethed with rage. "You're a monster."

"No—" Caliban grinned. "I tell the truth. You just don't want to hear it."

"Will you shut the fuck up?" the White-Haired Boy cried out in anger as he lunged toward the three-dimensional rendering of his father, his fist flying through his face.

Caliban cackled at the sight. "Better work on that right hook."

And with that, he hung up. The image of Caliban collapsed into a pile of blue pixels on the circular disk. The White-Haired Boy ripped open the door and stormed out of the office, his face beet red, tears streaming down his cheeks. And then, he stepped into the hallway only to find the other boys. Some of them whispering to each other. Others beginning to laugh. Number Twenty-One even going as far as to turn his fingers into a gun and pantomimed blowing his brains out. The White-Haired Boy watched in horror. Because in that moment, he knew they had heard everything. Trying to stem the tears, he rushed down the hallway as the other boys grew louder, his walk quickly turning *into a run. And just as he reached the end of the hallway and rounded the corner, he saw him—Fearless.*

"Hey. Thirteen," Fearless said, clocking the raw emotion on his face. "You OK?"

They locked eyes for a moment. The White-Haired Boy still tried to fight back the tears for as long as he could—he wanted to be tough. For his father. For Fearless. For himself. But there was only so much he could take. And so, the tears began to pour down his face once more. He wished that Fearless would hug him. He needed someone to tell him that everything was going to be alright. But he knew neither would happen. And so, he began to run. Through the hallways. Past the sleeping quarters and the pits. Down the tunnel and up the stairs back through the dry cleaner where the Korean women continued to iron clothes, not giving the heartbroken little boy with tears running down his face a second glance.

The White-Haired Boy stumbled out the front door and onto the streets of East Tharsis. He squeezed his eyes tight. He convinced himself that if he tried hard enough, that he could wake himself up from this nightmare. He would wake up in downtown Tharsis, in his bed with the baby blue blanket and matching pillows. He would lay there for a moment, listening to the sound of his mother softly singing "La Vie en Rose" in the kitchen as she made blueberry pancakes. Just like she did every Sunday morning. He took a deep breath.

"Wake up," he softly whispered. "Just wake up."

But then, he started to cough. The acrid air singed the back of his throat. A cruel reminder that this nightmare was his new reality. East Tharsis was a prison. And his father was the warden, sitting above the yard while the prisoners fought for their lives.

The White-Haired Boy opened his eyes and slowly turned back to the dry cleaner and stood before one of the large shop windows that were covered in graffiti and stained grey from the soot in the air. But in it he did not see his own reflection. He saw his father's. The monster who lived in the high-rise. The one who sent him to this place. The one who could've saved his mother. The one who would not shed a single tear now that she was gone. He just stared back at the White-Haired Boy with those same cold, lifeless eyes. Until—

He grinned.

The White-Haired Boy's eyes began to change. The whites were tinged with a crimson hue. He had never felt this before. The feeling wasn't just anger. It was something else. Something deep inside him that made the blood vibrate in his veins. It felt like something else entirely.

Rage.

The White-Haired Boy charged at the reflection and struck the window with his fist. Thud. *The glass spiderwebbed. He took in his fist, where shards of glass stuck out like thorns on a rose. And then struck the window again.* Thud. *The shards dug in deep into his skin as new ones took hold. Then again.* Thud. *He continued to punch the glass. The skin was beginning to tear away. The hand becoming more mangled with every strike, when—*

The owner of the dry cleaner ran out through the front door. He screamed at the White-Haired Boy in Korean, furious at what he had done to his window. Until his eyes ticked to The White-Haired Boy's hand. He gasped at the sight. The skin had been torn back so much that the bone was starting to show.

Then all at once, the White-Haired Boy seemed to wake up. The whites of his eyes once again held their pearly hue. He took in the splintered window, utterly confused at how or what had happened. Then, his eyes drifted to his hand. He marveled at it for a moment. He knew that it should hurt, but he felt nothing. The blood continued to drip from the wound and onto the sidewalk like a leaky faucet you can't quite fix.

Drip. Drip. Drip.

He locked eyes with the owner. Then whispered, "Where am I?"

Suddenly, all at once, the pain came rushing back and the blood loss took its toll.

And the White-Haired Boy collapsed onto the sidewalk.

-SIX-

"Midnight Protocol"

"**W**ould you slow the fuck down?"

Fearless clipped in his seatbelt and pulled it tight. He gripped the door handle for dear life, his knuckles bright white. After their brush with death, he would have thought that Vicious would go back to driving like a grandmother with his hands at ten and two. But he did the opposite. He hammered the gas, swerving in and out of traffic as he raced to get out of Tharsis. Cheating death hadn't humbled Vicious; it adrenalized him.

"My father keeps a small ship at a private spaceport outside of Tharsis." Vicious continued, "We can be out of Mars orbit by midnight."

Fearless threw him a hard side-eye, careful to keep the other eye on the road. "You keep driving like this we're not going to be alive by midnight."

"What would you have me do then, huh? Sit back, have a Kudo and wait for the next assassin from the Europa Crew to take a shot at me?"

"Alright, let's just think about this for a second." Fearless took a breath, then rolled out his theory. "You're positive no one saw you last night, right?"

Vicious nodded. "Positive."

"Then we have to consider the possibilities here. It could be the Europa Crew, sure. But we can't rule out the Neptune Cartel, Slade's biggest competitor. Or a low-level dealer who was fed up with her taking forty percent off the top. Hell, for all we know, it was an inside job."

Vicious scoffed. "That's absurd. Who in the Red Dragon would want me dead?"

"You *are* an asshole."

Vicious gritted his teeth. He wasn't in the mood for jokes. "What's your point, Fearless?"

"My point is, if you—*we*—get on a ship, we're gonna have to pass through the astral gates, where our identities will be logged and recorded. And if you don't think there will be another asshole waiting on the other side to put a bullet in your—*our*— foreheads, then frankly you deserve to die."

Vicious grumbled. He was right. "Fine. We stay here. On Tharsis. But we trust no one. It's just you and me from here on out. You hear me? Nobody."

Fearless took this in. He was right. It was a fair point. For all they knew, it could be an inside job. Anything was possible. Then, it occurred to him. He turned to Vicious. Raised an eyebrow.

"There is one person we can trust."

The old iron fire escape creaked beneath their feet. They were seven stories up and it felt like at any moment the entire thing could come crashing down and it would be curtains for the Red Dragon's least famous janitors. Vicious and Fearless knelt on either side of a small apartment window. It was dark inside.

Vicious looked into the pitch black apartment and then whispered to Fearless. "We couldn't have just called?"

Fearless angry-whispered back at him. "And let whoever is trying to murder you track our location because you were stupid enough to use your cell phone? *Absolutely not!*"

"Well *excuse* me! I've never had anyone try to *murder* me before."

"Clearly!"

Fearless held up his hand to shush Vicious. He could hear something coming from inside the apartment. They listened closely. They could hear a soft moaning coupled with the repetitive *thud thud thud* of a headboard hitting the wall.

Fearless's jaw dropped like a teenager. "She's getting laid!"

"We should go." Vicious motioned to the fire escape's ladder. "This is weird."

"Who do you think she's banging?"

"I don't care! Can we go, please?"

Fearless cupped his hands around his eyes, attempting to see inside. "You don't think it's Spider, do you?"

"Why do you care so much?"

Fearless scoffed. "I don't."

Vicious grinned a shit-eating-grin. "Hol-y shit. You *like* her, don't you?"

"I don't like *like-like* her. I just like being *around* her."

"Because you *like* her!"

Fearless began to spin. "You say a *word* to Goldie about this and I *stab you—*"

WHOOOOOOOOSH!

The window flew open so fast it nearly broke off its hinges. In the evening breeze, seven stories up stood Goldie. Her body hastily wrapped in a bathrobe, her hair tussled. And although her cheeks were awash with a post-coitus glow, the shimmer quickly gave way and was replaced with an angry crimson.

"What in the hell are you two sick fucks doing standing outside my bedroom window?"

Fearless grinned, but Vicious quickly interjected, before he could say something that would get them both thrown off the fire escape.

"Look, Goldie. We got a situation."

Goldie shook her head. "Tell the girls you're architects. Or dolphin trainers. I don't care. I can't help you get laid tonight." She grabbed the window frame and began to pull it back down. Vicious stuck his hand out and stopped it. He looked her in the eye. Sincere.

"A real situation."

Goldie sighed. She looked back into her dark apartment, then back to Vicious. "Give me five minutes."

Vicious nodded. "Thank you."

They sat at a small kitchen table, three glasses and a cheap bottle of bourbon between them. Fearless's eyes wandered to the refrigerator. Pictures clung to its surface with the help of small flower-shaped magnets. A daisy held a picture of a family barbecue. A tulip held a picture of four friends with their arms draped around each other's shoulders. He wondered what it would be like to be a part of her family. To have her friends become his friends, too. To be able to paper their refrigerators with images of their shared history. But his mind couldn't wander for long, as he was interrupted by:

"I owe you one, Hugo. Thanks."

Goldie hung up and placed her cell phone on the table. She poured herself three fingers of bourbon and downed it quickly. Vicious watched as she placed the empty glass back on the table. He motioned to it.

"I'm going to assume that drink wasn't a celebratory one."

Goldie shook her head. "That was my guy inside the Europa Crew. The drunk you beat the shit out of? He's dead."

Vicious looked to the floor. He slowly shook his head. For a moment, it was as if he felt remorse.

Goldie continued. "His name was Nicky Cortez. He just joined their outfit. Was set to be initiated next week."

Fearless interjected. "Then that rules out the Crew as the shooter. Ain't no way you're sending an assassin to shoot up Slade's place over some baby errand boy—"

"Not quite." She took a breath, then continued. "Nicky Cortez has an older brother. Darien. He's a capo in the Crew and from what I'm told, he has the clearance to authorize something like this. It doesn't mean he did it. But we can't rule them out just yet."

Vicious sat back in his seat. "Shit."

Fearless poured himself a few fingers of bourbon. "*Shit* is right."

Then, as Fearless threw back his bourbon, Goldie stood up and walked to the pantry and pulled out a pack of popcorn. She popped it into the microwave and turned it on. Then sat back at the table.

Fearless's eyes narrowed, bewildered at the snack choice. "Popcorn? *Now?*"

She held up a finger. As if she was telling them to wait one minute. When, suddenly—

Pop. Pop. P-pop. P-pop-pop.

Goldie lowered her voice. "You two should both know that the Red Dragon is *always* listening." She leaned forward. "Now, we can't rule out the Europa Crew, but we also can't rule out that this was an inside job."

Fearless turned to Vicious. He loudly cleared his throat. *A-hem.* As if to say, *told you so.*

Vicious whisper-snapped at him, "Shut up, Fearless," then turned back to Goldie. "What makes you think it's an inside job?"

Goldie glanced at the titanium briefcase tucked underneath the table. "Did Dodd tell you what you were carrying?"

Vicious shook his head. "Of course not. Figured it was cash. Diamonds, maybe."

"Not quite."

Fearless and Vicious traded a glance, confused. Goldie explained.

"Three days ago someone broke into a medical lab on Venus where scientists were developing a top secret synthetic stimulant for the military known as HEX1516. Word is, it's so pure it can keep a soldier up for days on end without the side effects of cocaine or speed. When the cops arrived, they discovered that a single hard drive was missing. On it were the step-by-step instructions on how to manufacture HEX1516 in mass quantities."

Vicious perked up. "And you think the Red Dragon's involved?"

"I don't think, I know. When you used to steal diamonds for a living, you make a few friends in the high-end security business.

Just so happens that one of these friends built the security system for the lab. His back was to the camera, so they didn't capture his face. But they did get his piece sticking out of his waist. A Glock 19 Gen 5 9mm with a coiled dragon on the bottom of the clip."

Fearless and Vicious both reached into their waistbands, pulled out their respective Glock 9mms, and ejected the clip. On the bottom of each was a small coiled dragon etched into the surface, just as Goldie had described.

Vicious smirked. The pieces were slowly coming together. "So, what you're saying is, the Red Dragon stole the drive from the lab to hand over to Slade so she could mass produce the solar system's next big party drug—until someone decided to make a play for it."

Goldie nodded. "Exactly."

But Fearless wasn't convinced. This didn't quite add up. "Listen, it's a great theory, especially since you know I was the one who suggested the inside job thing first, but that's neither here nor there—"

Vicious rolled his eyes. And so did Goldie.

Fearless continued, "But why the hell would Dodd send two janitors on their *first job* to deliver the most valuable case in the entire solar system? It doesn't make any sense."

Goldie shrugged. "Maybe that's why he did it. No one would ever suspect you two idiots of carrying a case like that."

They were interrupted by a loud *DING!*

Fearless motioned to the kitchen. "Popcorn's done. And unfortunately, so is this conversation."

Goldie scowled. "That wasn't the microwave." She picked up her cell phone off the table. Her eyes ticked to the screen. They widened. Then widened some more. She quickly looked up to Fearless and Vicious—absolutely terrified. "You both need to leave, *now*."

But they didn't budge. Fearless looked to her, confused. "What are you talking about?"

Goldie quickly stood up. "Right the fuck now, let's go!"

Vicious and Fearless hopped up to their feet, briefcase in tow, as Goldie frantically ushered them back through her bedroom and pushed up the window that led out to the fire escape.

Vicious turned back to her. "Goldie. What the hell is going on?"

"The Red Dragon just activated the zero protocol—"

Goldie reluctantly turned her cell phone toward them. On the screen was a picture of Fearless and Vicious, side-by-side. Below the photos was bold text. The Red Dragon's version of a wanted poster. It read:

WARNING. THE ZERO PROTOCOL INITIATED HAS BEEN ACTIVATED FOR THE FOLLOWING MEMBERS: FKA "FEARLESS," FKA "VICIOUS." YOU ARE HEREBY AUTHORIZED TO KILL ON SIGHT.

Vicious swallowed nervously. Then said, "You were right. Dodd thinks we murdered Slade and stole the hard drive."

Goldie motioned toward the open window. There were tears in her eyes. "You have to go. I can't help you anymore. If they find out you were here, they'll kill me, too."

Vicious nodded. "I understand. Thank you for everything."

But Fearless didn't share his sentiment. He pointed the briefcase at Goldie. "We're not leaving until you tell me how to open this case."

Goldie looked shaken. "What? I don't know how to open it."

Fearless grew angry. His normally laid back cadence now laced with rage. Maybe he was doing it from fear. Or maybe he knew it was the only way to get what they needed.

"We're on our own now. And the only leverage we might have, the only thing that *might* keep us alive, is in this fucking case. So tell me who *can* open it. Or we sit here. And come sunrise the Red Dragon lights this whole fucking place up."

Goldie waffled for a moment, then grabbed Fearless's hand. She grabbed a ball-point pen off a nearby nightstand and began to write on his skin, pressing a little harder than she should.

Fearless recoiled. "Ow, what the fuck?"

Goldie pressed harder. Making sure to dot her I's and cross her T's. Fearless looked at the back of his hand where an address was scribbled in blue ink. It read:

615 STONE

He stared at it, puzzled. "What is this?"

"That's where you'll find Pouncey. She's the best safecracker in the solar system. If she can't open that case, no one can."

Fearless nodded. "Thanks."

Vicious climbed out the window onto the fire escape. Fearless followed. When, Goldie called out to him.

"Fearless?"

He turned back. "Yeah?"

"You ever threaten me again and I will slowly dismember your body and scatter it around the solar system so no one will ever, *ever* be able to find you."

Fearless grinned. *That* grin.

"Promise?"

Fearless and Vicious quickly descended from the fire escape and into the dead-end alley behind Goldie's apartment building where they had left Dodd's town car. They hustled toward it. Given that they were now sworn enemies of the Red Dragon, they were eager to get the hell out of there. And fast. They reached the town car where Vicious fumbled in his pants pockets for the keys, but found nothing. Fearless impatiently pulled on the passenger door handle.

"Would you hurry up?"

Vicious continued to feverishly dig through his pockets. "Where the hell are they?"

"What do you mean, where are they?"

"The keys. I don't know where they are. I can't find them!"

Fearless's eyes nearly fell out of their sockets. "Are you seriously telling me that we're number one on the Red Dragon's kill list and you can't find your fucking car keys??"

"They were just here a minute ago, I swear!"

"You know what, screw it. I'm just going to kill you myself for being such a moron."

Vicious patted the lapel of his suit jacket and heard a familiar *clink*. A wave of relief rushed over him as he reached inside his suit jacket to reveal the keys. He held them high.

"Got 'em."

Vicious unlocked the door and opened it wide, when something caught Fearless's ear. It was a familiar sound. A kind of metallic grinding. *Flick. Flick. Flick.* Fearless turned to the open end of the alley, where a fire-red ember burned bright. A cigarette. He softly whispered to himself.

"*Spider...*"

Vicious's eyes slowly ticked to Fearless. Then to the open end of the alley where the cigarette burned bright. He too knew instantly who it was. "Shit." He quickly turned back to Fearless. *"Get down, now!"*

BRAAAAAAT-TAT-TAT-TAT-TAT!

A hail of gunfire burst from the muzzle of two Sig Sauer MCX submachine guns, briefly illuminating the alley and the two assailants who held them. *Spider and Karma*. Fearless and Vicious dove to the ground and furiously crawled as the town car was shredded by MCX's .300 AAC blackout shells, raining shards of glass and metal fragments down on them.

"How the fuck did they find us so fast?" Fearless cried out as he struggled to put a fresh clip into his 9mm.

"Goldie fucked us!" Vicious snapped back, as he did the same.

"How dare you! She would never!"

"See! You *do* like her! I knew it!"

"Fuck you!" Fearless growled, as he racked the 9mm slide. *KA-CHUNK!*

"Are you ready to do this or what?!"

Vicious nodded. As Fearless raised three fingers. *3... 2... 1...*

Fearless and Vicious rolled out from the front of the town car and moved along either side. They each popped their respective chrome handle, swinging the heavy metal door's outward in order to form a standing bulletproof barricade. Each raised their 9mm high and fired upon their new found Red Dragon foes in unison. *Bang-bang-bang-Bangbangbang!* And even for a couple janitors, it was a sight to behold. Fearless and Vicious were in perfect sync, going toe-to-toe with two of the Red Dragon's best. Spider and Karma momentarily fell back, giving them just enough time to get inside the town car.

Vicious turned the ignition, as Fearless reached for his door. But he quickly shook him off. *"No! Keep it open!"*

The town car kicked to a start. Vicious threw the car into reverse and mashed the accelerator. The throaty V-8 engine roared to life as they whipped backwards down the alley. Vicious clocked the rearview mirror, where Spider and Karma stood pat with the MCXs in hand. The muzzles flashed in the mirror as they emptied their clips upon the town car yet again.

BRAAAAAAT-TAT-TAT-TAT-TAT!

But as they reached the end of the alley and the town car emerged from the darkness, Spider and Karma saw the fruit of Vicious's ideas in real time. The speed at which they were traveling had created an immense amount of drag, enough to keep both doors open and giving the town car a T-shape that filled the entire alley. As this hulking, winged beast descended upon them, Spider cried out into the night.

"Get the fuck out of the way!"

The two storied Red Dragon assassins quickly dove out of the way, just narrowly missing being split in half by the town car's doors. Vicious reversed into the street, cutting across traffic and into the other lane, where he threw the town car in drive and punched the accelerator—causing both doors to shut simultaneously.

Inside, Fearless could barely believe what he had just seen. It was as if his mostly insecure sometimes hot-tempered friend had turned into the world's greatest stunt driver at the blink of an eye.

"Where the hell did you learn to drive like that?!" Fearless cackled.

Vicious grinned as he white-knuckled the steering wheel. "Race car camp."

"Did you say, *race car camp*?"

Fearless stared back, his jaw slack. Vicious did a double take at him.

"What? I used to go every summer!"

Fearless's eyes narrowed, incredulous at the thought. "How rich are you, man?"

Vicious chuckled as he took the nearest exit and guided the town car onto the freeway that ran alongside Tharsis City. He swerved in and out of traffic, continuing to press the accelerator to the floor as he put some distance between them and the Red Dragon's finest.

"We're going to need a place to lay low tonight. You grew up on these streets. Is there anywhere that we can hide tonight where the Red Dragon won't be able to find us?" Vicious asked.

Fearless chewed on this for a moment. "Yeah. I know a place. But I'm telling you right now, it's not exactly a five-star getaway."

"What? What are you trying to say?"

"You're a little fancy, that's all."

"Me? Fancy? I'm not fancy."

"You're a little fancy. It's not a big deal. You just are."

"I am *not fan*—"

BRAAAAAAT-TAT-TAT-TAT-TAT!

Another barrage of bullets strafed the town car. Vicious clocked the rearview mirror, only to find that Spider and Karma's all black Land Rover Defender 90 was nearly bumper to bumper with them.

"Fuck! That's not possible!" Vicious said, as he quickly jerked the wheel right into the other lane, momentarily riding the shoulder as he accelerated past a half-dozen cars and zipped back into the lane.

"I told you it wasn't Goldie!" Fearless quipped.

"We were out of their sight when we got on the highway! There's just no way they'd be able to find us that quickly!"

Fearless shrugged. "Maybe it was a lucky guess?"

"Lucky guess my ass." Vicious grumbled. He mulled it over

for a moment, when it occurred to him. Vicious chuckled. *Of course.* "We're in Dodd's car."

Fearless furrowed his brow. "No shit."

"He's a capo. Red Dragon headquarters knows the location of all of their most senior members at all times. It's a matter of security."

"Which means?"

"There's a tracker on this car."

Fearless's eyes narrowed. He already knew what was coming next. So he didn't bother to ask. He just waited for Vicious to say it.

"On the bottom."

Fearless stared back at him. "And how do you suppose we get said tracker off the bottom of the car?"

Vicious winced. "Well, we can't exactly stop, can we?"

Fearless boiled. "Oh, so you want *me* to get it off the bottom of the moving car??"

"I can't get it, I'm driving!"

"Fuck you! Let me drive, then!"

"I'm the better driver!"

Fearless scoffed. "Why? Because you went to race car school when you were twelve?"

Vicious snapped back proudly. "Yes!"

BRAAAAAAT-TAT-TAT-TAT-TAT!

Another round of bullets rang out. Fearless and Vicious instinctively ducked, as the rearview mirror was blown to pieces. The windshield was peppered with bullets, leaving a splintered spider web in its wake. It had appeared that time, unfortunately, was not on their side.

Fearless grumbled as he unsnapped his seatbelt. "Fine! I'll do it! But keep the car straight, will you?"

He climbed out of the passenger window, shoulders first. The ferocious highway wind whipped through his hair. He quickly turned to the Defender behind them, firing off a half-dozen shots to buy himself some time.

Bangbangbang-bangbangbang!

The Defender's tires screeched on the pavement as it quickly swerved out of the line of fire and fell back a few car lengths. Fearless quickly took advantage of the opportunity and bent at the waist. He turned and shouted back to Vicious inside, "Hold my legs!"

With one hand holding tight onto the side-view mirror, and Vicious's right arm clutching somewhere around his ankle, Fearless slowly shimmied his body down the side of the car's exterior. The heat rose from the asphalt below. He could feel it on his face. A day's worth of sun and rubber tires slowly searing his cheeks. And as he reached the bottom of the chassis, he poked his head under— to find a tracking device, with a blinking red indicator light. The only problem was, it was planted below the trunk.

"Ah, shit," Fearless muttered.

CRASH!

The Defender slammed into the driver's side of the car, pushing the town car horizontally across the highway. Fearless dangled by the side-view mirror, like a sloth hanging from a single tree branch. He looked up to the mirror, grateful that Dodd refused to trade in this old piece of shit. Because, fortunately for Fearless, this town car was an older model town car with mirrors made entirely of chrome that were bolted into the frame, unlike the new ones made of fiberglass that were merely glued.

"What did I say about holding onto my feet!" Fearless shouted to no response, as Vicious managed to gain control of the town car which was now in the midst of a dangerous high speed game of cat and mouse. Fearless quickly formulated a plan. In order to get under the trunk, he would first need to get on top of the car's hood. And so, he reached up with his right hand and grabbed hold of the support pillar that connected the roof to the windshield. He slowly pulled himself up, wedging his left foot into the open passenger window for support—and then, in one go-for-broke move, flung his body onto the car's hood! Just as—

CRASH!

The Defender slammed into the town car yet again, causing Fearless to slide across the hood, from one side to the other, nearly falling off the edge but managing to hold on. Fearless locked eyes with Vicious behind the wheel.

"What are you doing on the hood?" Vicious cried.

"You just worry about keeping it steady!" Fearless snapped back.

Fearless slowly army-crawled up the windshield and onto the roof. When, he looked to his right, and saw the Defender coming in for another body slam, which would surely be the death blow, but he managed to draw his 9mm and hold it flat against the roof—

Bangbangbang!

Fearless could only squeeze off three shots, but they were enough to send the Defender flying across the highway and momentarily out of sight. Fearless moved across the roof, but stopped. His eyes ticked to the trunk. In order to see under the trunk, he was going to need something to hold onto. And with the trunk closed, it would be physically impossible to hold onto it while looking underneath. Then, he got an idea.

Fearless shouted to Vicious. "Pop the trunk!"

"Do what?!" Vicious called back through the blown rear window.

"Just do it!"

WHOOSH!

The trunk shot open and began to flail violently in the wind. Fearless slowly found his bearings and rose to his feet. In order to get into the trunk, he would have to jump over it. And so, Fearless took a deep breath—*and leaped over the open trunk door,* his feet landing flat inside the trunk! Fearless quickly fell to his knees and held onto the bumper as he bent at the waist. And now he was finally able to see under the trunk, he saw it. The blinking red tracker. Fearless reached for it—but it was too far! His fingertips grazed the tip of the tracker. It was so close he could actually touch it.

And then the Defender roared back into view. They were now behind the town car and closing in quick. Fearless reached into his waistband and raised his 9mm. He aimed it at the Defender's windshield—when he realized the solution to his problem.

Fearless flipped back under the town car. He lined up the tracker with his 9mm—*bang!*—and blew it off the town car's undercarriage, scattering it across the highway! Then, Fearless flipped himself back into the trunk and laid on his back. And with his remaining bullets, he took aim at the encroaching Defender. He drew them in, waiting for the Defender to make contact.

Bangbangbang!

Fearless pumped three bullets into the driver's side of the windshield. Blood splattered throughout the interior, as the Defender careened across the highway and into the guardrail where it came to a stop with a sickening crunch. Spider and Karma had to be dead.

Fearless lay on his back. The town car's trunk still open,

flailing in the wind. The stars shimmering in the sky above him. It occurred to him that he'd never seen the stars in Tharsis City before. Everything was so bright all the time—all the buildings, all the digital billboards—that it washed out the sky. Fearless reached into his jacket pocket and pulled out a pack of cigarettes. Placed one in his mouth. Lit it. He took a long drag.

Then slowly exhaled. And for a moment, he was at peace.

Chirp-chirp. Chirp-chirp. Chirp-chirp.

Fearless and Vicious sat on the hood of the bullet-ridden, windowless town car on the outskirts of Tharsis City, overlooking a water purification reservoir. They had decided to hide out there for the night, trading pulls from a bottle of whiskey Dodd kept in the car as they watched steam slowly dance off the surface of the emerald green water. The water on Mars was poisonous. It was too acidic to even smell, let alone drink. In order to make it suitable for human consumption, it needed to be treated with the same chemicals they used to clean old swimming pools. It was what gave the water its emerald hue. The government claimed it was safe, but the residents of Tharsis City refused to drink it. They voted to have their water flown in from Europa instead, where it was naturally occurring and pure like it once was on Earth. The city didn't know what to do with the leftover green water, so they piped it out to East Tharsis. Just like they did with everything else that gave you cancer.

"What's this one called?" Fearless asked, referring to the repetitive chirp.

Vicious looked to his cell phone. "This one's called crickets. Whatever the hell that is."

"Are you playing that off your phone?"

"Yeah. Why?"

"Can I see it?"

"Sure."

Vicious handed him the phone—and Fearless immediately chucked it in the reservoir. It sunk to the bottom like a stone. Vicious sat there, his jaw slack as Fearless dressed him down.

"I just nearly died on the highway trying to get a tracker off a moving car. I will be damned if I die because you gave up our location because you wanted to listen to crickets on your cell phone."

Vicious cringed. "Sorry." He motioned to Fearless's cell phone that he clutched in his hand. "Aren't you going to toss yours in, too?"

"No."

"Why not?"

"Because I turned my cell signal off."

"Are you fucking kidding me? Why didn't you just turn mine off?!"

Fearless glared at him. "Because I can't trust you to not turn it back on, that's why."

Vicious shook his head. He took another pull of the whiskey and winced as it went down. He stared out the emerald water for a moment, hypnotized by its slow, mechanical churn. Then turned to Fearless.

"How'd you know about this place, anyway?"

Fearless chuckled to himself. "I used to sleep here sometimes when I was a kid. No one bothers you out here. Everyone thinks the smell gives you cancer."

"Doesn't it?"

"I guess we'll find out. Someday."

Vicious chuckled, too. Fearless was his best friend. But sometimes it felt like he knew nothing about him. Throughout their friendship, they had avoided most of the tough questions. But as they were stuck sitting on the edge of a potentially poisonous water reservoir with a hit placed on their heads, he figured now was as good a time as ever to ask.

"What was it like, you know, growing up on the streets?"

Fearless shrugged. "Cold."

Vicious pressed him. He wasn't getting off the hook that easy. "No, but for real."

"I guess I don't know what you mean?"

"Alright, look. Let me put it this way. My father was never a good person. And he got even worse after my mother died. But even on the hardest nights, when I would lie in bed and cry myself to sleep, I knew he was in the house. Somewhere. Even if I hated him. I still had him. So I guess my question is, what's it like to know there's no one else but you?"

Fearless took a deep breath. And an even bigger swig of the whiskey. He let it singe his throat, then spoke.

"You know the feeling of seeing a tiger in a cage? Where you can't quite believe what you're looking at, you know, this beautiful creature that you have no reference for. You've seen one, sure. On TV, maybe. But when you see one up close, you can't really process what you're looking at. Because you don't know what it's like to be around one everyday of your life. How it acts. How it feels. Heck, how it smells. That's what it's like when I see a family. I feel like I'm at the zoo, watching something I'll never quite understand. And I've been chasing a feeling I don't even know ever since."

Fearless shrugged. Then took another swig. "It's why I joined the Red Dragon. And you see how that's worked out for me."

Vicious could hear the bitterness in his voice. "Listen, Fearless… I'm sorry about—"

But Fearless wouldn't let him finish. "Save your apology. What happened, happened. And now, it is what it is. We just gotta get through it. One day, I'll probably do something I regret. And we'll have to get through that, too."

Vicious took in his words. It was a wiser side of Fearless. One that he was just now getting to know. Fearless took his suit jacket and balled it up. He placed it between his head and the windshield and closed his eyes.

"Get some sleep. We're going to this Pouncey bright and early tomorrow—"

Vicious didn't say a word. He just nodded. He was lucky to have a friend like Fearless. He'd probably never have another one quite like him. And so, he too tucked his jacket behind his head.

And drifted off to sleep.

-SEVEN-

"Right Hooky"

"**W**e want blood! We want blood! We want blood!"

It was Saturday night and the crowd that had gathered at the Pits that evening was dressed even more outlandishly formal than usual. Men wore tailored tuxedoes with tails and top hats to match. Women wore form-fitting sequined dresses that they had usually reserved for a night at a charity gala. Bankers. Real estate magnates. An arms dealer or two. They were all here. Because Saturday night at the Pits was the social event of the week.

The White-Haired Boy didn't so much dance around the ring as he scurried. His right hand was wrapped in a crude bandage, the blood seeping through. It was his first fight—and he was absolutely terrified. Not that the crowd's chanting and insatiable thirst for bloodshed made it any better. He wondered what they would do if he died. Would they even care? Or would they just cheer? He didn't want to know the answer. And so he had decided that the only way to stay alive was to deploy the only survival tactic he knew—running for his life.

"Come on! Hit me! Make Mama proud!"

Number Twenty-One, the boy with the homemade tattoo, chased the White-Haired Boy around the ring like a farmer trying to snatch an anxious chicken from the coop. Every time Twenty-One had him cornered and ready to strike, the smaller, more agile White-Haired Boy somehow managed to squirm his way out from underneath him and to the other side of the ring.

Number Twenty-One began to lumber. He was drenched in sweat. Exhausted. He looked to the crowd in frustration. The mood was beginning to shift. They too were frustrated. The chanting had subsided. And was replaced with a chorus of boos.

Ding-ding-ding!

The referee stepped in between the two fighters. The third round had come to an end. And so had the fight. There would be no winner tonight. In the Pits, the concept of a draw did not exist. There were only winners and losers. And unfortunately for both boys, they were losers—each of them two more losses away from being kicked out on the streets.

The White-Haired Boy sat on the bottom bunk. The sweat rolled down his body and began to pool on the surface of the mattress below him. He didn't care if had to sleep on a cold, wet bed that night. He was just happy to be alive. Then, out of the corner of his eye, he clocked the chess piece. It was sitting on the window ledge where he had placed it on the day he arrived. It was mocking him. He could hear his father's voice. How disappointed he was. How he was ashamed to have a son like him. The one who always runs away from a challenge. The one who will never, ever be a real man like him.

"Hey—Mama's boy."

The White-Haired Boy glanced up from his inner monologue. The voice was coming from Number Twenty-One. He stood before the White-Haired Boy, his fists still clenched. His jaw locked in a scowl. Behind him were two other boys who wore a similar snarl. The White-Haired Boy swallowed in fear. He had managed to stay alive in the ring, but he wasn't so sure that this encounter would have the same outcome.

Number Twenty-One glared at him. "What the fuck do you think you were doing out there tonight?"

The White-Haired Boy shrugged nervously. "I don't know."

"You don't know?" Number Twenty-One chuckled. "That's funny."

Number Twenty-One slowly stepped toward him. He cracked his knuckles. The White-Haired Boy's eyes ticked to the sleeping quarters' lone entrance, but the two lackeys with Number Twenty-One quickly circled around the bunk on either side like a gang of hyenas trapping their prey. There would be no outrunning anyone this time.

"Because, what it looked like to me, was that you were trying to embarrass me tonight."

The White-Haired Boy tried to reason with him. "I wouldn't do that, I swear—"

"Well, that's too bad. Because you did *embarrass me. And now I have a loss on my record. Which means I'm two losses away from being back on the streets." Number Twenty-One motioned to the other boys. "So me and the boys decided that we're going to have a little makeup fight. To make sure you don't go and embarrass anyone else."*

The two other boys each grabbed the White-Haired Boy by

the arm and lifted him up off the mattress. They stood him in front of Number Twenty-One. He grinned. The White-Haired Boy's eyes frantically scanned the sleeping quarters for any shred of help. But all the other boys just looked away. Either they were too scared to help, or they agreed with Twenty-One. He wasn't sure what was better.

Until, his eyes locked with the Irish Boy. Twenty-Two. The one who had shown him the ropes that first night. There was a glint of compassion in his eyes. And for a split second, it looked as if he was going to intervene on the White-Haired Boy's behalf. But then, he just shook his head and said, "Sorry, mate."

CRACK!

Number Twenty-One struck the White-Haired Boy so hard in the face that you could hear his cheek bone splinter. The force of the punch sent him flying back onto the mattress. The other two boys quickly collected the White-Haired Boy and brought him back up to his feet. His face quickly swelled up, the skin already beginning to turn black.

Number Twenty-One inspected his handiwork. "That one is going to need some surgery to fix. But surely Daddy will pay for that, won't he?"

He cackled as he raised his fist and wound up to strike the White-Haired Boy again, when someone grabbed him by the wrist, mid-punch!

Number Twenty-One looked to his fist. It was as if it was floating in the air. It seemed impossible. His eyes ticked to the hand holding him back, slowly traveling up the chiseled forearm, past the elbow to the shoulder, up the neck where they came to rest upon his face.

Number Twenty-One whispered in terror. "Fearless…"

Fearless didn't utter a word. He just stared at Number Twenty-One with those deep brown almost black eyes. He looked utterly terrifying. He looked like he'd come here to kill someone. Maybe he was going to. Suddenly, Fearless took Number Twenty-One by the wrist and quickly twisted it behind his back. With his free hand, he gripped the back of Number Twenty-One's head and slammed it into the metal frame that separated the top bunk from the bottom.

It reverberated with a thunderous TWANG!

Number Twenty-One fell to his knees, his now split forehead bleeding in his hands. Fearless quickly turned his attention to the other two boys, who stood before him. Terrified. He looked them up and down. He slowly raised a fist to his face. Then looked them in the eye. And whispered:

"Boo."

The two boys quickly ran off. Fearless looked around the sleeping quarters to the other boys who just a moment ago would not even look in the White-Haired Boy's direction.

"Anyone else feel embarrassed? Anyone?"

The boys softly murmured. Fearless turned his attention back to the White-Haired Boy. Even after properly dismantling Number Twenty-One and his lackeys, he didn't show a lick of emotion. He just lowered his voice and softly said, "Meet me out front in five."

The White-Haired Boy coughed as they walked down the sidewalk. He had only been in East Tharsis for a week, but it felt like his breathing was getting worse. Fearless looked at him and chuckled.

"You'll get used to it."

The White-Haired Boy rubbed his throat. "Get used to what? Dying a slow death?"

"You're not dying. You're adapting. The air here isn't as pure as it is in the rich part of town. Some people actually say it makes your lungs stronger."

"Who says that?"

Fearless chuckled. "I don't know, they're probably dead by now."

The White-Haired Boy laughed. He was relieved to be out of the Pits for the night. Like a weight had been lifted off his shoulders. But there was an elephant in the room. Hell, there was a blue whale in the room. Then, he turned to Fearless and said, "Why did you help me tonight?"

Fearless took a deep breath. "I don't know. I guess we have more in common than I thought."

"Like what?"

"Well, for one thing, we're both orphans."

The White-Haired Boy furrowed his brow. Confused. "I hate to break it to you, but I'm not an orphan."

Fearless shook his head in disgust. "Shit. You might as well be. Your mom hated your dad so much that she tried to kill herself."

"That's not why she did it," the White-Haired Boy croaked. A lump in his throat forming. "She's sick. Has been for a long time. If I was there, I could've helped her. I know I could have."

Fearless clocked his crudely bandaged hand. "By the looks of that hand, seems like you were pretty damn upset that someone else didn't help her, either."

The White-Haired Boy tucked his hand away. Embarrassed. He still wasn't sure what happened the day before. It was as if someone else was in control of his body. He had never felt anything like that. And he certainly didn't want to talk about it.

"Something like that," he replied eventually.

They walked in silence for a moment. Fearless took a deep breath. Then said, "Look, I heard the way that guy talked to you over the intercom. We all did. That's not a dad. Shit, that's not even a human being. That's pure evil right there. You'd be better off never going back to that place."

"I'm not sure I ever will."

"Well, you could always live here." Fearless motioned to the homeless refugees they passed that had overtaken the sidewalk. They built small shelters for themselves out of whatever they could find. Tarps. Boxes. An insulated cooler that they used to ship syn-fish, if you were really lucky. The White-Haired Boy noticed two small children sitting outside a tent. A small fire built in a waste basket was crackling between them. Their parents were inside, using a makeshift kitchen to cook a small pot of rice. The sight made the White-Haired Boy sad. An entire family confined to a tent on the street.

"Here? Even the Pits seem better than living like that."

Fearless shrugged. "It's not as bad as you think. Street people are nice. They share resources. Look out for each other. It's much more of a community than those pricks who live in those high-rises downtown."

The White-Haired Boy thought about Fearless's earlier choice of words. "Wait. You mean... you lived, here?"

"Yeah. Right here on this street." Then motioned to a few more streets. "And also there. There. And oh, there."

"What about your parents?"

Fearless chuckled. "What parents? I never knew them. I

don't even have the slightest memory of them. Not even a flash of a hug or an ice cream cone on a hot summer day. The only thing I know about them is that they left me in front of a night club. Not a firehouse. Or a convent. Or even a grocery store. A night club. *Do you have any idea how cruel you have to be to leave a baby in front of a night club and hope for the best? They might as well left me in front of oncoming traffic."*

The White-Haired Boy searched for the right words, but there was nothing you could say to someone who had been through something unimaginable. "I'm sorry."

Fearless shook his head. "It is what it is."

The White-Haired Boy chewed on this for a moment. He knew it was rude to ask, but he was dying to know. "What was it like? You know... living on the streets."

Fearless brushed him off. His answer was curt. "Cold."

The White-Haired Boy could tell he didn't want to talk about it. And quickly changed the subject.

"So, where we going?"

Fearless grinned. "The Sneaky Lizard. Where else?"

They rounded the corner of the sidewalk. A half block ahead of them was a bright green neon sign in the shape of a cartoon lizard that hung above a red door. The lizard had a mischievous look on its face, as if it was trying to forewarn you that nothing good ever happened behind these doors.

The White-Haired Boy turned to Fearless. "That's a bar."

Fearless smirked. "No shit."

"What are we going to do in a bar?"

"What do you think?" Fearless began to walk towards the red door. He motioned for the White-Haired Boy to follow. "Don't worry. I've been here a million times, just trust me."

The interior of the Sneaky Lizard, like the front door, was bathed in deep red. The lights were repurposed from an old film development lab on Earth, which gave everyone's skin a bright crimson hue. The air was thick with cigarette smoke and the noxious fumes of the bootleg liquor that they mixed in the back. Somehow, it was still better than breathing the air outside the door.

The White-Haired Boy followed closely behind Fearless as he confidently pushed through the crowd. The patrons were a rowdy bunch. A mix of crooks, scumbags and refugees that had scrounged up enough coin to buy a drink. And no one in this place was trying to have just one. The White-Haired Boy tried to play it cool. The adult strangers that surrounded them looked mildly surprised to see two adolescents in the bar, but something told him that it wasn't the strangest thing anyone had seen in this place.

Fearless confidently approached the counter and flagged down the bartender. The White-Haired Boy stood next to him. He fidgeted as he nervously glanced around the room. He whispered, "How many times did you say you've been here before?"

Fearless feigned doing the math in his head for a moment, then said, "Zero."

"What? Are you kidding me right now?"

"Been here? Sure. Been inside here? No."

The White-Haired Boy's eyes nearly fell out of his head. "We could go to jail!"

Fearless scoffed. Then laughed. "Don't be so dramatic. The cops don't come to East Tharsis. It's basically the Wild West out here."

The White-Haired Boy continued to protest, until the bartender interrupted their squabble. She had a mess of bright green hair and more curves and confidence than either of their teenage minds had ever seen, and for that matter, could fully comprehend.

The bartender took in the bruises and scrapes that dotted their faces and raised a curious eyebrow. "Rough night?"

Fearless smirked. "You don't even know the half of it." He raised two fingers. "Two. Of the good stuff."

The Bartender reached below the counter and pulled out a bottle with a yellow label with a red, fire-breathing dragon on it. Kudo. "We only serve one thing. We make it here."

"What is it?"

"Can't tell ya. It's a secret recipe. But it'll put hair on your chest. Guaranteed."

The White-Haired Boy glanced at Fearless. He softly shook his head as if to say, no way are we drinking that. Fearless grinned. Then turned back to the green-haired bartender.

"Make it a double."

"You two got ID?"

Fearless shrugged. "Do we need them?"

The bartender considered this for a moment. "Fine. I'll serve ya. But if Rico asks, it wasn't me. Capiche?"

Fearless slowly nodded. "Capiche."

As the bartender turned away to fill their glasses, The White-Haired Boy grabbed Fearless by the arm. He was concerned. "Who's Rico?"

He shrugged. "How the hell should I know?"

Fearless reached into his pocket and pulled out a thick, colorful roll of woos in various denominations. He peeled off a few bills and placed them on the counter. The White-Haired Boy eyed the roll, surprised. "Holy shit. How much is that?"

Fearless glanced at the woos. "I dunno. Enough. I guess."

"Where'd you get that much cash?"

Fearless sighed. "The Pits. Rich people slip it to me sometimes after a fight. It's blood money."

The White-Haired Boy clocked his uneasiness. "If you make that much money, then why do you still fight? You could go get an apartment in the city or something."

Fearless considered this for a moment. Then shrugged. "The streets are the only family I've ever had. I'd miss it too much, I guess."

The bartender placed two glasses of Kudo before them. She glanced around the room, then lowered her voice. "Listen, I shouldn't be telling you this... but I'm doing a private show in the back room tonight. Normally it's two hundred woos a pop. But I'm willing to give you a special discount. Fifty woos each."

Without hesitating, Fearless peeled off a few more bills and placed them on the counter.

"Keep the change."

The bartender winked and stuffed them in her cleavage. "See you boys in a few."

The White-Haired Boy's eyes ticked to Fearless, in awe of his confidence. Fearless handed him one of the glasses of Kudo, and said, "Here's to new friends."

The White-Haired Boy couldn't help but smile. "To new friends."

Clink! *They touched glasses and threw the Kudo down their throats. They recoiled, struggling to keep the mystery liquor down. After a moment, they both managed to swallow it. The White-Haired Boy wiped the leftover liquid from his lips.*

"Tastes like gasoline."
Fearless winced. "I think it was."

The White-Haired Boy and Fearless sat in a small room the size
of a photobooth on an old brown leather bench that was meant
for one adult, its yellow foam filling bursting through the seams.
In front of them was a glass window with an accordion shade.
The White-Haired Boy turned to Fearless. Confused.
    "Are you sure we're in the right place?"
    Fearless shrugged. "I think so. It was either this room or the
bathroom."
    WHOOSH!
    The accordion shade quickly whipped up to the top of the
window frame. On the other side of the glass was a small room
with nothing in it but a single folding chair. In it sat the bartender,
wearing nothing but the shock of green hair that sat atop her
head. A bit of gin joint jazz began to crackle through a lone
speaker mounted in the corner of the room. The Bartender began
to gyrate on the folding chair, performing a seductive dance that
didn't have much rhyme or rhythm at all.
    The White-Haired Boy looked to Fearless, their jaws equally
slack. It was the first time that he had seen a real, live naked
woman. And by the look on Fearless's face, he took it that it
was his new friend's first time, too. They began to laugh, it was
a nervous yet excited giggle, the kind of sound that young boys
tend to make at this sort of thing. It was a blissful minute, one
that the two of them would remember forever.
    Boom-boom-boom!
    The door to the small room rattled on its hinges. It forcefully

swung open, revealing a thin man who wore his greasy black hair in a tight ponytail. He took in the two kids before him, less than pleased.

"What the fuck are you two doing in here? Minimum age is eighteen. I'm going to need to see some ID or I'm calling the cops.

The White-Haired Boy froze in fear. Fearless spoke for the two of them. "Rico, I presume?"

"Yeah, I'm fucking Rico. Who the fuck are you?"

Fearless confidently stood and offered his hand to shake. "Name's Double Tap."

Rico crunched his brow as he extended his hand, confused. "Double tap, what?"

"Your nut sack, you dumb fuck!"

Fearless quickly withdrew his hand, then struck Rico in the groin! Rico doubled over with a deep groan, giving the two boys a brief window to escape. Fearless quickly turned to the White-Haired Boy and motioned to the door.

"Let's go!"

But the White-Haired Boy was too busy taking in the naked bartender, desperately making a mental note of all her wonderful shapes and curves. Fearless rolled his eyes and grabbed him by the wrist, ushering him towards the door. The White-Haired Boy craned his neck as they passed Rico, shouting to the bartender as they exited—

"I'll never forget you!"

The two boys stumbled down the dark hallway that led to the sleeping quarters, drunk on a cocktail of Kudo and teenage hormones. Their delirious giggles echoed throughout the hallway as the recounted the night's events, a night that the White-Haired Boy would not soon forget.

When, suddenly, Fearless let out a soft cry. He was doubled over. His jaw clenched. The White-Haired Boy grabbed his friend by the shoulders, trying to keep him upright. That's when he saw it. The blood. It was pouring from Fearless's abdomen. The White-Haired Boy's eyes frantically searched the hallway for an assailant. And that's when he saw him. Standing in the shadows. It was Number Twenty-One. His split forehead was haphazardly stitched back together with a needle and thread. In his hand was an eight-inch hunting knife. The majority of which was covered in blood. Which meant Fearless's wound was deep.

The White-Haired Boy could feel the blood pulsing in his veins. His fingertips pulsated. It was a primal response. One he hadn't felt before. He didn't feel the need to run away. Not this time. His body wanted him to do something else. It wanted revenge.

Crack!

With blinding speed, the White-Haired Boy struck Number Twenty-One with his fist in the forehead along his stitches. The larger boy stumbled backwards, clutching his forehead. He cried out in pain, his hunting knife falling to the floor. The White-Haired Boy advanced on him, throwing a low-kick to his knee cap, dislocating it. Number Twenty-One slumped to the floor. It was the fight they never had.

The White-Haired Boy picked up the hunting knife and wiped Fearless's blood off on his shirt. He stood over the defenseless boy. Ready to strike.

Number Twenty-One raised his hand. "Wait... Please... I wasn't tying to kill him... I swear..."

But the White-Haired Boy was out of mercy. He knelt down next to Number Twenty-One. And raised the hunting knife high in the air. Ready to plunge it in his chest. When—

Thwap!

Someone grabbed him by the wrist. It was Fearless. He slowly shook his head. "He's not worth it."

The White-Haired Boy slowly lowered the knife. He lingered over Number Twenty-One for a moment. Considering his options. "Fine. I won't kill him—"

His eyes ticked to the tattoo on the other boy's arm. The crude skull and crossbones. It shimmered with sweat in the darkness. The White-Haired Boy smirked. He had an idea.

"I'm just going to take a souvenir to remember him by."

And then, the White-Haired Boy plunged the hunting knife into his arm and began to savagely carve out the faded tattoo. It would be a slow, methodical process. After all, he didn't want to leave any ink behind.

Number Twenty-One began to scream.

Then screamed some more.

-EIGHT-

"POUNCEY"

They had been promised robots. Robots that could terraform inhabitable moons. Robots that could build skyscrapers in a sea of liquid methane. Robots that would turn an acidic atmosphere into breathable air. When the government broke ground on Mars, they promised it would be the first and last planet terraformed by humans, a process which had cost countless civilian lives. They were told that the field of robotic innovation was moving at an incredible pace. But in the end, the only robots humanity got were robots that could mix drinks. And even then, they still made for shitty bartenders. Which is what made the sight of one of the loathed bartending robots turned safecracker so remarkable. Especially in a shitty little pawn shop in a shitty little place like East Tharsis.

Fearless and Vicious stood on the other side of the counter, mesmerized. The robot had humanoid features with latex skin stretched over its metal skeleton, which gave him a nightmarish facade. In one hand, it held a drill that was currently obliterating the locking mechanism of a heavy steel safe. In the other, a cocktail shaker. It turned its head toward them. It knew it was being watched.

"What'll it be, cowboy?" The robot spoke with the high-pitched twang of a Southern school girl.

Fearless cleared his throat. And whispered to Vicious. "That's a dude, right?"

Vicious deadpanned, entranced by the robot. "I'm not sure about anything at this point."

A gruff female voice called out from the other side of the room. "I see you've met Bernard."

Pouncey limped into the room. She had a robotic leg from the knee down, repurposed from Bernard. Her silver hair was slicked back, which gave it an almost chromium quality. Likely somewhere in her mid-sixties, she wasn't the dashing safecracker they'd come to expect from the movies. She looked like a pirate who had sailed every corner of the solar system and could most certainly hold her own, even at her age.

Fearless was genuinely terrified of her. Managing only a simple, "Hi."

Vicious took the lead. "I take it you're Pouncey."

She mulled this over in her head for a moment. "That depends who sent you."

"Goldie."

Pouncey chuckled wistfully, as if remembering a past lover. "Well, in that case, yes, I am Pouncey. How's my protégé doing? Still knocking off diamond dealers in the rock district?"

Fearless and Vicious traded a glance. Clearly she didn't know *who* Goldie worked for these days and they weren't about to out their friend.

"Goldie's in the import-export business now," Vicious said as he placed the titanium briefcase on the table. "And she told us that you might be able to open this."

Pouncey ran her hand over the case as if it was a fine fur, admiring its texture and metallic coat. "Ah yes, the McCallister X-7 attaché. Made of pure, single origin titanium with double magnetic tungsten-reinforced locks that require two separate three-digit alpha numeric codes that change every fifteen minutes. It's waterproof, fireproof, bulletproof—and if you had one, nuclear bomb proof. It's utterly impenetrable."

Fearless raised an eyebrow. "So can you open it or what?"

"No."

Vicious recoiled. "What? Goldie said that if anyone can open it, it's you."

"That's true. But *that* case has a vibration-sensitive failsafe. Try to drill into it and even the steadiest of human hands will set off an internal infrared flash that will incinerate anything and everything inside."

Fearless chimed in. "Like a hard drive?"

"Exactly like a hard drive."

Vicious took a deep breath. "Well, do you know anyone else that can open it?"

She smiled. "In fact, I do." And motioned to the robot behind her. "Bernard."

Bernard turned to them and repeated what seemed like the only phrase he knew. "What'll it be, cowboy?"

Fearless cringed. "That never gets any less weird."

Vicious brushed him off, continuing their negotiation. "And how much is it going to cost *Bernard* to open it?"

"Fifty thousand woo."

Fearless interjected, shocked. "You want fifty thousand woo? To open a fuckin' briefcase?"

She smiled and nodded. Unfazed. "Yes. I do."

"Even though the robot is going to do all the work."

"Yes."

"But he's a *robot*."

Pouncey's eyes narrowed as she took in Fearless. "And who do you think programs the robot?"

Vicious cut off Fearless before he could do any more damage. "OK, listen, Pouncey. I'm gonna level with you. We don't have fifty thousand woo. And we need it done *today*. To be perfectly frank, opening that case is a matter of life and death to me."

She smiled. A big, sincere grin. "Well. Then I wish you well in the afterlife. Thanks for stopping by!"

Fearless held a finger up to Pouncey. "Just give us one second, would you?" He grabbed Vicious by the arm and led him to the opposite corner of the pawn shop, out of earshot. Fearless lowered his voice.

"Look, I know you don't want to, but why don't you just call him and ask for the money?"

Vicious looked at him quizzically. "Call *who*?"

"Your dad."

"What? No. Is that a joke? And say what? *Hi Dad, I killed a drunk in a moment of blind rage and now it turns out that the Europa Crew put a hit on my head, although we can't be sure it was them because we don't have any actual evidence, which is why we need to open an impenetrable briefcase to verify whether or not a lucrative hard drive is inside in order to determine the possibility that someone in our own organization was trying to kill us to obtain it.*"

Fearless chewed on this for a moment. Then said, "Yeah, pretty much."

"We don't have that kind of relationship. Or any relationship for that matter. So the answer is no."

From the other side of the room, Pouncey's voice rang out. "You know, there is one favor you could do me."

Vicious turned to her, intrigued. "What kind of favor?"

"A fifty thousand dollar favor. But… there's a catch. It's no questions asked. Just a yes or a no. Right now."

Fearless and Vicious traded a glance. Pouncey was their only hope. And they didn't have much of a choice.

Vicious turned back to her. "Fine. We'll do it."

Pouncey looked them up and down. Then shook her head, as something had just occurred to her. "Those clothes aren't going to work. Neither is your car. In order to go where you're going, you'll need a cover. And I think I have just the thing. Meet me around back."

As Pouncey disappeared into the back, Fearless raised an eyebrow to Vicious—*just what exactly are we getting ourselves into?*

Pouncey stood next to a white work van. The word RICKY'S was emblazoned across the exterior in hot electric pink writing, as if it was the cover of a 1980s workout video. Fearless and Vicious stood on the other side of the rear parking lot with their arms folded. Whatever they were about to get into, they weren't happy about it.

Vicious motioned to the van. "What the hell is *that*?"

Pouncey grinned. "*This* is your cover."

"It's a *van*."

"Indeed it is," Pouncey said as she gave the exterior an affectionate pat. "The other day, some kid came in and pawned this catering van he stole."

Vicious grumbled. "What's the job?"

"Glad you asked. Tonight, the Sapphire Gala, the most coveted ticket in all of Tharsis City, is taking place at the home of the Mo Hadid in the Waterford Estates, the rightful heir to the throne of what used to be known on Earth many years ago as the Ottoman Empire and who is currently one of the wealthiest people in the entire solar system."

Vicious raised an eyebrow. "What's the catch?"

"The catch is that Mo owes me a million woo." Pouncey gritted her teeth. Her demeanor suddenly turned bitter. "Bring Mo to me and in exchange I'll open your briefcase."

Fearless interjected. Skeptical. "So, you want us to kidnap this guy Mo. Easy. But, uh, one quick question— how the hell do you expect us to get into the *Sapphire Gala* in the *Waterford Estates*, of all places?"

Pouncey grinned mischievously as she turned and opened the van's back door. She reached inside and grabbed two crisp white button down shirts. Each of them had a pink bowtie dangling from the next. Its hue matched the van's exterior perfectly.

Fearless deadpanned. "You have got to be shitting me. You want us to pretend to be caterers?"

Her eyes narrowed. "Yes. I do. Do you want me to open the case or not?"

Fearless turned to Vicious and whispered. "Caterers? What is this? A bad heist movie?"

Vicious grumbled back. "You got a better idea?"

Fearless mulled this over for a moment. "Not really, no."

Vicious turned back to Pouncey. "Fine. We'll do it."

"Terrific." Pouncey grinned as she approached them. She held out both hands. In one hand were the keys to the van. In the other was a small tablet. She handed both to Vicious.

"This tablet has everything you need to know. I'll take care of the rest."

Vicious took the keys and tablet with a nod. He turned to exit the parking lot, motioning Fearless to follow. "Let's go."

Pouncey called after them. "Oh, and fellas—"

They slowly turned back to her. She grinned.

"Be careful. Mo's a feisty one."

The Waterford Estates was the most exclusive neighborhood in all of Tharsis City—and maybe the entire solar system. If the glittering skyscrapers and their marble-accented penthouses downtown was considered "new money," then the Waterford Estates was "old money." *Very old.* Located high in the Martian hills that looked down upon the glittering Tharsis skyline, it was a gated community with fortified walls and its own private security team so heavily armed that it could fight off an insurrection with ease. The thirteen homes within its walls were immaculate family compounds, full of priceless heirlooms and works of art that were passed down from generation to generation of the descendants of the kings, queens, lords, and barons who resided in them. The residents were the last vestige of Earth-born royalty in the solar system—and they were determined to keep their bloodlines moving forward. At any cost.

A half-dozen cars waited in line at the estate's main entrance, which featured a twenty-foot tall stainless steel gate that when closed formed a solid gold "W." At the front of the line, a team of security guards were in the midst of performing a bomb sweep of a flower delivery truck. The driver had his hands on the truck and his legs spread while he received a full, more-than-intrusive pat down.

Halfway through the line of cars, Fearless and Vicious idled in the white catering van. They had since traded in their ruffled suits and were now wearing the crisp white dress shirts with matching pink bowties. Fearless tugged at the neck of his shirt as he took in his new wardrobe in the rearview mirror.

"I look ridiculous."

Vicious rolled his eyes. "Will you get over it? It's just a bowtie."

"To *you*. To me it's a prison sentence."

Feeling anxious, Fearless craned his neck to see around the other cars. He cringed as he took in the flower truck driver, who had the scarred look of a man who had just been through a twenty-four-hour police interrogation for a crime he didn't commit. He turned back to Vicious.

"Going a little hard on the flower boy, don't you think?"

Vicious took in the sight of the security guard and the assault rifles they clutched in their hands with trepidation. "Security's clearly not taking any chances tonight. That's for sure."

Fearless motioned to the tablet in Vicious's hand. The one that Pouncey had given them.

"You got a picture of this Fat Mo? I wanna know what we're dealing with here."

Vicious handed Fearless the tablet. He tapped it on and clocked the photo on screen. Fat Mo was anything but fat. She was a petite woman of Middle Eastern descent who wore her hair in one long elaborate braid. She didn't wear makeup, and, from what Fearless could tell, she didn't wear any jewelry either. Her nickname was an odd choice, given that she likely weighed maybe one hundred pounds soaking wet.

Fearless turned to Vicious with an incredulous glare. "*This* is Fat Mo?"

"That's what the file says. What were you expecting?"

"Well, I don't know—someone fat?"

Vicious shrugged. "Just because her nickname is Fat Mo doesn't mean she has to be fat. Take Skinny Vinny for instance. We call him skinny but he's actually fat. It's the opposite."

Fearless let out an exasperated exhale. "We call Skinny Vinny 'Skinny' *because* he's fat. Which makes it funny. It doesn't work the other way around."

Vicious rolled his eyes. "OK, fine. What about Nico Nine Fingers? We call him Nine Fingers because he can't shoot worth shit. Not because he actually has nine fingers."

"What does that have to do with calling an obviously skinny person like Mo, fat?"

"It doesn't. I'm just giving you an example."

"Well it's a shitty example."

Boom boom boom!

Two armed security guards appeared on either side of the van. They motioned with their assault rifles for the two to exit the vehicle. Fearless turned to Vicious with a glint of sarcasm in his voice.

"Well, if the Europa Crew or the Red Dragon doesn't kill us, these assholes *definitely* will."

Fearless and Vicious climbed out of the van. The security guards directed them to place their hands along the hot pink lettering of the van's exterior. One of the security guards approached them and procured a small handheld tablet. "Vendor name?"

Vicious motioned to the bright pink lettering beneath his hands. "Isn't obvious?"

The security guard wasn't in the mood for chit-chat. "You want to work the gala or not, asshole?"

Vicious sighed. "Ricky's Catering."

The security guard slowly scanned the tablet, "You're in luck. On the list."

Fearless breathed a sigh of relief. And softly whispered to Vicious. "You know, I kind of thought Pouncey was full of shit, but—"

"Where's the rest of your team?" the security guard snapped.

Vicious was caught off guard. "What do you mean, *team?*"

The security guard motioned to the tablet. "Says here there's supposed to be twelve caterers. Where are they?"

Fearless grumbled. "I take it back. Fuckin' Pouncey…"

Vicious stammered as he tried to drum up an excuse. "Oh, well, about that, the thing is, the other guys—"

Fearless could see he was drowning. So he did what he did best. Lied.

"Are on their way. In a separate van. My partner… *Julius* and I here," Fearless motioned to Vicious, then turned back to the security guard, "are the advanced strike team. We go into the event first, establish a perimeter, optimize hors d'oeuvre passing routes, plant our flag, so to speak. Then we radio back and relay that information to the rest of the team so they hit the ground running when they arrive. You look to be some sort of highly paid, highly decorated private mercenary, I'm sure you of all people would understand this kind of clandestine operation."

The security guard's eyes narrowed—and then he put the tablet in his back pocket. He tapped his earpiece and spoke softly, "Got two coming in," then turned back to Fearless. "Go ahead before I change my mind."

Fearless turned to Vicious. And winked.

The catering van rumbled down the long driveway to the Hadid Estate, which in itself was excessive. Lined with imported California palm trees and a built-in waterway that ran down the center, the driveway featured a coordinated water fountain show that rivaled the Bellagio Casino in Las Vegas. And to think, that was before you even arrived at the home itself.

"*Holy shit.*" Fearless whispered with a childlike wonderment as he glanced out the passenger window. The Hadid Estate was not a home. It was a palace. Neoclassical in style, the exterior was constructed entirely of marble and was surrounded by grand, Corinthian pillars that wrapped around the estate. Spotlights illuminated the exterior, so brightly that it could be seen from miles away. It was a home fit for a Greek god.

Vicious steered the van into the motor court, where a security guard directed them to the side of the home. There, dozens of vendors and their trucks were lined up, unloading their goods for the evening: Exquisite flower arrangements. Dozens of lobsters and tins of caviar packed on ice. Top shelf alcohol stacked by the case. Pastries and cakes that were so elegantly decorated that they looked like works of art. It was as if a royal wedding would be taking place that evening, not simply a charity gala.

Fearless and Vicious stepped out of the van and took in the churning hospitality machine around them. Standing at the side-door that led into the house was a high-strung event coordinator with a ponytail pulled tight. She clutched a clipboard tight, furiously checking off vendors and directing them where to go inside the house.

Fearless nudged Vicious. And motioned to the door. "Looks like we got another potential roadblock."

"Just follow my lead," Vicious replied, as he opened the van's back door to reveal a large, rectangular-shaped cooler. He grabbed one side of the cooler by the handle. He motioned for Fearless to grab the other. Together, they carried the cooler towards the side-door, with Vicious leading the way. But as they got closer to the door, Vicious began to shuffle his feet and emitted a deep grunt with every step.

Fearless stared back at him. Eyes wide. He whispered, "What the hell are you doing?"

Vicious gritted his teeth. "What did I *just* say about following my lead?"

Fearless' eyed the cooler. "It's *empty*."

"*No shit!*" Vicious angrily replied, as he angrily motioned his head towards the side-door where the event coordinator stood guard.

Fearless's eyes ticked up to her. And then it clicked. *Oh. Right.* And so, like Vicious, he began to grunt and shuffle his feet. They made their way towards the side-door, the two of them bellowing and howling as if they were a pair of competitive weightlifters in the middle of a dead lift.

"Excuse me, where do you think you two are going?" the event coordinator asked with a stern tone, blocking the entrance.

Vicious motioned to the cooler. "I've got ten dozen premium cuts of Wagyu beef steak right here and we need to get it inside and into proper refrigeration, immediately. We've got no time to waste."

"Well, lucky for me, I do." The event coordinator chirped as she scanned her clipboard. "I don't see any Wagyu on my list."

Fearless raised a subtle eyebrow to Vicious, who quickly covered. "That's because this was a special order. From Ms. Hadid. Called me herself."

Her eyes narrowed. Extremely skeptical and less than enthused. "Ms. Hadid, a lifelong vegetarian and prominent animal rights activist, called you—"

Vicious smiled with an especially confident shit-eating grin. "Julius. The butcher."

As she continued her interrogation. "Julius, the butcher, in a pink bowtie, and ordered one hundred and twenty Wagyu steaks for this evening personally, even though the menu has been set for months now and consists of vegetarian and seafood options. Do I have that correct?"

"That's correct."

"I don't believe you."

Vicious scoffed. "Excuse me?"

"I don't believe you." The Event Coordinator motioned to the cooler. "Open it."

Vicious shook his head. And chuckled. "Let me get this straight, you want me to open this cooler of rare Wagyu beef, from cows that were imported from Earth, where they now live on the planet's floating islands on a diet of specially grown Japanese grass, before they were cut, wrapped, and placed in this cooler, packed with eighty pounds of dry ice to ensure it was kept at a perfect twenty-eight degrees Fahrenheit to preserve flavor, and now, you want me to *open* said cooler, out here, exposing the meat to the Martian air and potentially degrading the quality of the meat by a full letter grade before the *Sapphire Gala* just to prove a point?"

Vicious's words of warning landed on the event coordinator. She mulled this over for a moment. Then motioned inside.

"The walk-in refrigerator is located in the southeast corner of the kitchen."

Vicious smiled. "Thank you. Myself, and the succulent cuts of Wagyu, appreciate it."

They hoisted the cooler back up, and continued their shuffling and groaning act as they walked inside the estate and into the industrial kitchen bustling with vendors and chefs alike. Vicious directed traffic as they maneuvered the empty cooler through the throng and into the walk-in refrigerator in the far corner of the kitchen. "*Out of the way! Out of the way!*"

They stepped inside the walk-in refrigerator and locked the door behind them. Fearless turned to Vicious, positively giddy. "That was *incredible*. How do you know so much about Wagyu beef?"

Vicious shrugged. "When I was a kid, my father got into a screaming match with a chef at a five-star restaurant about the way he stored his Wagyu. I guess sometimes it pays to be a rich asshole."

Fearless chuckled as he loosened his pink bowtie. He closed his eyes as he rubbed his neck. "*Goddamn*, that feels good."

"Shit," Vicious quipped.

Fearless opened one eye. "Shit, *what*?"

"We blew our cover. We're not caterers. We told that woman with the clipboard that we're butchers. And they're sure as hell not going to let two butchers walk around the Sapphire Gala in cheap shirts and pink bowties."

"So what do we do?"

Vicious took a deep breath. And exhaled. His breath turning into a white cloud of moisture in the walk-in refrigerator.

"We're going to need some more formal attire."

-NINE-

"The Sapphire Gala"

The sun had set on Tharsis City and with it, the home of Monique Hadid. The guests slowly began to trickle in, one by one, each arriving in a car more expensive than the next. However, none of these guests would be driving themselves. They had chauffeurs, ones that were required to stay parked outside the estate for the entire evening, and, more importantly, don a half-decent black suit and tie at all times.

Hiding in the dark catering van, Fearless and Vicious discreetly watched as the drivers dropped off their guests at the estate's main entrance and then parked their cars along the edge of the driveway's synchronized fountain. Each driver then exited their cars and stood by them, where they would remain until the evening was over.

"Look at these guys," Vicious marveled. "They drive these rich assholes around all day and then have to stand by their cars all night while their bosses party. What kind of job is that?"

Fearless chuckled. "That sounds a hell of a lot like what we do, Vicious."

"At least we're going somewhere with our lives."

"Are we, though?"

Vicious considered this. It was a fair point. So far all the Red Dragon had brought them was a lot of long nights disposing of dead bodies and a brush with death at the hands of an assassin of unknown origin. He cracked his neck. "Alright. Let's make this quick. Find someone your size. Meet on the mezzanine level. Got it?"

Fearless nodded. He quickly exited the van and quietly made his way toward the long line of high-end cars and their chauffeurs standing guard outside them. He moved along the passenger side of the cars, careful to keep a low profile to keep himself hidden and only stopping to size up the chauffeurs. *Too tall. Too short. Too muscular. Too thin.* Until finally, he found a match. The driver of a classic black Rolls Royce Corniche. He was just a kid. About Fearless's age. With a slender build and a shock of black hair. If it was any other night, Fearless thought, perhaps they could have met at a bar. Struck up a conversation. They would have a beer. Or probably three. Maybe they would have become friends. But tonight was not that night. He wondered if he'd ever have a night like that ever again.

The young chauffeur lit a cigarette. He took a drag and exhaled a plume of smoke into the Martian night. When, suddenly—

Fearless silently wrapped his arm around his neck, hooking the chauffeur with his elbow and applying just enough pressure to put him to sleep. His body went limp. And he began to snore. Fearless plucked the cigarette that dangled from the kid's mouth. Took a drag. And exhaled a plume of smoke. Then dragged his body into the darkness.

From the home's mezzanine level, Fearless and Vicious, now appropriately dressed in their respective chauffeur's suits, peered over a railing that looked down onto the grand atrium where the gala was being held. One hundred and fifty guests, each hand-picked by the Sapphire Gala's board of directors mingled about in the event's required black tie formalwear. A stage anchored the room, where a twelve-piece jazz band played an upbeat, brassy piece while drone-waiters zipped through the crowd with trays of perfectly balanced champagne flutes and bites of caviar. They were taking in how the other half lived from their bird's eye perch, when an elegant young woman in a flowing, shimmering gold ballgown took the stage. This was Monique Hadid, the last surviving family member of an empire that once ruled the known world. The jazz band's ditty softly came to a stop as the crowd showered her with praise in the form of a standing ovation. She took a moment to acknowledge them with a polite wave, then stepped up to the microphone.

"Friends, family, colleagues, and all the esteemed guests from across the many industries that continue to make Tharsis City thrive, on behalf of my family, I would like to welcome you to our home in celebration of the one hundred and twenty-second annual Sapphire Gala..."

Fearless chuckled. "Fat Mo. The nickname doesn't make any sense." He craned his neck, admiring her figure. "But that dress makes a *lot* of sense, if you know what I mean."

Vicious scanned the crowd as Mo continued her speech. His eyes ticked to a man in an ill-fitting suit standing in the corner who discreetly toggled an earpiece. But it wasn't just him. There was another man by the bar. Two more situated on either side of the stage. Vicious counted at least a dozen of them spread throughout the atrium, then turned to Fearless.

"Apparently, the only thing Fat about Mo is her wallet. She's got an army of security guards watching her every move. I counted at least six heavies, all of them in constant communication. She never leaves their sight. Not for one second."

But all Fearless could do was smirk. "Well, we'll just have to go to her then, won't we?"

The sea of guests parted as Monique Hadid descended the home's grand staircase, her security detail flanking her on either side. Her gold ballgown softly swayed as she made her way through the crowd toward the bar situated at the center of the atrium. As she reached the counter, the twenty-something year old bartender stood stiff with nerves, ready to take her order when a familiar voice chimed in.

"She'll have a scotch. Something over fifty years old. From Earth. But nothing from a port barrel, of course, which she finds far too sweet." The voice belonged to Fearless, who leaned against the bar. Monique took him in, impressed with his approach. She glanced at her security detail, who peeled away to give her some private time. Monique turned to Fearless. Her lips curling to a smile.

"Impressive. But you forgot one detail." She turned to the bartender. "One ice cube—" Then back to Fearless, "To take the bite off."

Fearless raised an eyebrow. "An ice cube? In a fifty year old Earth scotch? A sin."

"It's only a sin if you don't finish it."

Fearless called out to the bartender. "Make it two." Then turned back to Monique. He grinned. *That* grin. It was electric between them. They held each other's gaze as the bartender returned with their tumblers of scotch. Fearless clutched his tumbler, then raised it to her.

"To you. To tonight."

They clinked glasses. And took a satisfied sip. Monique took him. Her eyes narrowed, intrigued by the forwardness of this mysterious stranger.

"I didn't get your name?"

Fearless took another sip of scotch in order to buy himself a few more seconds. His eyes flicked to a bottle of Johnny Walker perched on the shelf behind the bar. Then back to Monique.

"John. John Weston."

She offered her hand. "Monique Hadid."

"I'm familiar," Fearless said, as he softly kissed her hand.

"And what do you do for a living, John Weston?"

Fearless thought quickly. "I'm in the high-end liquor distribution business."

She smiled. "Ah. That explains how you were able to pull off that party trick."

"I wouldn't call it a party trick. It's more of a skill. I like to think what a person chooses to drink will tell you a lot about who they are."

"And what is my drink telling you about me?"

"That you're going to take me upstairs."

Monique raised an eyebrow at his cocksure attitude. "Is that so?"

Fearless grinned. "That's right."

She took a sip of scotch as she contemplated this for a moment, then leaned close to him in order to whisper in his ear, just out of the range of her security detail.

"Five minutes. The east wing. Past the elevators. Third door on the right."

Fearless motioned to the security detail nearby. "What about them?"

"Don't worry. They'll leave us be. For however long it is we'll need." Monique winked at Fearless as she finished off the rest of the scotch, then turned to a nearby guest waiting to greet her. Fearless turned and slowly walked away from the bar. From across the room, Vicious approached and met him in stride.

"Well?"

Fearless grinned. "I'm meeting her upstairs in five minutes."

"Nice work. I'll hide in the room. We'll take her down when she's distracted."

Fearless cleared his throat. "Yeah, listen, so about that. This chick into me. Like *really* into me. So, I'm going to go in solo. And I'll let you know when we're, uh, finished."

"Are you shitting me?"

"She's like the third richest person in the solar system. And she's *hot*. Besides, you're the one who dragged me into this mess. The least you can do is let me have a little fun before we die. Potentially."

Vicious grumbled. "Fine. I'll wait down here. By the bar. Don't make me wait too long."

"Don't worry," Fearless grinned as he continued toward the grand staircase that led to the upper mezzanine. "I will."

Fearless took off his suit jacket and set it on the antique four post bed. He ran his hand across the bed's crisp linens, they were cool to the touch. They *felt* expensive. He slowly sipped his scotch as he paced around the immaculate bedroom, taking in the twenty foot ceilings and the way the plush carpet felt beneath his feet. He wondered what it would be like to wake up in a place like *this* every morning. If people like her enjoyed it. Or if they just had grown so accustomed to living in such opulence that it all had become normal. Whatever normal meant to them, that is.

"I see you've found it, Mr. Weston." Monique slowly closed the door behind her. She smiled as she slowly strolled toward him. Fearless took her in. The truth was, something about her intimidated him. Maybe it was her lifestyle. Or her confidence. Whatever it was, it felt different. And Fearless liked different.

"I'm surprised your security detail wasn't waiting here for me," Fearless replied.

"Like I said, they give me my space when I need it. Besides, they're more than happy to stay down by the bar and have a few drinks on the clock. Trust me."

Monique grabbed Fearless by the tie and softly kissed him. Then, to his surprise, she softly bit him on the bottom lip, drawing the faintest amount of blood. Fearless raised an eyebrow. *This* was not what he expected. She forcefully pushed him onto the bed on his back. They began to furiously kiss as she climbed on top of him, their clothes quickly coming off in pieces and landing on the plush carpet below. Then something caught her eye. Fearless followed her gaze. She was staring at his suit jacket, the one he had left on the bed. The inside of which was now on full display. Along with the initials that were embroidered inside it.

DLO.

143

Monique slowly turned back to Fearless. "I thought you said your name was John Weston."

Fearless knew she had him dead to rights. Unfortunately for him, their sexy-time had come to a close. And it was time to carry on with the mission at hand. *Kidnapping Fat Mo.*

"It was. Downstairs, at least."

Monique quickly reached for her fire red, five-inch Louboutin stiletto. She cocked it high above her head, ready to strike. Fearless clocked it with a slight shrug. Surely, it would sting. But how much damage could a luxury shoe really inflict? When, to his surprise, he heard—

Ching!

A thin, however menacing three-inch blade emerged from the stiletto's heel. *Shit.* Fearless barely had time to react, managing to catch the shoe's heel as the tip of the blade danced over his jugular vein. He gritted his teeth. She was stronger than he expected. *Much stronger.*

"Would you just chill out?! I'm not going to kill you!"

Mo pressed the heel harder into his neck. "Then what the fuck are you doing here, huh?"

"I was just going to kidnap you! *That's all.*"

Mo's eyes narrowed. "Who sent you?!"

Fearless struggled to catch his breath. "I wish I could tell you, but it's kind of a need-to-know basis!"

"I think I fucking need to know. Tell me or I'll bleed you out all over this hand-woven, imported linen!"

Mo pressed the tip of the blade into his skin. Blood began to slowly trickle out of Fearless's neck, drop by drop…

Fearless gurgled. She didn't leave him much choice. "Alright! It was Pouncey! OK? Pouncey!"

Just the mention of the name hit Mo like a sledgehammer. She loosened the stiletto's grip on Fearless's neck and rolled off of him. Fearless quickly dove off the bed and onto the floor. He scrambled across the carpet on all floors and then popped up to his feet. A safe distance now between them. "Are you insane?! Who tries to stab someone with a shoe?!"

But Mo didn't react. She just laid flat on her back, staring at the ceiling. Her eyes began to well with tears. "Why would Pouncey want to *kidnap* me?"

Fearless furrowed his brow. "How the hell should I know? It was a job."

"How much?"

"What do you mean, how much?"

"How much did she offer you to kidnap me?"

Fearless winced. "That's not important."

Mo slowly turned her head toward him. The way she glared at him would put the fear of God in any mortal man. "Tell me how much. Or I will scream. Then all six of my security guards will burst through that door. And blow you to pieces."

Fearless took a deep breath. And relented. "Fifty thousand woo."

Mo let out a primal, guttural cry. The kind of cry that a toddler emits in the middle of a toy store when they don't get their way. A cry, by design, that is used to alert every human being and animal with ears in a five-mile radius.

Fearless ran to her side. Not to comfort her—but to cover her mouth and somehow muffle the screech that was pouring from her. He pleaded with her, "Will you shut up?!"

Mo continued to bellow through Fearless's hand. "Iftee owsound ooo? Ats it?"

Just then the bedroom door swung open. And in that moment,

Fearless's life flashed before his eyes. But the images he saw weren't of his family. Or friends. Or people in general. It was of food. Mostly.

"What the *fuck* is going on in here?"

The concerned voice belonged to Vicious. He cocked his head sideways, confused by the sight of Fearless holding his hand over a crying woman's mouth as she lay on a bed.

Fearless breathed a sigh of relief. "Thank God it's you."

Vicious motioned to Mo. "What are you doing to that poor girl?"

Fearless crossed his arms in frustration. "Nothing! *Clearly.* Because the past two times I *actually* thought I was going to get laid I had my wallet stolen and almost got stabbed. So, frankly, I'm a little hurt and also starting to doubt that anyone is ever going to love me."

Vicious stared back, wide-eyed. "OK, look, we can talk about your... *issues* later. Because right now, I need you to explain to me what the hell is going on before Mo's security gets suspicious and kills all three of us."

Fearless took a deep breath. "Look. I just tried to explain to Mo here that I wasn't here to *kill* her. I was here to *kidnap* her. Next thing I know, she had this super sharp scary shoe to my neck that was also a knife and demanded to know who sent me, so I said Pouncey, and then she freaked out."

Mo began to bellow again. Fearless sighed. "Like this."

Vicious approached them and carefully sat next to Mo on the bed. "Look, Mo. Obviously there's some history between you and Pouncey. Is that right?"

Mo snotted as she nodded her head.

Vicious continued. "Well, what if I told you, we could bring you to Pouncey—and you two could sort this out on your own?"

Mo chewed on this for a moment as she wiped away her snot. "I'd like that. But, the um, the thing is, my security team won't let me leave the compound alone."

"Surely you could sneak out the back?"

Mo shook her head. "This house is covered in cameras. By the time we stepped foot outside, they would shoot you dead on sight. I'm a prisoner here. That's how my parents wanted it. They want me to be alone. *Forever.*"

Fearless and Vicious traded a glance. They looked at each other knowingly, as if to say, *there is one other option.* Vicious turned back to Mo.

"Do you think you'd fit inside a cooler?"

Just before sunrise, the catering van pulled into the rear parking lot of the pawn shop. Pouncey was waiting for them, arms folded, Bernard at her side. Their faces shared a similar look—they weren't expecting much from them.

Fearless and Vicious exited the catering van. The bags under their eyes, like their feet that slowly shuffled across the parking lot, were heavy. It had been a long night. Pouncey slowly shook her head.

"Well, well, well. Look who it is. Those aren't the faces of two men who were successful, wouldn't you agree, Bernard?"

Bernard slowly shook his head. *No.* Even the robot was bagging on them. Until, Fearless and Vicious opened either side of the catering van's rear doors. They reached inside and pulled out the long cooler and set it on the asphalt. It furiously rocked from side-to-side.

Pouncey took in the cooler, concerned. "I told you to kidnap *Mo*. Not bring me back some kind of wild animal."

Fearless gritted his teeth. "Well, as it turns out they're one and the same."

He kicked open the cooler, and out popped Mo. She feverishly staggered around the parking lot in her gold ballgown, the purple mascara running down her face. She let out an angry, raspy snarl as she directed her rage at Fearless and Vicious.

"What the *fuck*? You said I'd be in that *stinky* cooler just until we left the house! Not until we drove all the way to… where are we again?"

Pouncey chimed in. "East Tharsis."

Mo continued to rage, "All the way to East fucking Tharsis!" But then, it occurred to her who the voice across the parking lot belonged to. "Pouncey?"

Pouncey softly smiled. "Hello, dear."

Mo ran over to her. They embraced and held each other tight. The two of them stroking each other's hair and crying in between deep, passionate kisses. Vicious slowly turned to Fearless, absolutely dumbfounded by the sight.

"I was not expecting… this."

Pouncey turned to them with tears streaming down her face. "Thank you for reuniting us. You see, Mo's family never approved of our relationship. They said I was too old. Too poor. Not good enough for their Monique. They hid her away in that compound with a team of security guards who were not meant to protect her, but to keep her locked up, and us apart, forever."

Fearless stared back, dumbfounded by the realization. "Glad we could help."

Vicious cleared his throat. "Not to sully your star-crossed reunion here, but I believe we had a deal."

Pouncey smiled. "But of course."

Fearless and Vicious watched intently as Bernard took a magnesium oxide torch to the titanium briefcase's locking mechanism. The torch burned bright blue as his hand moved in a perfectly steady rhythm, unaffected by the heat.

Vicious's eyes turned to Pouncey, who stood nearby. "You're *sure* he's not going trip that failsafe and destroy what's inside?"

Pouncey scoffed at the notion. "Of course not. Bernard is the best in the safe-cracking business. After all, I *am* the one who programmed him. I've given him everything I know."

Fearless grumbled. "Once a shitty robot bartender, always a shitty robot bartender. If you ask me."

Click. The briefcase unlocked. Bernard slowly backed away. And announced the completion of the task at hand. "*Here you are. Next round's on me, Cowboy.*"

Fearless and Vicious traded a glance. *Holy shit.* The moment of truth had arrived. They slowly approached the case. Vicious took a deep breath. Then slowly opened it. They peered inside. But they said nothing. Neither of them a single word.

Pouncey approached. And glanced inside the case. She slowly turned to Fearless and Vicious.

"I take it that's not what you were expecting find."

In a fit of rage, Fearless took the briefcase and threw it against the wall. Its contents scattered across the floor. There were dozens of them. Each identical. Mo slowly bent down and picked up one of the items. She looked at it curiously. It was roughly the size of a pack of cigarettes, with the word BICYCLE written across the top in dark blue ink. Below it, a bright red spade. A hard drive, this was not.

She turned to Fearless and Vicious curiously. They looked as if they had seen a ghost.

"Playing cards?"

~TEN~

"ANTICIPATION"

They called him Dr. Teeth. He visited the Pits once a week on Sundays in order to patch up any injuries or lingering ailments the boys had received during the weekend's fights. He was exceptionally tall and wore a bowler hat that he never, ever took off. The boys liked to joke about what he was hiding underneath that hat. Was it a terrible haircut? Or a nasty scar? Or, perhaps, did he have a metal plate inserted into his head as a child after an accident and had to wear a hat in order to block out the old FM radio signals that his head picked up from Earth? Whatever it was, Dr. Teeth looked every part a villain in a James Bond film. Unfortunately, he was anything but and had earned his nickname because he was a dentist. Humpty couldn't convince an actual medical practitioner to come do back-office treatments on his boys, so he found the next best thing. A dentist without a conscience.

"That doesn't look like a fight wound," Dr. Teeth said, as he examined the knife wound on Fearless's abdomen that he had received from Number Twenty-One. It was about two inches *long and bright pink, the beginning stages of an infection setting in. Fearless was laying on his side on an old couch that was currently being used as a makeshift exam table. Next to it was a floor lamp with the lampshade removed, which was standing in for a proper medical light.*

Fearless shrugged. "You wouldn't believe the fingernails on this kid if I showed you."

Dr. Teeth didn't appreciate the sarcasm. "You know that I'm obligated to report any suspicious injuries to Mr. Lucky, right?"

"The only thing that's suspicious," Fearless quipped, "is that hat you never take off."

"Hold still." Dr. Teeth grumbled, as he began to stitch up the wound. Fearless's eyes ticked to the White-Haired Boy, who sat in the corner. They shared a smile, the two now partners in crime and loving every second of it. Until—

The Irish Boy, aka Number Twenty-Two, stuck his head in the door. "Hey, Humpty wants to see you two when you're done."

Fearless grumbled. "Ah, shit."

"You sure it was just some fingernails?" Dr. Teeth chuckled.

"Shut up and keep sewing, Teeth," Fearless replied with an ice cold glare. His eyes ticked back to the White-Haired Boy sitting in the corner and winked. The White-Haired Boy looked down to his feet, trying not to laugh.

Humpty sat behind his old steel desk with a deep scowl. It was Sunday. And you never wanted to see Humpty on a Sunday. That's because it was his only day off during the week. The boys had heard he spent his entire Sunday at church, attending mass three to four times in a row. Sometimes he'd stay after to have a meal with the priests, or stay late into the night wiping down pews and putting hymn books back in their correct places so they would be ready for the next morning's mass. Some of the boys said they heard he was in the seminary before taking control of the Pits. Others said he spent his entire day off with God in order to try to wipe his conscience clear. Maybe both were true.

"I'm sure you two have already heard that Number Twenty-One was attacked last night," Humpty growled at Fearless and the White-Haired Boy, who were seated across from him on the other side of the desk. The two of them traded an over-the-top, faux-shocked glance that was so full of pearl-clutching shit that a portrait should've been commissioned to hang in the museum of bullshit.

"Wow, I had no idea, that's just terrible, sir," the two of them responded, in almost perfect unison.

"Save me the horse shit, fellas," Humpty snapped. "I don't know if you two were involved, but I'm willing to bet you know who was. So if you want to come clean, come clean now. Because if I find out after the fact it was you, the consequences aren't going to be pretty."

Fearless and the White-Haired Boy turned to each other and flashed a dramatic furrow of the brow, coupled with an overly serious shake of the head.

"No sir, we don't know who could do such a thing," Fearless said. "But I'll tell you what, I'm going to keep my ear to the ground. Both of us will. And together we'll bring these perpetrators to justice."

Humpty glared back, less than enthused. "I've got my eye on you two. You're dismissed."

Fearless and the White-Haired Boy rose from their chairs and headed for the door, but before they exited, Fearless turned around.

"Number Twenty-One still planning on fighting me this weekend?"

Humpty nodded. "He says his arm feels fine. So yes, he is."

"Well," Fearless grinned. "It should be quite the show."

The White-Haired Boy stood before a piece of training equipment that the same time looked ancient and downright alien in nature. It was a donation from a Chinese man who once owned a kung fu studio in East Tharsis. Built out of a single post of wood, it was a training dummy which had three foot-and-a-half long wooden pegs that jutted out from the post at various heights. The pegs represented an opponent's arms and legs, and the various positions and lines of force they created.

The White-Haired Boy stood before it, bemused. "What the hell is that?"

"This is a wing chun dummy," Fearless said. "Doesn't look like much. I was skeptical at first too. But Chinese fighters have trained in kung fu on these for centuries. Turns out it's one of the best opponents I've ever faced."

The White-Haired Boy scoffed. "I thought you said you were going to help train me? I've never even seen anyone use this thing."

"That's because the other boys don't know what the hell they're doing. Whaling on a punching bag for ten minutes is only going to make your knuckles sore. Ten minutes with the wing chun will make you a better fighter, guaranteed. The best fighters don't just train. They evolve."

The White-Haired Boy sighed. "How does it work?"

Fearless positioned himself in front of the wing chun dummy and began to go through a series of choreographed moves. He blocked one of the arms with his right wrist, then struck the dummy with his left palm. He repeated the move with the left wrist, sticking with the right palm. He slowly cycled through the three pegs, block-strike-block.

"The dummy represents your opponent," he said as he moved. "When you block their advance, you have an opportunity to strike the area they've left vulnerable. However, when you strike, they have the opportunity to strike you as well." Then, he began to move faster. The pegs responded to his attacks, like an opponent would, but Fearless never let the peg touch his body. He moved with such fluidity and grace that his hands seemed to roll over the pegs like drops of water.

The White-Haired Boy was less than impressed. "I thought this thing is supposed to teach me how to fight?"

Fearless shook his head. "Fighting isn't about knowing how to fight. It's about knowing how to anticipate. And from what I saw during your first fight, the only anticipating you did was anticipating when to run for your life."

The White-Haired Boy shrugged. "I was scared."

"You were scared because you didn't know what to expect from your opponent. You weren't scared of him. You were scared of the unknown. This dummy eliminates the unknown."

The White-Haired Boy took a deep breath and stood in front of the dummy. He tried to mimic Fearless's series of movements, but he was clumsy and awkward.

"Again," Fearless commanded.

The White-Haired Boy started over. The second time around was a little better, but not by much.

"Who's your opponent tomorrow night?" Fearless asked.

"Twenty-Two. The Irish Kid," the White-Haired Boy replied with a sheepish shrug.

"That Irish Kid has the fastest hands in the Pits," Fearless said bluntly, as he motioned to the dummy. "We're going to have to do this all night if you're going to have a shot. Again."

The Pits were sticky with humidity. It clung to everything. The fighters. The fans. Even the dirt was turning to mud. Usually the Pits were cooled with air conditioners to keep the bettors happy and continuing to gamble. However, tonight the air conditioning had broken down. Which left everyone involved extra irritable.

The White-Haired Boy was dripping with sweat. He continually wiped it from his eyes as he looked out into the crowd. He scanned the risers for a particular face, the one who had sent him to this horrid situation in the first place—but he wasn't there. Part of him was relieved. But part of him couldn't help but be disappointed.

"Hey! Are you listening to me?" Fearless scolded.

The White-Haired Boy snapped out of his search and shook the sweat from his eyes. He turned to Fearless, who was acting as his corner coach tonigh,t and nodded. He tried to put on a confident face, but on the inside he was absolutely terrified.

"Remember what I said. Don't react to him. Anticipate him!"

Ding!

A single bell rang out, signaling to the fighters that the first round was about to begin. The White-Haired Boy tapped his gloves together and trotted to the center of the ring. The Irish Boy met him there—and gave a subtle nod.

Ding! Ding! Ding!

The fight began. Fearless was right, the Irish Boy had incredibly fast hands. He peppered the White-Haired Boy with a flurry of quick, precise jabs that quickly backed the White-Haired Boy into his corner. He was utterly incapable of fighting back, the Irish Boy was far too fast. His only option was to hold his gloves high and block the flurry of blows as best as he could.

"Get out of the corner! Run for your life!" Fearless shouted.

The White-Haired Boy absorbed a few more blows, then managed to duck under the Irish Boy and escape back to the center of the ring. The White-Haired Boy looked frantically in Fearless's direction. Fearless responded with a calming hand, silently telling his friend to relax his nerves. And then, he mouthed his mantra again.

"Don't fight. Anticipate."

The White-Haired Boy nodded. He danced in the center of the ring, waiting for the Irish Boy to come to him. His opponent followed suit, peppering the White-Haired Boy with two quick jabs—but the White-Haired Boy somehow dodged them!

The Irish Boy advanced on him again, throwing two quick lefts, then a right—but again, the White-Haired Boy danced and dodged out of the way!

Suddenly, the sparse crowd in the risers began to stir. It had seemed that this strange boy with all-white hair, the one who literally ran out of the ring during his previous fight, was beginning to turn the tide.

Frustrated by the crowd's support of his opponent, the Irish Boy moved in for the kill shot and threw a hard right jab—

When the White-Haired Boy, channeling the wing chun, raised his right wrist and blocked it! And just as Fearless taught him, he followed the block with an immediate strike to the Irish Boy's solar plexus, sending him stumbling backwards!

The crowd roared!

Fearless pumped his fist as he shouted from the corner, "That's it! Keep pressing!"

The White-Haired Boy advanced on the Irish Boy, firing off a perfectly executed block-strike-block-strike combo! The Irish Boy was on his heels!

The crowd began to turn feverish. They began to chant. "Finish him! Finish him! Finish him!"

The White-Haired Boy's lips began to curl to a smile. This was the moment he had been waiting for. The moment where everything would change, the moment where he would become a man—

And as he threw a block, he slowly wound his arm back in order to gain enough momentum to knock out his opponent once and for all...

The Irish Boy clocked the White-Haired Boy's mistake—and saw his window. And while the crowd's darling was winding up, the Irish Boy delivered a clean uppercut right to the White-Haired Boy's jaw.

Crack!

The White-Haired Boy twisted through the air like a bruised, blood-spitting whirling dervish—and careened face first into the dirt.

Unconscious.

Snap! *A pair of hands cracked a capsule and waved it under the White-Haired Boy's nose. He was laying on a bench in the post-fight locker room. He slowly stirred at first, then feverishly sat up and violently waved his hands in front of his face, trying to diffuse the smell.*

"What the hell is that smell?" *the White-Haired Boy coughed.*

"You know, they used to be called smelling salts." *Fearless shrugged.* "But to be honest, I think it's just a bunch of really, really bad for you chemicals."

The White-Haired Boy chuckled and wiped his watering eyes. "Did I win?"

Fearless chuckled. "No. Fuck no, you didn't. You got knocked out cold. But! For a minute there, you had old Irish on his heels. The bettors in the stands were absolutely shitting their pants."

"Why are you so happy, then?" *the White-Haired Boy asked.*

"Because," *Fearless smiled,* "you anticipated. And when you anticipated, you started to win. Now all you have to do is take that into your next fight and I think you have a real shot at winning."

The White-Haired Boy clocked a fight schedule that was written on a large blackboard nearby. On it was a full breakdown of the week's fights. Who's fighting who. Win-loss records. Betting odds. Everything.

"I've got Sixteen next," *he muttered.*

"Sixteen!" *Fearless clapped his hands.* "That kid has the slowest first step I've ever seen in the Pits. You could beat him!"

The White-Haired Boy smiled sheepishly. "You think?"

"I don't think. I know. The next fight is yours."

The next morning, the White-Haired Boy and Fearless woke up early to begin training. Lately, they were always by each other's side—and it was becoming apparent to the other boys that the two of them had formed a close friendship. It wasn't unusual for the boys to become friends during their stay in the Pits. After all, they were suffering together. However, what made this friendship unusual was that it was Fearless. And Fearless didn't like anyone.

"Hey, you two," a boy called out to them. "Humpty wants to see you in his office."

Fearless and Vicious traded a confused glance.

Again?

"I'll keep this quick," Humpty said, as he loudly slurped a bowl of spicy noodles over his desk, the orange broth flecking his shirt with droplets. "Due to recent events, there's been a change to the fight schedule."

Fearless and the White-Haired Boy once again found themselves on the other side of Humpty's desk. Their eyes ticked to each other with a confused stare, until Fearless spoke up for the two of them.

"What do you mean, recent events?"

Humpty blotted his mouth with a napkin. "I'd thought you'd heard?"

The boys shook their heads. They hadn't heard anything.

"Number Twenty-One. He left this morning. That wound on his shoulder got so infected that he couldn't raise his right arm. It's too bad, really. I thought he had a shot at the title this year."

Fearless furrowed his brow. "But I was supposed to fight him next."

"That's right," Humpty said. "Hence the change of plans. You've got a new opponent."

Fearless scoffed. "Who?"

Humpty speared a pile of noodles with his chopsticks. Then grinned. He didn't have any evidence that the new found friends were involved in the attack on Number Twenty-One. But he was going to punish them anyways.

"He's sitting right next to you."

-ELEVEN-

"JOKERS WILD"

The air stunk of synthetic fish. In a new world where it felt like anything was possible, it turned out that the only thing that human beings learned to grow with some sort of success on Mars was fish. Mostly because the red soil on Mars was toxic. It was full of chlorine, which killed any crops or plants that humans tried to grow. The government tried all kinds of ways to fix it, like using dusting ships to spray the planet with highly concentrated doses of Vitamin C to neutralize the chlorine, and when that didn't work, detonating carbon bombs in hopes of completely changing the elemental makeup of the soil. Hell, they even tried to bring in dirt from Earth. But nothing worked. All the plants just continued to die, year after year.

Which is why the majority of biologists and horticulturists started growing synthetic meat in labs instead. But it never seemed like they could get that quite right either. Red meat looked the part, but tasted like high-end dog food. Poultry actually tasted the closest to the real thing, but it would spoil within hours, leading to a wave of salmonella poisonings that nearly ended civilization, at least on Mars. Fish, however, not only looked the part, but tasted like it too. The only downside was the smell, which was akin to a salmon fillet brought home from a restaurant in a to-go container, only to be forgotten and left to languish in the back of the refrigerator for months.

"It stinks up here," Vicious muttered, as he stood at the edge of the fish factory's roof with a pair of binoculars to his eyes.

"Well, *you're* the one who wanted to stake out Dodd's apartment. I warned you that he lived across from the fish factory. Which *stinks*. So, stakers can't be choosers," Fearless replied.

"That's not the expression."

Fearless shrugged. *Whatever.* He was seated in a folding chair with the titanium briefcase open on the ground next to him. Discarded empty packs of playing cards littered the roof. Fearless opened another pack and selected a card. A king of hearts. He held his lighter beneath it and set it ablaze, watching as the dour face of the sovereign slowly melted away.

Vicious lowered the binoculars and turned back to him. "Are you going to do that all night or you going to help me?"

Fearless motioned to his eyes. "Only one pair of binocs."

"I meant that we could work in shifts."

"I don't know, that kind of sounds like a *you* job. I don't think I'd be very good at it."

"So you're not going to help? At all?"

Fearless ignored him as he reached into the deck and pulled out another card. A joker. He took in the cartoon court jester and his bright red jumpsuit. His motley pattern hat, like his shoes, had bells on them. Unlike the stern king, he wore an animated grin on his face. It was as if he was trying so hard to be noticed, to stand out in this fifty-two card royal family.

"You know, I kind of feel bad for the jokers," Fearless said. "There's four kings in a deck. Four queens. Four jacks. Four aces. Four of everything else. But there's only two jokers. And for the most part, people just throw them away. Like they're nothing."

Vicious took the joker from Fearless's hand and whipped it off the roof. Fearless looked to his empty hand, then to Vicious. "What the hell is your problem?"

Vicious stood over him. He was doing a slow burn. "What's my problem? *What's my problem?* You're my problem!"

Fearless pointed to his chest with a dubious look in his eye. *Who, me?*

"Yes! You! We've been up here all fucking day waiting for Dodd to get home and all you can do is sit on your ass and light cards on fire!"

Fearless stood up. Then stepped up to Vicious. "What would you have me do, huh? This is boring as hell! Do you want me to stand there next to you and say *the eagle has landed* or whatever it is you say on stakeouts when your target finally shows up? Would that make you happy?"

Vicious clenched his jaw. He didn't take kindly to the sarcasm.

But Fearless kept at it. "Hey, I got another idea—how 'bout we high-five when we see him! Now *that* would be swell!"

Vicious drove both of his palms square into Fearless's chest and pushed him to the ground. Fearless glared back at Vicious in disbelief. And then, in one fluid move, he hopped back up to his feet. It was a brief, albeit impressive reminder of his innate athleticism that he rarely showcased.

Fearless rolled up his sleeves and approached Vicious. He clenched his fists tight. "You wanna go? Do you? Because I promise you this isn't going to end like when we were kids."

Vicious's eyes narrowed. "What's that supposed to mean?"

"You know *exactly* what it means."

There was a fire in Fearless's eyes. He was usually excruciatingly unflappable. As cool, calm, and extremely nonchalant as they come. But clearly, the push had set him off. Vicious had gone too far. Vicious exhaled. He took a moment to collect himself. "Alright, look, I'm sorry."

"Don't pull that shit again," Fearless grumbled as he sat back down in his folding chair. He reached down and grabbed a new pack of cards out of the case. And began to light them on fire.

Vicious paced in front of him. "I'm just frustrated, alright? None of this makes any sense. Why would Dodd fuck over Slade, of all people, like that? She's been the Red Dragon's number one drug distributor for *years*. There's no one better than her. And then, you get your hands on the formula for a new party drug and instead of handing the hard drives over to her to manufacture, you send her a briefcase full of playing cards and hire an assassin to shoot up the place and make it look like the drop went south?"

Fearless considered this for a moment, then replied with a matter-of-fact tone, "Yeah, pretty much."

Vicious pressed him. "But *why*?"

Fearless lit an ace of spades on fire. He shrugged as he watched it evaporate into the Martian night. "Isn't it pretty obvious? Slade's expensive."

"I don't buy it. That's a hell of a lot of theater to cut out the middle man."

Fearless sighed. "Think about it. This new party drug is going to take the solar system by storm and make everyone involved pretty goddamn rich. If you have those hard drives with the formula on them, you don't *need* Slade. You can manufacture the drug *yourself*. Which is going to *really* piss off all the other cartels. So what do you do? You take out Slade and make it look like couple of disgruntled janitors were trying to get rich, then when you find out they're still alive, you turn the entire Red Dragon against them to save face."

Vicious slowly walked back to the roof's edge. Something about the whole scenario still wasn't sitting quite right with him. He put the binoculars to his eyes again, then softly whispered to himself. *"If you want to cut out the middle man, then just cut out the middle man..."*

Fearless approached and stood next to Vicious. "Look, Dodd's a fuckin' moron. But the plan was genius, really."

At that moment across the street, the light turned on in Dodd's fifth floor apartment. He stumbled drunkenly inside, a teased-haired blonde in a leopard print bodysuit on his hip. With him were two armed Red Dragon heavies. The kind of guys who have different brass knuckles for different days of the week. Vicious passed the binoculars to Fearless, who took in the scene.

"The eagle has landed, alright. Looks like he's got a couple new friends, too. And I don't mean the stripper in the leopard print. Hiring two heavies is an odd choice for a guy who has the entire Red Dragon looking for us right now, which means either he's paranoid, or—"

"He's scared."

Fearless slowly nodded in agreement. "What's our next move?"

"Let's go give him something to be scared about," Vicious said with a grin that was worthy of his name. He was going to enjoy this. He turned and headed for the roof's maintenance door nearby, then called back to Fearless over his shoulder.

"Call Pouncey. Tell her we're going to need that catering truck."

The next morning, Fearless and Vicious waited in the catering truck outside of Dodd's apartment building. Empty coffee cups littered the dashboard. Vicious hadn't slept all night, his eyes locked on the front door and the doorman who guarded it. Fearless, on the other hand, slept soundly with his feet up on the dashboard. So soundly, in fact, that he hadn't even noticed the three times that Vicious had left the van and come back with coffee. Vicious marveled. Fearless didn't sleep like a baby. He slept like a bear hibernating in a soundproofed bomb shelter.

Just after sunrise, Dodd emerged from the apartment building's lobby with the two heavies at his side. Vicious thought they looked formidable from the roof of the factory, but now seeing them up close, he realized that they were likely a combined six hundred pounds. One wore a dual holster strap that held twin fully automatic mini-Uzi submachine guns. The other brazenly carried a sawed-off shotgun slung over his shoulder like a medieval knight carrying a sword.

Vicious shook Fearless awake. "Wake up. Dodd's on the move."

Fearless mumbled, lost in a dream. "*Mr. Crab... Please... I mean you and your people no harm... I come in peace...*"

Vicious pinched Fearless's arm. *Hard.* "*Fearless.*"

He startled awake and rubbed his arm. "Ow what the hell, man?"

"Good morning." Vicious motioned to Dodd's security detail. "They look like Red Dragon heavies to you?"

Fearless's eyes narrowed. "Red Dragon heavies don't carry in the open like that. Those two are hired guns. Black market heavies, maybe."

Vicious slowly began to put the pieces together. "So Dodd not only upgrades his security detail after the shootout at Slade's, but he hires them from outside the Red Dragon. What does that tell you?"

"That Dodd doesn't even trust the Red Dragon right now."

Vicious shook his head. "I'm telling you, something's not right."

Dodd and his heavies piled into a town car idling in the front of the apartment building. It was an older Earth model, much like the town car that Vicious and Fearless drove before it was obliterated at the hands of Spider and Karma on the highway. Just sight of the car infuriated Fearless.

"You've got to be shitting me. The guy's car gets stolen by *us* and he gets the *exact* same old piece of shit as before?" Fearless stewed for a moment, then turned to Vicious. "You think the air conditioning works?"

Vicious shrugged, "Does it matter?"

"To me, yes."

"Then probably."

Fearless shook his head. "*That motherfucker.* Screw kidnapping him, let's just *kill* him."

Vicious chuckled. "Keep your nine millimeter in your pants. We got a long day ahead of us."

As the town car pulled away, Vicious put the catering van in gear. They tailed the town car from a distance as Dodd went about his day, in search of a window of opportunity to abduct their old boss. Finding a window to pull it off without the knowledge of his new security detail, however, would prove easier said than done.

Dodd's first stop was breakfast at Tiny Mel's Big Diner, where Fearless and Vicious watched from the corner of the parking lot as their former boss sat in a window booth and ate five well done strips of synthetic bacon with a side of double well done hash browns. "A breakfast crime that should be punishable by law," Fearless said. The heavies never left his side, including when Dodd spent twenty-five minutes in the bathroom—which Vicious noted was "absolutely disgusting, but also kind of hilarious, if you think about it."

Post breakfast, Dodd's next stop was at the concrete company, which just the idea of trying to infiltrate, let alone entering in order to kidnap a Red Dragon capo, was a truly moronic undertaking. Or, as Fearless noted during their five-hour stay across the street where they waited for the new town car to emerge, trying to abduct Dodd from inside the concrete company was like "strapping a bunch of Venus Wagyu to your human meat sack and trying to poach a cub from a pack of starving lions in the middle of the jungle." Vicious disagreed, countering that it was more like "covering yourself in honey and then trying to kidnap the queen bee from the hive." However, this didn't make sense to Fearless, "because bees make honey," so technically, "covering yourself in honey might actually give you a cloaking-like ability" and thus, "abducting the queen bee would actually be easier than with the meat sack." Vicious didn't actually care about this, but Fearless couldn't stop dreaming up hypothetical food-based kidnapping scenarios, including swimming in a pool of chum full of bloodthirsty great white sharks. The problem was, he couldn't decide if the sharks would be "too distracted by the abundance of chum" and "not even notice you in the pool," and if this was "actually a better cloaking system than the honey and the bees thing," and at some point the thought of it totally overwhelmed Fearless and he fell asleep. Vicious was relieved and was grateful for some quiet.

Dodd emerged from the concrete company just after two o'clock and promptly headed to the River Club, a private members only eatery located on the 80th floor of the Diamond Tower in the Tharsis City financial district. Dodd stayed inside with his security detail until approximately four o'clock and emerged drunk, having had four dry gin martinis served up with a double twist, as was his preference. A trip back to his apartment followed, where he napped until six o'clock, rose for a quick takeout dinner of synthetic sushi and departed the apartment building at eight o'clock, on the move yet again.

Fearless furrowed his brow as he watched the town car weave through Tharsis. It was something about the amount of left and right turns, the streets they used, the shortcuts they took. It was as if he *knew* where Dodd was going. He could feel his blood starting to boil. Mostly because he had made the drive himself, so many times, after dropping Dodd off for the night at his apartment. And then, the town car came to a stop, right where he knew it would in front of—

Ana's Bar.

"I *knew* it. I *knew* he was going here tonight," Fearless seethed. "That greasy, wannabe gangster scumbag doesn't even deserve to drink the stale urine in the urinals at Ana's Bar. You don't think he has a table, do you? I'll kill myself if they gave a fake-ass gangster like Dodd his own table."

Vicious took in the main entrance of Ana's for a moment. And then, it hit him.

"It has to be Ana's. That's where we grab Dodd."

Fearless scoffed. Then chuckled. And followed that with a *chortle*. "You have *got* to be kidding me, right? Like, you're not actually serious right now, are you?"

Vicious reasoned with him. "Look. You saw—Dodd goes throughout the day with those heavies. There's not a single second that they leave his side. Hell, they were by his side while he was taking a *dump* at the diner. I know Ana's isn't the best choice, but it's our *only* choice."

"Hell, why don't we just climb in bed with him at the end of, too!" Fearless detonated. "Look, Vicious, I love you, but we couldn't get into Ana's on a *normal day*, even if we wanted to. And let us not forget the fact that we're currently the Red Dragon persona non grata. At this point, we'd probably have a better shot of walking into the Elder Temple than Ana's."

Vicious looked back out the window at Ana's main door. He watched as various gangsters entered. Not all of them were Red Dragon, but the majority were. But no matter the crime family, they all had one thing in common. They brought girls. Lots of *girls*.

Vicious grinned. "Girls."

Fearless raised an eyebrow. "Excuse me?"

"Girls don't have a problem getting in Ana's, right?"

"I guess not, why?"

Vicious continued. He grew giddy at the idea. "What if we sent in a girl? No, two girls. And we convinced them to seduce Dodd. Meanwhile, you and I could take out those heavies.

And the girls bring Dodd back to my father's penthouse where we're waiting."

Fearless considered this. "I'm not going to lie, that idea isn't half bad. Actually, it's damn good. One problem. Where the hell are we going to get two girls, at this hour, who are going to agree to do this for us, for zero money?"

Vicious sunk in his chair. And so did Fearless. They both stared ahead. Defeated. They were left without any options. Dodd was untouchable. *Or so it seemed.*

They both slowly turned their heads to the opposite side of the street. To a place where they might just find the girls they're looking for. Another bar. Their bar.

The Bar.

Knock. Knock. Knock.

Fearless and Vicious stood in the dark alley outside the backdoor to The Bar, when the door opened—and Felix, the bartender with the tattooed hands, emerged. He was a welcome sight to them. They didn't have many allies left in Tharsis City.

"I'm just going to assume that if you're coming in through the back you're in some hot water," Felix said, with a fair amount of concern.

"Scalding, if we're being honest." Vicious peered through the open back door. "Look, Felix—you remember those college girls from the other night, the ones who we bought that bottle of champagne for?"

A bewildered smirk crept across Felix's face. "Those two hustlers that claimed they were college girls so poor saps like you will buy them drinks? *Yeah.* I think I remember them."

Fearless grumbled. "I *knew* it."

Vicious brushed him off. "Any idea where those two live, Felix?"

"Not a clue," Felix replied, still wearing that same smirk. He motioned back towards the bar. "But I do know that they're sitting in the corner of the bar right now, just like they have been all week."

Fearless and Vicious traded a glance. Luck, for once, was on their side. Vicious turned back to Felix.

"Any way you could give us fifteen minutes in your private room with them?"

Felix grinned. "Sure thing. I'll tell them there's a couple of high rollers back there that want to buy them another vintage bottle of champagne." Then, he looked to Fearless with an irk in his eye. "Your tab's still open, by the way."

Fearless rolled his eyes. "I'll settle up with you once I get my stolen wallet back from the blonde one."

Fiona and Penny approached the private room with an extra bounce in their step. Felix had told them that two wealthy businessmen had been admiring them from across the bar. And instead of just sending them a drink like any regular schmo would, they bought out the entire back room for the evening and put a bottle of 2010 Dom Perignon on ice in order to get to know them better. But when they opened the door, they found the room was empty.

"*Sit*," Vicious ordered.

Recognizing him, the girls quickly turned to leave—but Fearless slammed the door shut and blocked the exit. The girls slowly retreated to the center of the room, terrified by the realization that they were trapped in a room with the two men they had gone home with the other night.

Fiona, the blonde who stole Fearless's wallet, spoke up. "Listen, *assholes*. Whatever it is you think you're doing right now, I can promise you that you're going to regret it."

Vicious rolled his eyes. And sighed. "It's not what you think it is."

Fearless chimed in. "Except for my wallet. That part is what you think it is. Which is that I want it back."

Fiona scoffed. "Are you fucking kidding me? That's what this is about?"

Fearless doubled down. "Yes, yes it is."

Penny interjected, disgusted. "Let me get this straight, you tricked two women into going into a private room and locked the door behind you to confront them about a missing wallet? You need a therapist." And then turned to Vicious. "*Especially* you."

"Look, it's not about the wallet, alright?" Vicious reassured them. "We have an offer to make you."

Fiona glared back at him. "Locking us in a backroom at a bar is a pretty fuckin' creepy way to make us an offer, don't you think?"

Vicious motioned to the long dining-room table in the center of the room. "Sit. Please."

The girls traded a glance—then reluctantly sat down on the far end, putting a fair amount of space between them.

"Thank you," Vicious calmly said. "Are you familiar with the bar across the street?"

Penny, the quieter one with the auburn hair, spoke up. "Sure. It's that gangster joint, right?"

Vicious nodded. "Yes. It is. Right now, there's a man inside that bar that my friend and I need to spend some quality time with. The problem, you see, is that the two of us can't get into Ana's—"

Fiona gritted her teeth. "Because you're losers?"

Fearless interjected. "You had sex with this loser, thank you very much."

Fiona chuckled. "No, we didn't."

Fearless scoffed. "*Yes*, we did."

"I mean, that depends on what you call *sex*. Because the kind I have doesn't involve you passing out on top of the bed the moment we walked in the bedroom. You were snoring like a Labrador. And then, at one point, you started mumbling in your sleep. Something about a giant crab?"

Fearless turned bright red. He fell silent. Vicious tried to hold in his laugh with all his might. But it only made it worse. And then, it emerged from his throat—a loud *snort*.

Fearless slowly turned to Vicious and whispered. "*It's not funny.*"

"*It's pretty funny.*"

"*Would you just get on with the meeting, please.*"

"Sorry." Vicious collected himself, then spoke for them both. "Look, we can't get in because our rank within our organization isn't high enough. But women don't have a problem getting in."

Fiona began to put the pieces together. And began to negotiate with Vicious. "So let me get this straight. If I'm hearing you correctly, you want us to help you *kidnap* this guy?"

"More like... *lure him* back to my penthouse," Vicious countered.

"What's in it for us?"

"We forget about the whole wallet thing. We're even."

Fiona scoffed. "*Please*. The only thing in that wallet was a few receipts for Big Jae's noodle bar. That place sucks. You can have your wallet back."

Vicious took a deep breath. "We don't have any cash to offer you."

Fiona mulled this over for a minute, until she turned to Penny and whispered in her ear. They shared a chuckle and a nod. Then turned back to Vicious. "There is something. A landscape on the wall of the living room. An abstract of a sunset."

Vicious scoffed. "That's a Rothko. From Earth. It's priceless. And doesn't belong to me. Absolutely not."

Fearless leaned over and whispered to Vicious. "Fuck the painting. Give it to them."

"It's my *father's*."

"Would you rather have your dad be pissed off that a painting went missing from his penthouse he's never slept in or would you rather *die*? Your call."

Vicious gritted his teeth. And turned back to the girls. "Fine. You have a deal."

Fiona and Penny shared a satisfied grin for a moment, until Fiona turned back to the two of them. "So, what's the plan?"

"We'll be in your ear every step of the way." Vicious reached into his pocket and procured a small black case with an earpiece inside. He slid it across the table. "Dodd will be at Ana's tonight."

"A little short notice, don't you think?" Fiona snapped back.

Vicious clenched his jaw. "You want the Rothko or not?"

"Fine," Fiona replied. Then, she grinned. "We'll just need a few minutes to get changed into more... *appropriate* evening wear."

———•———

Fiona and Penny didn't walk into Ana's Bar. They *strutted*. Dressed in matching bright red body-hugging, short sequined dresses, they forewent the long line full of bustling twentysomethings hoping to get in. They confidently approached the surly doorman, who guarded the entrance with a velvet rope and a scowl. But Fiona and Penny didn't let either stop them. Literally. They opted to pretend like they owned the place and attempted to walk right in—

"Hold up right there," the doorman said, with a raised hand. "There's a line."

Fiona flashed him a coquettish grin. "That's cute," then motioned to Penny. "But we don't do *lines*."

The doorman didn't flinch. "Well I *do*. This is *Ana's*. And if you ain't got a table, you get in line. Now get to the back of the line before I call security."

Penny anxiously pulled Fiona aside, making sure to stay within earshot of the doorman. "Just call Dodd, will you? He'll come out front and get us."

"I don't know, he *hates* when I do that. But I guess I don't have a choice."

Fiona was reaching for her cell phone, when the doorman interrupted. "Did you just say you're with *Dodd*?"

Fiona smirked. "That's right."

"My apologies, then. Right this way, ladies." The doorman lifted the velvet rope and motioned to the door. "Welcome to Ana's."

Inside, Penny and Fiona passed through a small, dark lobby. A small line had formed in front of a Dutch door where an employee stood. The girls passed by, assuming it was a coat check—until the gangster at the front of the line placed his chrome .357 Magnum on the counter. And in exchange for the handheld howitzer, the employee handed him a ticket. This wasn't a coat check. Not even close. It was a *gun* check. And if you wanted to get inside Ana's you had best follow the rules or risk permanent banishment.

Fiona and Penny traded a tense glance—perhaps this job was *slightly* more dangerous than they had bargained for. But there was no turning back now. Especially when there was a genuine Rothko waiting for them on the other side of the deal. And so they headed for the double doors that led into the club's main dining area; they could hear the muffled sound of big, brassy jazz reverberating from the other side. And as two security guards standing on either side of the doors opened them simultaneously, they stepped into:

Inflamed nightclub nonpareil. The lighting was all deep ocher and cigarette smoke, swirling above the high-back booths and blue-velvet-tufted banquettes. On stage, there was a nine-piece jazz band humming away. Fiona and Penny cut through the main dining area, passed the tables reserved weeks in advance. The clientele appeared decidedly sketchy. It wasn't a Red Dragon bar. But they were tolerated. Just like the rest of the thieves and pirates who had to check their guns at the door if they wanted to do business.

And although the gangsters who came there tonight were from all different background and organizations, some of them friends, some of them sworn enemies, there was one universal truth—inside these walls, life was *damn* good.

Fiona and Penny made their way towards the long, polished mahogany bar that anchored the room. They posted up by the counter, where they ordered two double single malts apiece. The first to shoot quickly to calm their nerves. The second to neutralize any nerves that were still left standing.

Fiona's eyes ticked to Penny. "You ready for this?"

Penny gave a hesitant nod. She wasn't quite sure if she'd *ever* be ready for a night quite like this, but then again, *what choice did they have?*

Fiona reached into her purse and removed the earpiece from its case and placed it in her ear. Almost instantaneously, she heard a voice. It was Vicious.

"Dodd prefers a corner booth. He'll be seated with two strapped heavies on either side. Dodd will be the guy in the middle drinking a gin martini."

Fiona clocked him. Her eyes ticked to his drink. "Double twist?"

"That's him."

Fiona winced as she looked Dodd over. He was sweating, as was his custom. A bead of sweat slowly trickled from his sideburn, the liquid turned black from the cheap boxed hair dye he had used that afternoon. He was the frog prince of Ana's palace, but no amount of kisses would turn him back into a dashing cavalier. And for that, Fiona could only manage a single word.

"Gross."

Vicious continued with his instructions. *"Now listen closely. You are to approach Dodd's table, but do not speak until spoken to. When Dodd addresses you and asks who you are, you tell him that you are a gift. Sent from the Neptune Cartel. Now, once he accepts, don't waste time. No staying for a drink. Tell him you have a car waiting out back. In the alley. And that all three of them are welcome. Understood?"*

"Yeah, I got it. But the earpiece has to go."

"Absolutely not. We need to be your voice on the inside."

"Then let us be your eyes," Fiona softly quipped back, keeping her voice down at the ever crowding bar. "Because you know how we end up dead? When your gangster boss sees a fuckin' earpiece in my ear."

Fiona waited for a reply, but there was only silence. She took a deep breath. And waited some more. Until.

"Fine."

Fiona grinned. "See you boys on the other side."

Fearless and Vicious stood in the dark. The alley that ran behind Ana'sBar was particularly decrepit, as far as alleys went, overrun with the rats and roaches who camped out all night to get a taste of the scraps of the five-course tasting menu that evening. It was also wet. *Very wet.* Dozens of air conditioners from the apartment building opposite Ana's faced the alley, spewing thick beads of condensation onto the pavement below. In short, it was an absolutely miserable place to be standing on a Saturday night.

A cigarette dangled from Fearless's mouth. He sparked a lighter to it, but it was quickly extinguished by a droplet of air conditioner water. Fearless grumbled. He flicked the soggy cigarette to the pavement. He was bitter. Extremely so. He turned to Vicious, whose face was twisted into an equally rancorous expression.

"We've been waiting two hours for these girls. And I can't even smoke."

Vicious clenched his jaw. "They'll come through for us. They're probably just tied up. Just give it time."

Fearless chuckled. Then shook his head. "For a guy who's a pretty dark motherfucker, you sure do have faith in people. Because I can *guarantee* you those two chicks are inside having the time of their *fucking lives* and have already forgotten about the two assholes waiting for them in the alley."

"What is your *obsession* with Ana's? It's just a *bar*. Who cares!"

"I care!" Fearless snapped back. "Ana's is the only reason I joined the Red Dragon!"

Vicious scoffed. "You told me that you joined the Red Dragon for me."

"Of *course* I told you that. It's because that's what you needed to hear. Just like every other pep talk I have to give you when you're feeling sad. To be honest, you're fucking miserable!"

Vicious motioned towards the alley's entrance. "If I'm so miserable, then why don't you leave? Go ahead! No one's forcing you to be friends with me! I was only friends with you in the first place because I felt bad for you."

Fearless threw his hands in the air and stomped off. "Well in *that* case, I'm out. Good luck getting yourself out of this jam *alone*."

Vicious called after him. "Better alone than with you. *Douchebag*."

"*Prick*—" Fearless snickered, but the dig was cut short, as he walked directly into a three-hundred-pound brick wall that smelled of cheap cologne and expensive whiskey. The man didn't even flinch. As Fearless slowly looked up to find:

One of Dodd's heavies, standing before him in the alley. Fearless gulped. The heavy, who he had only seen from a distance, was somehow bigger than he could have possibly imagined. And just as Fearless clenched his fists in what surely would be a futile effort to defend himself, the heavy spoke.

"Amn tis bathroo is et, an. Sh. Er am I."

The heavy, to Fearless's surprise, was drunk. *Hammered. Pissed. Properly shit-faced.* All of them, combined. He wobbled as he spoke, his feet performing a delicate dance as they tried to keep this behemoth upright. His eyes were glassed over. And at one point, he started to snore.

Fearless slowly turned back to Vicious, eyes wide, who offered a silent shrug. Fearless turned back to the heavy, put two fingers in his chest and sent the mammoth bruiser tumbling into a nearby pile of trash, where he continued to snore.

When, from the backdoor emerged Dodd, his arms draped around Fiona and Penny. He too, was in the midst of a roaring blackout. The two girls dragged him into the alley, his chin softly bobbing against his chest as he softly mumbled incoherent nonsense.

Fearless took in Dodd, and with it the girls' work, with total disbelief. "Holy *shit*. What did you do to these poor motherfuckers?"

Fiona shrugged. "Well, we followed your instructions until we realized that Dodd's security weren't about to let him walk into a dark back alley. So we took matters into our own hands."

Penny chimed in with a smirk. "And by that we mean tequila. Mostly."

Vicious whispered, so as not to disturb Dodd, "Wait. Where's the other heavy?"

Fiona motioned back to Ana's. "Passed out in the booth. Pissed himself too. You would think these big guys could hold their liquor. But it's actually the opposite."

Vicious couldn't help but grin. "Nice work."

"Thanks." Fiona sighed, as she motioned back to Dodd. "Now are you two going to help us or do we have to load him in the van, too?"

-TWELVE-

"80 Floors Up"

It was just before dawn. The air smelled of synthetic bacon crackling on the stove. It didn't share the same savory, salty smell of its pork cousin. Rather, it was sweet. It was a peculiar choice for bacon, of all things. The engineers who designed the scent described it as a "more satisfying olfactory experience." But to those who remembered the real thing, this new sugar-sweet scent was an imposter. To them, it smelled the way cherry candy tastes saccharine, rather than tart like a fresh cherry.

Fearless was one of them. He couldn't recall the way bacon tasted, or, for that matter, ever eating it in the first place. But in his memory, he could smell it. It was hard for his brain to even make sense of it all. How a scent could linger in his prefrontal cortex, lying dormant for years until it was presented with the smell of the imposter. He'd like to think that a mother cooked it for him as a young boy. Or a grandmother, even. Back when pork was still imported from Earth, from real pigs that grazed on grass that grew from the ground. It was a pleasant mystery that his brain would never solve. And maybe that was enough.

"Is that burnt yet?" The sound of Vicious's anxious voice interrupted his peculiar day dream. Fearless quickly snapped out of his haze and continued to push the syn-bacon around the pan, the strips charred to pinkish grey crisp.

"Just about," Fearless replied. He didn't address Vicious. He just kept his eyes on the syn-bacon. Expressionless.

Vicious clocked his sullen tone. "Listen, I'm sorry about last night. I didn't mean that thing I said about only being friends because I felt bad for you. That wasn't right."

"I'm sorry I called you a prick."

"Apology accepted."

Fearless mulled this over for a moment, as if rescinding his apology. "You *were* kind of being a prick, though."

Vicious shook his head. Then chuckled. He knew that half-hearted, half-assed apology was all he was going to get from Fearless. So he let him have this one.

"Yeah. I was."

Fearless forked the syn-bacon onto a plate. The charred strips landed on the plate with an audible *ting-a-ting*. He turned to Vicious with a smile. "Think this will wake him up?"

Vicious grinned. "Yeah. I think breakfast in bed should do just the trick."

Fearless and Vicious made their way across the penthouse. There was a thick fog that morning, one that reached all the way to the penthouse. A grey cloud lingered outside the floor-to-ceiling windows. But as the sun began to rise, it illuminated the red Martian soil on the ground and bathed the entire apartment in an eerie, cerise glow.

They turned down a long hallway. It was lined with various paintings and other works of art. Vicious stopped in front of an empty space on the wall. Dust outlined the frame where the Rothko once hung. He sighed. "God, I loved that painting."

Fearless shrugged. "Never understood what the fuss was about, I guess. All art is some guy throwing some shit at the wall and hoping it sticks."

Vicious could only shake his head as they continued down the hallway, their bare feet slowly sliding across the cool marble floors.

"Can I ask you a question?" Fearless asked with a hint of trepidation.

"Sure."

"How far are you planning on taking this?"

Vicious took a deep breath. "As far as I have to."

The drool slowly dribbled from Dodd's mouth. He was seated in the living room, crudely tied to an antique dining chair. There wasn't any rope to be had, or duct tape, so they had used belts to secure his wrists and ankles. They belonged to Vicious's father, constructed of the finest tanned leathers from the hides of animals that hadn't existed in decades.

Vicious and Fearless took in the capo. There sat the man who had once held so much power over them. The one who ordered them dead. And now, he sat in a puddle of his own piss, helpless.

For a moment, Fearless wondered if he was dead. Part of him wished he was. For his sake. Because what was about to happen to Dodd was going to be inhumane. And he would deserve every moment of it.

"Time to wake up."

Vicious held a piece of charred syn-bacon below his nose to rouse him. Dodd slowly began to stir, mumbling incoherently about the night before. His eyelids fluttered. Slowly at first, but then he brought the room into focus.

"Where the fuck am I?" Dodd's voice cracked as he spoke. His throat singed by the long night of inhaling tequila and cigarette smoke.

"Don't you recognize the place?" Vicious slowly paced behind Dodd. "After all, you seemed to know *so* much about it. You seemed to know so much about *me,* just because you knew my address."

Dodd's eyes frantically searched the room for the voice. "Listen, I have money. Lots of money. We can work something out! I-I drank too much last night. OK? I-I don't know how I got here. Or who *you* are—"

Vicious slowly kneeled down next to Dodd so they were eye level. He spoke to him in a comforting matter, as if he were a doctor addressing a child who was about to get a vaccine.

"Sure you do."

Dodd recoiled in fear. All at once, the blood drained from his face. It was as if he had seen a ghost. Maybe, he had.

"*Vicious...*"

Vicious grinned. The darkness was no longer riding shotgun. No longer was it bubbling beneath the surface. *It* was here. And *it* was the one leading this interrogation.

"Good morning, *sunshine.*"

Dodd immediately began to panic, tugging at his restraints. Trying to break free. But it was no use. As it turned out, the belts were as effective as they were expensive. He frantically looked around the room, for a way out, for someone, for anything until his eyes landed on Fearless.

"Fearless! You gotta help me! You can't let him do this!"

Fearless lit a cigarette. And took a drag. He leaned against one of the floor-to-ceiling windows, the fog clouds outside of which were now blood red. He stared into them, pondering Dodd's words.

"Can't let him *do what,* Dodd?"

Dodd motioned to his restraints. "This! *This! Look at me!*"

Fearless exhaled a plume of smoke. And nonchalantly approached the chair. "But he hasn't done anything yet. As far as I can see, my friend here has merely tied you to a chair with some luxury leather accessories. It could be worse. All things considered."

He took another drag as he slowly paced to a modern leather armchair nearby. He equally slowly sat down, crossed his legs and held the cigarette high between his index and middle fingers— channeling his inner Audrey Hepburn, sans the cigarette holder.

"It's not as if he, say, sent you on a job with a briefcase full of playing cards."

Dodd's eyes widened. He tried to speak, but the words wouldn't form.

"You didn't think we could open the case, did you? *Oops,*" Vicious opined as he pulled his Red Dragon issued 9mm from his waist. He ejected the empty clip from the handle. And began to slowly load it with bullets. One by one. And turned to his partner.

"Fearless, how many toes do you think Dodd has?"

Fearless played along and carefully looked his bare feet over. "Oh, ten, I reckon."

Dodd clocked the handgun and quickly realized where this was headed. And he was running out of time. "Look, boys, this is all just a *big* misunderstanding."

Ka-chunk! Vicious racked the slide. "Huh. Is that so?"

"Yes, I swear, I can explain!"

Vicious placed the 9mm's muzzle on Dodd's big toe. "Then *explain.*"

Dodd's lower lip trembled at the sight. "OK. *Look.* The Red Dragon was working with Slade on a deal for a new party drug. The negotiation wasn't going well. The Elders wanted to get the deal done. So they told me to have a couple guys deliver a case. I didn't know what was inside. I swear!"

Vicious turned to Fearless. They traded a glance. Then turned back to Dodd.

"Wrong."

BANG! Vicious squeezed the trigger and blew off Dodd's big toe!

Dodd howled in pain. "Motherfucker! You motherfucker! Fuck! Fine! *Fine!* The briefcase was my idea!"

Vicious pressed to the big toe on the other foot. "Why us, then?"

Dodd struggled to catch his breath as the blood poured from his foot. "What are you talking about. I just needed a couple guys to deliver the fuckin' case! You were available!"

BANG! Vicious blew off the other toe! And Dodd howled louder.

"Wrong answer! Who sent the assassin, huh? Was it the Europa Crew? Did they put you up to this?"

Dodd's eyes began to flutter. A pool of blood formed on the floor. "No…"

Vicious *screamed* in frustration. "Bullshit!"

BANG! Vicious blew off one of Dodd's toes!

BANG! Then another!

BANG! And another!

Fearless looked down to his feet. The pool of blood had traveled all the way across the room. And was soaking into his shoe. "*Vicious*. I don't think he has the answers you're looking for."

Vicious locked eyes with Fearless. They were black. "Then we need to start asking in a different way."

He stood and grabbed the back of Dodd's chair. He dragged the chair through the pool of blood and across the marble floors, leaving two parallel red streaks in its wake. Vicious placed the chair in front of one of the floor-to-ceiling windows. He raised the 9mm to the glass.

BANG! The window shattered onto the floor!

The wind howled furiously throughout the penthouse. Vicious put his foot to the seat of the chair. And slowly tipped Dodd backwards on the two back legs. He teetered over the edge of the window, where the fog had since cleared to reveal an eighty-floor drop.

Vicious looked to Dodd. "I'm going to ask you one more time. Was the assassin from the Europa Crew or not?"

Dodd's eyes fluttered open. It was a sudden moment of clarity. Perhaps he knew between the blood loss and the streets of Tharsis City waiting below that he was going to die either way. He spoke slowly between labored breaths. "I hired the assassin. Off the black market. It was me."

Vicious was taken aback. The admission hit him like a sledgehammer. "What? But that doesn't make any sense. Why would *you* want *us* dead? We're just two janitors."

Dodd slowly shook his head. "Just you. *Just you.*"

"Me?"

Dodd slowly nodded as he tried to string the words together. He was fading. "I didn't know. Until. You told me. Where. You lived."

Vicious clenched his jaw tight. "I don't understand."

"Your... father..."

Vicious slowly cocked his head sideways. The darkness faded. The light once again filled his eyes. The eyes of a little boy. Who just wanted to be loved. "My father? What does he have to do with any of this?"

Dodd softly chuckled. He was surprised. "You... don't know... who you are?"

Vicious could see it in Dodd's expression. His lips slowly curling to a smile. That sneer. He knew he was telling the truth. That Dodd knew something he didn't. And he was enjoying every second of it.

"What do you know about my—"

FWIP! A bullet clipped Vicious in the shoulder!

Vicious cried out in pain as he tumbled backwards a few steps, clutching his arm. His head whipped back to Dodd as he realized his foot was no longer holding the chair steady. Vicious lurched for him—"*No!*"

But it was too late. Dodd fell backwards through the open floor-to-ceiling window. And in an instant, he was gone. *Vanished*. Vicious rushed to the edge of the window. He locked eyes with Dodd. For a moment, he looked peaceful as he free-fell those eighty floors. And just before he smashed into the pavement, where his bones would shatter into an inconceivable amount of pieces, Vicious could have sworn he saw Dodd smile.

"Get down!" Fearless shouted as he dragged Vicious down to the floor.

FWIP! FWIP-FWIP-FWIP-FWIP!

Gunfire peppered the penthouse through the open window. Fearless looked across to the building opposite them, where he could see the muzzle flash of a long range sniper rifle.

"Sniper!"

FWIP! A sniper bullet whizzed by Fearless's face, just ever so lightly kissing the tip of his nose. He held his hand to his face, making sure his nose was still there, then glanced at his palm where a few drops of blood were lightly streaked.

"Not cool!"

FWIP! FWIP! FWIP!

Fearless and Vicious army crawled across the marble floors as the sniper fire continued to rain down on them. They quickly retreated into the U-shaped kitchen, where a wall of seamless white-oak cabinetry hid all of the appliances and cupboards. The only thing the designers couldn't hide was the solid marble island in the center. Fearless and Vicious quickly took cover behind it, momentarily catching their breath.

"They almost blew my nose off!" Fearless shouted.

Vicious winced, clutching his shoulder. "Who is *they?!*"

Fearless motioned to Vicious's pocket. "You still have those binoculars?"

Vicious winced as he reached into his pocket and handed over the binoculars. Fearless peeked ever so slightly above the island's marble surface, the binoculars to his eyes. He slowly scanned the adjacent building where the gunfire came from, searching for a shooter. And, sure enough, he found him. The sniper was laying on his belly on the roof of the building with a military grade M40 bolt-action rifle with an infrared scope. He had concealed himself entirely in black, but had neglected one crucial element. He was wearing a two-tone black and gold Rolex on his wrist. They called him Blackeye. And he was the Red Dragon's most elite sharpshooter.

"Fucking Blackeye. I knew it," Fearless grumbled.

Vicious cocked his head sideways. "*Blackeye?* Our Blackeye? Are you sure?"

Fearless nodded. "I'd recognize that ugly ass Rolex anywhere."

"But that's impossible! The Red Dragon doesn't even know Dodd's missing yet!"

"They've probably had your penthouse under surveillance for days. Hell, if the fog didn't lift, you probably wouldn't have gotten shot," Fearless said, as he clocked Vicious's bullet wound. His shirt soaked in blood. "*Oh shit.* That doesn't look good."

"I'll be fine," Vicious said, pulling his shirt tight.

They heard the familiar chime of the private elevator. They turned to the digital placard that hung above the door and indicated what number floor the car was currently passing. The numbers were counting u —*8... 9... 10...—and fast.*

"Well, whoever *they* are—they're coming for *us*," Fearless concluded.

Vicious pointed to a nearby monitor discreetly built into the seamless white oak cabinetry. "Turn that on. The private elevator has a hidden camera on a closed circuit security system."

Fearless kept a low profile as he scrambled to the monitor. He tapped the screen and the monitor slowly came to life. On screen was a fish-eye view of the elevator car where four heavily armed men were crammed inside. Fearless's eyes narrowed, confused. He called back to Vicious.

"Those guys are *not* Red Dragon, I'll tell you that much!"

"Then who?" Vicious shouted back.

Fearless took in the image, searching for clues—when he saw it. One of the men had an intricate tattoo on the inside of his forearm. A Grecian woman in a flowing white toga riding a bull.

"Shit…" Fearless muttered.

CRASH! The monitor exploded from the impact of a sniper bullet!

Fearless dropped to the floor. A small piece of the monitor's glass screen stuck to his cheek. He plucked it out. *"Come on! Enough with the face shots!"* he bellowed.

Fearless quickly crawled back to his position with Vicious behind the kitchen island. "It's the Europa Crew. They got four guys on the elevator. Armed to the teeth."

Vicious softly muttered. "It can't be…"

"Well, *clearly*, it is! And I gotta tell ya, from what I've heard, they're not the nicest bunch!" Fearless scoffed, as he turned back towards the digital placard above the elevator. The numbers continued to rise.

21… 22… 23…

"We don't have time for this, Vicious!"

Vicious shook his head. Then locked eyes with Fearless. "Before he fell out the window, Dodd told me he hired the assassin to ambush us at Slade's. He got him off the black market. The Europa Crew never came to him."

Fearless was taken aback by this information. "But why would Dodd want *us* dead?"

"Not us." Vicious shook his head. "Just me."

Fearless cocked his head sideways. His face contorting with shock. *"You?"*

From across the room they heard the *ding* as the car reached the eightieth floor.

The elevator doors slowly parted and emitted that same delightful, lab-designed melody. The same one that played the night they took Fiona and Penny back to the penthouse for a nightcap. But this time, the melody took on a haunting quality.

Fearless reached into his waist for his 9mm, but it wasn't there. He cringed. And whispered to Vicious. "Fuck! I must have left my gun in the catering van!"

Vicious popped the clip from his 9mm to check his ammo, only to realize—"*Shit*. I'm out."

Fearless panicked. "Well what the fuck are we supposed to do now?!"

When, suddenly they were interrupted by a deep, raspy voice that echoed through the penthouse. "*Vicious... Vicious... Vicious... Tsk tsk tsk.*"

The voice belonged to Darien Cortez, the older brother of the drunk that Vicious had killed at Big Jae's Noodle Bar. Every inch of his skin was almost entirely tattooed with images of Greek gods and illustrated tales of their legend. A fresh tattoo was etched into his cheek. So new that it was still smeared with petroleum jelly to keep the ink from smudging. It was a name. *Nicky.*

Darien continued to pontificate. "You know, you would've gotten away with it, Vicious. You would've been home free. So let this be an important lesson to you. If you're going to kill someone, never use a credit card at the crime scene. And if you don't want the waitstaff to give up your personal information... always, *always* tip."

Three more members of the Europa Crew flanked Darien either side. They too were significantly inked up; one had gone as far as to tattoo a skull over his entire face. The end result was particularly menacing. But so was the Europa Crew. They were a relatively new crime family, having established themselves as a legitimate threat a few years back after they burned down a Red Dragon-controlled casino in the orbit of Jupiter and killed everyone inside. There wasn't a motive behind the attack. They didn't do it for the money. Or territory. Or even respect. They simply wanted to instill fear across the solar system. Their modus operandi was chaos.

Darien called out again. "I'm going to give you a chance, Vicious. A chance to show your face. A chance to admit why you beat my baby brother so bad that we had to have a closed casket funeral. And then, after I'm done with you, I'm going to give you the chance to beg for mercy."

But there was no response. Only silence. Darien quietly motioned to his men and directed them to conduct a sweep of the penthouse. The men quickly fanned out in opposite directions, each taking a different wing of the ten thousand-square foot luxury residence.

With a pair of jagged hunting knives in each hand, Skull Face took the kitchen. He slowly stalked towards the island, his eyes following the trail of bloody footprints that led behind it where Fearless and Vicious had hid from the sniper's fire. He rounded the corner and raised his weapons, ready to properly gut them only to find they were gone.

"Ah, shit," muttered Skull Face. He turned back to the marble flooring, analyzing the bloody footprints and attempting to discern the various directions that they seemed to be heading in...

When one of the seamless white oak cabinets silently opened behind him. There stood Vicious, standing in a walk-in pantry. He hovered behind Skull Face for a moment like a vampire. Then, he quickly struck, wrapping his hand around the thug's mouth and pulling him into the closet. Skull Face let out a muffled cry, but it was useless.

Crack!

Vicious snapped his neck and slowly dragged him into the walk-in pantry, unbeknownst to the rest of the Europa Crew. His jagged hunting knives skittering across the floor.

Meanwhile, two more tattooed men took the master bedroom. They carefully searched the room, checking in closets, behind curtains, even under the bed. They looked to each other with a shrug. No one seemed to be here, either. And just as they turned to leave, they heard a metallic *ting* coming from the adjacent master bathroom.

The two tattooed men carefully stepped into the bathroom, guns drawn. It was the size of a one-bedroom apartment, covered floor-to-ceiling in pristine imported white tile. An antique clawfoot tub sat in the center of the room. At the far end of the bathroom, a pair of white curtains softly billowed in the wind. The window was open. The men traded a glance and approached the open window. One took the lead and stuck his head outside.

"No fire escape out here. Just a ledge—"

Suddenly, an unseen hand grabbed the tattooed man by the neck of his shirt and pulled him out the window! The man screamed as he tumbled eighty floors to his death, the sound echoing throughout the expansive bathroom.

"Holy shit!" the remaining tattooed man cried out. He slowly backed away from the window, gun ready to fire. His hand trembled. He took another step back. The gun still trained on the open window. Then another step back. When suddenly, he backed into something. Or *someone*. The thug slowly turned around.

It was Vicious. He locked eyes with the man. And whispered. "*Boo.*"

The tattooed man stumbled backward in the other direction. He raised his gun to fire, but his trembling finger couldn't find the trigger. Vicious didn't even flinch. He continued to slowly pace toward the man. A maniacal grin on his face.

The man didn't realize that Fearless was emerging from through the window behind him. Fearless stealthily slipped into the bathroom and grabbed a bath towel from a wicker basket. He quickly unrolled it and in instant, had wrapped the towel around the man's neck like a plush, high-end linen garrote. Fearless slowly brought him to the floor as he choked the man out. *Dead.*

"Hell of an entrance," Vicious whispered, impressed.

"Thanks," Fearless whispered back with a shrug. "How many are left?"

"Just Darien. But don't forget about the sniper in the building across the street."

Fearless gritted his teeth. "Fucking snipers. They all think they're so fucking cool because they can kill a man from a mile away. But you know what I think? They're *pussies.* Any *dumbass* with a M40 and an infrared scope can kill a guy. Try killing a guy with a bath towel. Now *that's* impressive."

Suddenly, Vicious held a quiet finger to his lips. "Did you hear that?"

They both listened closely. For a moment, it was silent. Until—

Click-clack. Click-clack. Click-clack.

It was the sound of footsteps. And they were getting closer. Vicious turned to Fearless with concern. "Shit. Darien. What the hell do we do now?"

Fearless chewed on this for a beat. His eyes ticked to the open bathroom window, the curtains billowing idyllically in the breeze. He already knew the answer to the question he was about to ask. But he couldn't help himself.

"You still afraid of heights?"

Fearless and Vicious stood on the concrete ledge outside the bathroom window. It had occurred to both of them that the eeriest part about being eighty floors up wasn't the height, it was the silence. There weren't any street sounds at this height. No commotion. No chatter. No angry car horns blaring. Just the sound of the wind howling in between the buildings, daring you to make a mistake.

Fearless quickly shimmied across the ledge to a nearby access ladder that led to the roof above the penthouse. He too didn't care much for heights, but he found it best to get it over with quickly with as little thought as possible. Fearless climbed the ladder and pulled himself up onto the roof. He turned around, then quickly realized that Vicious wasn't behind him. He was frozen on the ledge.

Fearless called out to him. "Vicious! What the hell are you doing?! We need to move! Right now!"

But Vicious didn't budge. He just kept his back to the wall. And his eyes straight. He was paralyzed with fear. Barely able to even speak.

"I… I can't."

"What do you mean, you can't?!"

Vicious trembled. "My legs won't move, alright? I'm too scared!"

"Too scared? Are you fucking kidding me right now? After all the shit you've put me through this week, this is how it's going to end?"

Suddenly, something from the adjacent building caught Fearless's eye. A small flash of light. Fearless's eyes narrowed. He squinted at it. It seemed to be signaling them, like a mirror. *What the hell was that?* And then, he realized what it was. The morning sun reflecting off the scope of a sniper rifle. The shooter from the other building had spotted them. And he was lining up a shot.

"Shit," Fearless muttered to himself. He called out to Vicious on the ledge. "Vicious! Listen to me! The sniper has eyes on you! He's going to take the shot!"

Vicious didn't respond. He was full on catatonic, lost in the throes of a devastating panic attack. Fearless quickly descended the ladder from the roof and carefully shimmied back across the ledge towards Vicious.

"Seriously!" Fearless said as he approached. "Of all the shit that's happened the past few days, *this* is the thing that you're afraid of?!"

Vicious didn't even crack a smile. His eyes were locked straight ahead, his hands clinging desperately to the building behind. Fearless reached him and extended a hand.

"Come on!" Fearless shouted, the wind howling between them. "Take my hand!"

But still, Vicious didn't move. Fearless turned back towards the sniper. His left hand was on his scope adjusting its focus. One click. Then another. Then, he slid his right hand down the barrel towards the trigger. It seemed to Fearless that he was sadistically eking out the moment.

Fearless whipped his head back to Vicious. "Vicious, please!"

When, without warning, Darien emerged from the nearby bathroom window. His eyes flared as he saw Vicious on the ledge. "You can't hide from me, motherfucker!"

KA-CHUNK!

Darien pulled back the slide of a chrome-plated Desert Eagle and chambered a .50 caliber round. Fearless's eyes ripped back to the sniper, his index finger now resting on the trigger. He turned back to find Darien, who lined up his shot. The absurdity of the situation wasn't lost on Fearless. There he was, stuck on a ledge eighty floors up with a ruthless killer who was afraid of heights, while not one, but two gunmen were ready to shoot them dead. Barring some kind of divine intervention, they would surely die, one way or another.

And that's when Fearless saw it. Five floors below them. It was as if they were stranded at sea and at the last second, just before they were about to drown, they stumbled upon a lifeboat. But in this case, it was a basket-shaped rope-suspended scaffold used by window cleaners, about ten feet long and two feet wide. Just enough room for them to land.

With a mere fraction of a second to make a decision, Fearless wrapped his arms around Vicious, held him tight and jumped off the ledge!

Bang! The sniper fire rang out!

Bang! Darien pulled the trigger!

The bullets exploded where the pair had been standing, shattering the giant floor-to-ceiling windows behind them. Fearless and Vicious fell together as one, tumbling towards the platform as the shards of glass chased behind them like a swarm of angry bees.

THUD!

Fearless and Vicious slammed into the suspended scaffold with force. The scaffold, in turn, began to rapidly descend. Although they had somehow safely landed atop it, they were still continuing to free fall at pace. The scaffold consisted of four pulleys, one for each corner. Each emitted a high-pitched wheezing sound as the ropes quickly burned through their steel wheels.

SNAP! One of the ropes broke!

SNAP! Another rope broke on the opposite corner!

The scaffold teetered violently from corner to corner, threatening to dump Vicious and Fearless from its basket at any moment, when—

SNAP! The third rope broke!

The scaffold flipped vertically, then came to a hard stop, the entire apparatus dangling by a single rope. Vicious and Fearless were now hanging upside down, not to mention face-to-face, as they stared at the street below them. For a moment they remained silent, the scaffold gently swayed in the breeze.

"All things considered," Fearless said, "that went better than expected."

Vicious craned his neck to look around Fearless. "We're still a good twenty floors from the ground. How the hell are we going to get out of here?"

Fearless scoffed. "Well, to be honest, I didn't plan that far ahead because you were too busy shitting your pants on the side of the ledge!"

Vicious eyed the pulley and the single rope that was keeping them alive. Then, his eyes flicked to the open end of the basket, which faced the windows of the building. He had an idea.

"On the count of three, I need you to push off the glass with your feet as hard as you can."

Fearless rolled his eyes. "Oh, so now that you're not eighty floors up you got a plan, huh?"

"1… 2… *3*…!"

Fearless and Vicious pressed their bare feet against the glass, pushing the scaffolding out over the street. It slowly careened backwards towards the window, slamming into it with a dull *thud* and not even leaving a nick on the surface.

"I don't think that worked!" Fearless shouted.

"Again!" Vicious commanded. "1… 2… *3*…!"

The scaffolding swayed even farther from the wall this time and careened back towards the glass with even more force—but this time as it slammed into the building the window cracked in a scaffold-shaped spider web pattern.

"One more time!" Vicious yelled.

Fearless began to panic. "This feels like a bad idea!"

"And jumping into the scaffolding was a good one?" Vicious queried. "1… 2… *3*…!"

They both pushed with an audible grunt, the scaffold swayed like a massive pendulum, its stainless steel frame groaning and gaining momentum as it careened back into the glass one final time.

CRASH!

The scaffolding burst through the floor-to-ceiling window and landed in the middle of someone's living room. Fearless and Vicious groaned as they rolled out of the basket and onto the shattered glass that littered the floor.

"Are you… OK?"

The voice came from a ritzy man in a bathrobe, who was holding a cup of tea in one hand a hologram newspaper in the other. It appeared he was in far too much shock to be angry.

"No, no I don't think I am," Fearless moaned as he staggered to his feet.

The man took in their appearances. His eyes wide. "You two should *really* see a doctor."

Vicious glanced down at his shirt, which was now entirely drenched in blood from the sniper wound in his shoulder. Fearless gently touched the side of his head, then recoiled from the stinging pain that ran down his face. A huge shard of glass had pierced through the cartilage of his ear and was still dangling from it.

"Fuck! Ow! Fuck! How many face things can happen in one day?!"

Vicious turned to Fearless. "We should go, they're bound to figure out what floor we're on now."

They quickly turned to leave, the shards of glass crunching beneath their feet. When, Vicious stopped and turned back to the man in the bathrobe. He motioned to the catastrophic mess that littered the living room. "Oh, I uh, I live in the penthouse. I'll have someone come by later so we can discuss this… *situation*."

Fearless offered a grin. "Have a nice day."

And just like that, they were gone.

-THIRTEEN-

"THE GOOD DOCTOR"

Fearless never thought that sitting on a toilet could feel this good. But this wasn't just any ordinary toilet. This was the Toto Neorest Supreme Galaxy Edition. It featured a temperature controlled seat, a built-in bidet, a soothing massage function in three variable speeds, a noise cancelling soundtrack of rain falling in the Callisto jungle, and perfectly portioned one-thousand thread count toilet paper with a soothing chamomile scent. It wasn't just a toilet. It was an experience.

"Your free period has ended," a calming, female voice said. *"Please insert three woo to continue your Toto experience."*

Fearless's eyes ticked to a credit card reader mounted on the adjacent wall. It slowly blinked in neon green, waiting for payment. Instead, Fearless wacked the reader with the underside of his fist.

"Card declined," the voice said, in a frustratingly calm manner. Fearless grumbled and pulled up his pants. He opened the door and found Vicious standing bare-chested at the sink, attempting to wash the blood out of his shirt with hand soap. He

motioned to the enormous, five-star hotel lobby bathroom they had found themselves in.

"I would ask how you found this place, but I'm not sure I want to know the answer," Vicious muttered.

"Look, every kid who grew up on the streets knows that the hotels have the best public shitters in the city. This just happens to be the Taj Mahal of shitters," Fearless replied, joining Vicious at the adjacent sink and washing his hands.

The bathroom was opulent, fitted with black marble floors and antique gold fixtures. The kind of place that left a stack of small, rolled up hand towels on a platter in lieu of a paper towel dispenser. And, of course, featured top of the line toilets.

Fearless turned his head in the mirror, where he inspected the shard of glass wedged in his ear. "You think your friend will be able to get this glass out of my ear without leaving me looking like some kind of freak?"

"He's the best doctor I know." Vicious winced as he pressed a hand towel to his shoulder. It quickly turned red, soaked with blood.

Fearless took in the wound. He watched with concern as Vicious retrieved his damp shirt from the sink and carefully put it back on over the wound. It was clear to Fearless that he was in a tremendous amount of pain. On top of that, his face had turned a ghastly shade of pale. He had lost a significant amount of blood. The question remained, how much more could he stand to lose?

"You OK?" Fearless asked with more sincerity than usual.

Vicious gritted his teeth. "Fine. And I'll be a hell of a lot better once the good doctor patches me and gives something for the pain."

"Where in Tharsis does this guy live?"

"He doesn't live in the city. He lives out in Summerville."

Fearless laughed. "*Summerville?* You mean that suburb where all those Stepford Wives live? I thought you said this guy was a mob doctor who would use discretion."

Vicious slowly buttoned up his shirt. "Well, uh, he's not *exactly* a mob doctor."

"What do you mean?"

"He's a pediatrician."

Fearless's eyes nearly fell out of his head. "I'm sorry—are you telling me we're going all the way out to the suburbs, to your kid doctor friend's house, *unannounced* I might add, to ask him if he'll stitch up your bullet hole? You have *got* to be kidding me, right?"

Vicious turned to Fearless. "Look, he's helped me out in the past. And besides, you got a better plan? Because the way I see it, not only do we have the Red Dragon searching for our asses, but now we have to worry about the Europa Crew, too. We can't just call up some ordinary shot doc. It's too risky."

Fearless put a finger to his chin, faux-pondering this. "Hmm. And whose fault might *that* be? Because the way *I* see it, we'd only be dealing with *one* crime family who wanted us—sorry, *you*—dead if you didn't snap and kill Darien's brother at the noodle bar."

Vicious sighed. "That wasn't me."

"Really? Then who was it, Vicious?" Fearless asked in frustration. "Because it looked a hell of a lot like *you.*"

Vicious grew quiet. He stood with his palms on either side of the sink. He locked eyes with himself in the mirror. Then turned to Fearless.

"OK, it's not a *who*, it's a *what*. A feeling that comes over me. I can't turn away from it or escape it, no matter how hard I try. It does what it wants. And unfortunately, after the way Dodd spoke to me in the car that night, all it wanted was to annihilate anything in its path."

Fearless considered this for a moment. "The feeling. It's getting worse. Isn't it?"

Vicious slowly nodded. He didn't want to admit it. Part of him was ashamed. "If I could turn it off, I would. But I can't. It is what it is."

He motioned to a clock on the wall. It was just after one o'clock in the afternoon. "We should get going. When I called the doc from the lobby I told him we'd be there this afternoon." Vicious headed for the door—and opened it. He turned back to Fearless, who was still at the sink. "You coming?"

Fearless nodded. "I'll meet you at the van." He motioned back to the stalls behind him. "I wanna sit on that toilet one last time."

Vicious chuckled. "We all have our kinks, man." Then turned and exited through the door.

But Fearless remained at the sink. He bowed his head. He knew that all the murder and bloodshed from the past seventy-two hours was taking its toll on him. He wasn't like Vicious. He wasn't a killer. He was just a kid from the streets who was good at fighting and could shoot a gun straighter than most. And when you're good at those two particular things, and there's no family to help you make the right choices, life tends to steer you in a certain direction. Fearless wasn't sure that he was cut out for organized crime. But he wasn't sure what other option he had.

He took a deep breath. Then slowly exhaled. "*It is what it is.*"

Summerville was the first planned suburban community to be built in Tharsis City. It was the brainchild of Elton Creed, the founder of the immensely popular theme park Earthland that was built on an asteroid in the belt located between Mars and Jupiter.

The concept was simple: Summerville would be a suburban utopia reminiscent of the great Midwestern suburbs on Earth. A place where crime was practically non-existent, there was a different neighborhood barbecue to attend every night of the week, and kids could leave their bikes on the front lawn without fear that they'd be gone in the morning. Creed named the suburb after the summer season, not only because it was his favorite time of year, but because he believed that the concept of summer was a reflection of what the community could be—worry-free days, warm nights and of course, no school.

"This place always freaked me out," Fearless said as he gazed out the van's passenger window. Outside, they passed by identical colonial style homes one after another. Each had a white picket fence and what seemed like an impossibly green lawn. The only variation between them were their color, but even then, owners were only allowed to choose between various shades of white and beige.

"I don't know," Vicious shrugged. "I always thought it was kind of nice."

Fearless shook his head. "I take it back, your insatiable thirst for murder is no longer the thing that freaks me out the most about you. The fact that you think Summerville is 'kind of nice' definitely takes the cake."

Vicious shrugged. "I'm just saying, it looks like a nice place to settle down with a family one day."

"That would imply that you *actually* want to get married."

"Don't you?"

Fearless scoffed. "Absolutely *not*. A wedding is just a fancy funeral. You might as well take that one hundred thousand woo and bury yourself alive with it. Because that's what marriage is going to be like when you're stuck in a place like Summerville, going to baseball games on Friday nights and eating ice cream out of one of those big waffle cones that are dipped in chocolate. That's about as much excitement you get from marriage. No thank you."

"What about lifelong commitment and getting to know a human being on the most intimate level?" Vicious countered.

"What are you? My therapist? Besides, how are *you* going to get married? What are you going to tell your wife when that thing takes over and you slaughter the dog walker? *Sorry, hunny, I had a bad day at work and snapped?*"

"You're an asshole."

"Yes, I am, but *you're* delusional." Fearless looked back out the window. "Where does this doctor live anyways?"

Vicious pointed ahead. "Should be this next house on the right."

The van approached a perfectly spotless concrete driveway with a birdhouse-shaped mailbox that had a few pink balloons tied to it.

Fearless's eyes ticked to the mailbox. "What's with the balloons?"

Vicious shrugged as he pulled into the driveway where a half-dozen cars were parked. The van came to a stop and they hopped outside.

Fearless motioned to the vehicles. "How can a pediatrician afford this many cars?"

"Maybe he's really popular…?" Vicious said, trying to convince himself.

Then, Fearless stopped on a dime. He held a hand to Vicious's chest, slowing him down with him. "Did you hear that?"

"Hear what?"

And then, they heard it—the sound of children screaming in the backyard. Fearless slowly turned to Vicious. He was absolutely fuming.

"There's a *kid's birthday party* happening right now."

Vicious scratched his head. He motioned back towards the mailbox. "I guess that explains the balloons."

"You said you *called him* from the lobby."

"I said I *tried* to call."

"No, you did not! You said *called.* Are you *shitting* me right now?" Fearless snapped. He pointed to the flecks of blood that peppered his shirt. "We're covered in *blood*! And you want us to walk into a birthday party with a bunch of children, unannounced?"

Vicious tried to explain. "Look, I *tried* to call. But he didn't answer. What was I supposed to do? Leave a voicemail that said, *Hey Doc, long time no talk. Listen, I got fucking shot and I need you to pull the bullet out of me before I lose too much blood?*"

Fearless shook his hands at Vicious in a rage. "Yes! That's exactly what you should've done!"

Then, suddenly, the front door opened to reveal a balding, middle-aged man dressed in a pressed pink Oxford shirt with a bag of party trash in his hand. He closed the door behind him and headed down the front porch steps—then froze.

"Doc!" Vicious called out in a friendly tone.

The doctor took in the two blood-drenched men before him. His jaw went slack. He frantically looked back to his house to make sure that no one was watching, then quickly approached them.

"Vicious? What the hell are you doing here?" the doctor asked in an aggressive whisper.

Vicious tried to explain. "I know this is a surprise, but—"

"A *surprise?*" the doctor blurted out. "It's my daughter's sixth *birthday*!"

"Look, you're the only one I can trust. OK? I got shot in the shoulder and I lost a lot of blood. I just need you to stitch it up so I don't lose any more."

The doctor looked back to the house again to make sure it was clear, then turned back to Vicious. He motioned to his shoulder. "Let me see it."

Vicious pulled back his shirt to reveal the gaping bullet wound. The doctor recoiled at the sight. "Holy *shit*! What happened to you?"

"Sniper rifle," Vicious replied with a psychotic level of nonchalance as he motioned to Fearless standing next to him. "Doc, this is Fearless. My... *business partner*."

"Nice to meet ya," Fearless chirped as he motioned to his ear. "And I got this shard of glass stuck in my ear. If possible, I'd really like to preserve the shape. I've been told I have nice ears."

"What do I look like? A fucking plastic surgeon? I'm a pediatrician," the doctor snapped back. "Look. You shouldn't have come here. But since you're here, it's my duty as a health care professional to help you. Use the entrance on the side of the house. I'll meet you in my office. Third door on the left."

Vicious breathed a sigh of relief. "I don't know how to thank you, Doc."

"You can do it by not letting my wife see you inside the house. Now *go.*"

Fearless and Vicious carefully opened the side door and entered the house that echoed with the not-so-faraway sounds of children's screams and laughter. They quietly walked down a hallway lined with framed family photos. Fearless stopped and motioned to a photo where the doctor and his family wore matching ugly Christmas sweaters at a ski resort.

"Look at these assholes. Is that what really sounds nice to you about marriage? Matching sweater pictures?"

Vicious gritted his teeth. "Would you shut up and keep moving?"

Fearless's eyes narrowed as he studied the photo closer. "His wife is *bangin'* though."

"Her name's Hannah. She's an old friend."

Fearless turned to Vicious and raised an eyebrow. "What do you mean, *old friend*?"

"I didn't *mean* anything. Can we just go, please—"

From behind them they heard a stern female voice. "Excuse me? Can I help you two?"

Vicious cringed. He already knew who it was. As they slowly turned to find Hannah, the good doctor's wife. She wore a country club member uniform consisting of a bright pink polo and a matching pink skirt, with her hair pulled back in a ponytail so tight that it smoothed the wrinkles on her forehead.

"What are you doing here?" Hannah asked, her voice one of surprise tinged with a romantic familiarity.

"Hannah," Vicious said as he approached her. "I needed a

favor. The doc said he could help me out. I'm sorry that I didn't let you know beforehand. It's uh, it's been a long time."

"A few years, I think," Hannah replied with a coquettish grin. She pulled him close for a hug. Vicious winced in pain as they embraced.

"What's wrong? What happened to you?" she asked with concern.

Vicious clutched his shoulder. "It's nothing, really."

"Let me see it."

Vicious pulled back his shirt to reveal the wound. Hannah shrieked with panic as she laid eyes on it. "Come with me, right now. We need to get you cleaned up."

Hannah pulled Vicious into a nearby bathroom and closed the door behind them, leaving Fearless in the hallway alone. He threw his arms up in the air in frustration. "I also have a shard of glass in my ear but don't worry, I'll just fuck off and show myself to the doc's office."

Vicious and Hannah stood in a small half bathroom. The space would be tight for one person, let alone two. She opened up a cabinet underneath the sink and pulled out a First-Aid kit. She set in on the sink and began to remove its contents, setting aside spools of gauze and tubes of disinfecting ointment. Then, she turned and motioned to him. "Take off your shirt."

Vicious hesitated for a moment. There was a history between them and the last time he removed his shirt for her it was under *slightly* different circumstances. He carefully took it off and set it aside. Hannah applied some rubbing alcohol to a gauze pad and held it over the wound.

"This might sting," she warned him.

Vicious winced in pain as Hannah carefully blotted the wound with the gauze pad. She cringed as she continued to apply it to his skin. "Sorry, I'm trying to be gentle."

Vicious brushed off her apology. "It's fine, really."

"When was the last time we saw each other?"

Vicious pursed his lips as he racked his brain for an answer. "It would have had to have been the Callisto beach club, right?"

Hannah chuckled. Her cheeks turning a rosy shade of pink. "Oh yeah. *That's* why I don't remember."

Vicious couldn't help but laugh, too. "What were those drinks called? The ones that they served in a whole pineapple with two straws and a little pink umbrella?"

"A painkiller."

"That's right. It took me three rounds to figure out that there were two straws because they were meant for two people."

"What a terrible, *terrible* idea for a drink." Hannah laughed. She continued to carefully blot the wound, then secured a large bandage over it. She placed her hand on his bare chest for a moment, then slowly moved her hand down his body as she traced his abdominal muscles with her index finger.

"What happened on the beach that night, though—" she continued, her finger lingering on his waist. "That… was not a terrible idea."

Vicious began to breath heavy. Their bodies lightly touched. There was an electricity between them. It was as if at any moment they were going to rip each other's clothes off and pick up where they left off on that Callisto beach.

And then, they did.

—————

Meanwhile, Fearless stepped into the doctor's office and shut the door behind him. His eyes narrowed as he slowly scanned the room and realized it was decorated entirely in an aviation theme. Dozens of model airplanes and spaceships hung from the ceiling. Books on flying and pilot's guides filled a floor-to-ceiling bookshelf. In the corner of the room, there was a full-sized cockpit window-shaped bank of computer monitors in order to conduct flight simulations. It was at the same time impressive and somewhat creepy.

"The good doctor *sure does* like flying..." Fearless muttered to himself, as he began to poke around the room. He approached the doctor's desk and took a picture frame off the surface. Inside was a photo of the doctor with Hannah as they stood outside a F-18 fighter jet. They wore matching flight suits with a helmet tucked under their arm and a cheesy thumbs up with their free hand.

"Again with the matching outfits," Fearless grumbled as he rolled his eyes. "This is why I'm never getting married."

Fearless set the frame back on the desk, when something caught his eye—the desk's center drawer was slightly ajar. Fearless's eyes ticked to the door to make sure no one was watching, then back to the drawer. He carefully opened it, scanning its contents. It was mostly pens and loose change. A notebook. A few loose paper clips.

Until, his eyes clocked a small, shiny object. Fearless picked it up. It was a single key. It dangled from a keychain with an address printed on it. It read:

THARSIS PRIVATE AVIATION

HANGAR 4
BAY 10

Suddenly the office door opened. The good doctor entered with a trove of medical supplies tucked under his arm. However, he stopped dead in his tracks upon seeing Fearless standing behind his desk.

"What are you doing standing behind my desk?" he questioned.

Unbeknownst to the doctor, Fearless discreetly tucked the key into his back pocket. He motioned to the various planes hanging from the ceiling.

"Just checking out your toys here," Fearless responded.

The doctor scoffed at the word. "They're not toys, they're *models*."

"You a fly guy or something?"

"The term is aviation enthusiast," the doctor responded, his eyes scanning the rest of the office for something. Or *someone*. "Where's Vicious?"

Fearless motioned to the hallway. "Oh, we ran into your wife in the hallway. She took Vicious somewhere to get a jump on cleaning out his wound."

The doctor's eye narrowed. "What do you mean she *took* him somewhere?"

"I don't know, the bathroom, maybe?" Fearless shrugged off the question then motioned to his ear. "OK so, about my ear—"

The doctor cut him off. "*Fuck* your ear. They're in the bathroom together?"

Fearless cringed. "I take it you're upset."

The doctor turned and whipped open the office door so hard that it slammed into the adjacent wall and shattered a picture frame hanging behind it! He stomped out into the hallway with a scalpel clutched in his fist. Fearless clocked the medical blade in his hand. "*Goddamnit, Vicious!*" And chased after him.

The doctor rushed down the hallway to the half bathroom. He furiously jiggled the handle and banged on the door as he screamed, "*Vicious! Hannah! Open the door right now!*"

But the doctor didn't wait for them to follow through. Instead, he cocked his foot back and took aim at the door! *BOOM!* The door blew right off its hinges!

To reveal Hannah sitting atop the sink, her legs wrapped around Vicious, their tongues down each other's throats. As he was earlier, Vicious was shirtless with his pants undone. Hannah was in a similar state of undress, down to her bra, her skirt hiked above the waist.

Vicious turned to see the doctor, his eyes ticking to the scalpel in hand. "Doc, wait!"

Hannah too saw the blade. "*Matthew, no!*"

"You son of a bitch!" the doctor cried out in a jealous rage, as he swung the scalpel wildly at Vicious!

Swish! Swish! Swish!

Vicious narrowly dodged the blade as it cut through the air, but with the close quarters he currently found himself in, he was running out of room—and time. Hannah screamed, desperate to stop her husband from killing Vicious, but it was no use. The good doctor only saw red as he raised the scalpel high, ready to draw blood—

SLAP!

Someone grabbed him by the wrist. It was Fearless. "I wouldn't do that if I were you."

Fearless locked the doctor's scalpel-clutching wrist behind his head, then locked his other wrist behind his lower back, twisting his arms into a figure-eight style hold. He dragged the doctor into the hallway.

"Get your hands off of me!" the doctor cried.

"Not until you cool the fuck out. All of you!" Fearless replied, as he held the doctor tight. He turned to Vicious and Hannah, who were standing in the hallway half-dressed. "What kind of messed up suburban love triangle is this?"

Hannah turned to her husband. "Matthew, I'm leaving you for Vicious."

"Sorry, you're doing *what now*?" Vicious replied. Clearly this was news to him.

"Fine! I'm happy for you two!" the doctor shouted. "I knew I should have never given you a second chance after you two ran off to Callisto together while we were supposed to be on our honeymoon!"

Fearless let out a long, exasperated exhale. "OK, clearly this is *way* more complicated than I thought. Doc, look, I let you go, are you gonna be cool?"

The doctor sighed with frustration. "Yes, I'll be cool. I promise."

Fearless carefully let him out of the hold. The doctor rubbed his wrists as the four of them stood in the hallway, not entirely sure where to go from here.

"Mommy? Daddy? What are you doing?"

The four adults turned to find a little girl, age six, wearing a birthday crown. She looked at them with her head tilted like a puppy, her eyes wide and brimming with tears. She had been watching all along.

"Don't cry, sweetheart. Daddy's fine. These men are just some old friends that were just leaving," Hannah said, as she walked forward and took the little girl by the hand. "Let's go get you another cupcake."

Hannah and the little girl walked off, leaving Fearless and Vicious with the doctor.

"I take it that you're not going to be fixing my ear," Fearless asked.

The doctor pointed to the side entrance that they came through. "Get the hell out of my house."

Fearless and Vicious rode in the catering van in silence. Fearless drove while Vicious slept in the passenger seat. Fearless shook his head as he replayed the day's events over in his mind. For everything that Vicious had put him through the past few days, to Fearless this one was somehow the worst. It wasn't the fact that Vicious dragged him all the way out to Summerville and he still had a shard of glass in his ear, or the fact that he showed up unannounced to the home of an old friend whose wife he had previously slept with. It was the little girl that upset him the most. Fearless didn't come across kids much. Especially in their line of work. But upsetting a little girl on her birthday was a bridge too far for him.

Vicious stirred awake. He winced as he sat up. The pain in his shoulder had become more intense. The blood continued to seep through the bandage that Hannah had applied. He glanced outside the window. They were chugging along a dark stretch of highway, as the city skyline lingered in the opposite direction.

"I thought we were going back to the city to find another doctor?" Vicious asked.

Fearless stewed. "You can find yourself another doctor once we get off Mars."

"What do you mean find myself?"

"On your own. Alone. Solo. I'm out."

Vicious scoffed. "You're *out*? Out of what?"

"This job, this friendship, and this life. I can't do it anymore, man. I'm done. I'm gonna fly out to New Tijuana for a bit. And figure out my next step."

"Look, I'm sorry. We needed a doctor, I didn't think—"

Fearless cut him off. "Didn't think? Didn't think what? That the doctor wouldn't be excited to see the guy who fucked his wife on their honeymoon? Just like you didn't think about killing that drunk in the noodle bar?" Fearless shook his head. "That's the thing about you. You don't think about *anything*. You just think about *Vicious*."

Vicious scoffed. "So I fucked up. I fucked up a lot. Fine. But at least I'm trying to go somewhere with my life, Fearless. At least I'm trying to make something of myself. Sometimes I wonder if you'd rather just sit at a bar and drink yourself to death."

"Well, it sounds a hell of a lot better than whatever this is."

Vicious scoffed. "Yeah, and how the hell are you going to get to New Tijuana?"

Fearless held up the single key. "The doctor loaned me the keys to his ship."

"You *stole* his keys."

Fearless snapped back. "And you *stole* his wife. Twice. So do me a favor and don't lecture me about the morality of theft."

Ahead, a row of airplane hangars appeared alongside a small airstrip. Fearless yanked the wheel and as they pulled in, they passed a sign that read:

Tharsis Private Aviation
No Trespassing

Fearless and Vicious exited the catering truck and walked into hangar number four. There were dozens of aircraft lined up side-by-side, most of them low-end ships and planes, some of them ready to fly, others in various states of disrepair. On Tharsis many people still flew traditional airplanes for fun, as flying a ship through the astral gates and the solar system itself had been so heavily regulated that it had taken on a persona akin to driving on a highway. And as they reached bay number 10, they saw what would be their ticket off Mars, once and for all. Or so they thought.

"That *can't* be the ship," Fearless muttered.

Vicious cringed. "Well, that's not going to get you all the way to New Tijuana. Actually, I don't think it's going to get you past Phobos. Maybe Deimos."

The ship in question was what was more commonly referred to as a moon jumper. A small twin seater ship that was most commonly used by affluent people in Tharsis to get from the city to their vacation home on one of Mars's two moons. Any farther and you ran the risk of running out of fuel and floating in space until someone came along and gave you a fill up. And even then, you could be a waiting a *long* time.

Fearless sighed. "Let's take a look at what she's working with."

Inside, the plane didn't fare much better in terms of first impressions. The display was digital, rather than the industry standard holographic. The controls were rusted and their grips worn down. There were two seats in front and a bench in the back, all three with questionable looking seatbelts and tears patched with duct tape.

Vicious looked to Fearless. "She ain't pretty. Can you fly her?"

"Me?" The question took Fearless by surprise. "I thought you were flying it?"

Vicious laughed. "I can't fly. I never have before."

"You're telling me as a kid you went gravity sailing on Europa and to race car school but you never learned to fly?"

Vicious shrugged. "I don't like heights, remember?"

Fearless grumbled. It appeared his grand plan of escaping his current life had already hit a roadblock, when they were interrupted by a gruff voice.

"Can I help you two?"

Fearless and Vicious turned to find a man in his mid-sixties. His gravelly voice sounded like the result of an unfiltered three pack a day habit that he was using as a way to try and kick his other habit, whiskey.

Fearless got an idea. He motioned to the moon jumper. "Can you fly this thing?"

"Sure I can," the older man grumbled as he motioned to the grease stains on his shirt. "Can't you see that I'm the mechanic around here?"

"I'll give you a hundred woo to fly us to New Tijuana," Fearless offered.

The man chuckled. "Gonna take a hell of a lot more than a hundred woo to get there. You're gonna have to stop for a fill up on Deimos, and that's if the gas station is open. Astral gate fees are fifty woo each way. And that's before we factor in flight time and a tip, which will be *significant* to account for the fact that the plane doesn't belong to you."

Fearless turned to Vicious and whispered, "Give me your gun."

"What, why?" Vicious asked.

"Because I left mine in the van again."

Vicious rolled his eyes as he reached into his waistband and handed Fearless his 9mm. He cocked the slide back and pointed it at the mechanic.

"How's this for a tip?"

The man slowly raised his hands as he began to full on panic. "Holy shit. That's a gun. OK. Oh wow oh wow. Holy shit. *Holy* shit."

Vicious gave Fearless the side-eye. "That's the line you went with? *How's this for a tip?*"

"Fuck you," Fearless whispered, as he turned his attention back to Scotty. "Now get your ass in the cockpit."

But Scotty didn't budge, as he doubled over struggling to catch his breath. "Ooooooweee. I ain't ever been stuck up before. Oh boy. Holy shit. Wow-o-wow."

Fearless and Vicious traded a glance as if to say, *this is getting a bit dramatic.*

"What's your name, old timer?" Fearless asked with a far more polite tone.

He struggled to speak in between breaths. "Scott-ty. Scotty."

Fearless took a deep breath. Exhaled. Now he just felt bad. "Just get in the plane, Scotty. Will ya?"

And then, it happened. All at once. As was its custom.

Scotty puked.

The moonjumper rumbled uneasily down the runway. Scotty, who was drenched in sweat post puke, was at the reins. Vicious sat shotgun, as was his request because of his tendency to get motion sickness, which relegated Fearless to the back bench. Not that he was complaining, as the bench allowed him to kick his feet up and put his hands behind his head.

"Hold on to your butts," Scotty said as he turned the ship and aligned it with the runway for takeoff. "These old ships tend to get a little bumpy after takeoff."

"Thanks for the heads up but I tend to be asleep before takeoff." Fearless yawned. But then remembered that Scotty was *supposed* to be their hostage. "Oh, but uh, remember I got my eye on you, don't make any sudden moves, and so on and so forth."

Scotty pulled back the thrusters. The moon jumper sputtered to a start, but then quickly picked up speed as it lifted off the runway and into the air. As they ascended into the atmosphere, Tharsis City looked small. It was merely a cluster of buildings built inside a crater, surrounded by thousands of miles of barren red desert.

"We're coming up on the stratosphere," Scotty said. "Round here is about when things get—" But then, Scotty struggled to speak. He re-focused himself, then tried again. "When things tend to get—" He clutched his chest. "Tend to get—"

Scotty passed out cold on the controls.

The moon jumper began to rapidly descend! Scotty's weight was entirely on the ship's yoke, pointing it straight down. The ship's computer began to flash an array of warning lights while an automated voice commanded *"Pull up! Pull up! Pull up!"*

Vicious frantically tried to rouse the mechanic. "Hey! Hey! Scotty! Wake up, man!" But it was no use. He put two fingers to Scotty's neck to check for a pulse, but felt nothing. Scotty was dead.

Vicious looked to Fearless, who continued to lay eerily calm on the bench. "You murdered Scotty!"

Fearless opened one eye. His hands still relaxingly clutched behind his head. "How did *I* murder Scotty? He definitely just had a heart attack. I should have realized it by the vomiting, which is a pretty clear warning sign. "

Vicious desperately tried to pull Scotty's body off the yoke as the ship continued to descend, but he was too heavy. He turned back to Fearless and screamed, "Help me, would you! We're gonna die if we don't get him off the controls!"

Fearless shrugged. His eyes remained closed. "You know, I always assumed this is the way I'd go out."

"What the hell does that mean?"

Fearless explained. "I have dreams about this moment all the time. I'm on a ship, something goes wrong, the ship falls out of the sky and crashes and I die. Then I wake up. So now, we're in that scenario, and I've made peace with it."

"Made peace with?" Vicious snapped back. "Are you out of your fucking mind?!"

Vicious, on the other hand, had not made peace with shit. He was determined to live, one way or another. He looked out the cockpit windows, clocking their descent. The red sand of the Martian desert below was getting closer and closer by the second. They had mere seconds to pull up and change the course of their lives forever.

And then he got an idea. Vicious quickly unhooked his seatbelt and climbed across Scotty. His hand frantically searched the side of the pilot's chair for the manual slide release. He fumbled around, his hands dancing around it, until; he grasped it. He pulled the lever, sliding Scotty's chair back mere inches and giving himself just enough leverage to push Scotty off the yoke.

Instantaneously, the ship began to level out. But the red Martian dirt in the window was still coming in too fast. They had pulled up as far as they could. They were going to crash. But the question was, would their angle of impact be the kind that kills them, or the kind that only severely maims them?

"Brace for impact!!" Vicious shouted.

But Fearless didn't even flinch. His eyes remained closed. And he didn't utter a word. He just laid there, waiting for it all to be over. And just as the ship was about to slam into the ground, Fearless's lips slowly curled to a smile.

And then, everything went black.

–FOURTEEN–

"The Fight"

The broken asphalt crunched as the limousine slowly drove through the streets of East Tharsis. It wasn't unusual for a limousine to drive in this neighborhood. The rich often came through this part of town when they wanted a hire a prostitute or buy black market drugs. But this wasn't just any ordinary limousine. It had triple thick bulletproof windows that were tinted black. The frame was made of steel reinforced with ceramic plating. The tires were lined with Kevlar, making them impossible to deflate. This wasn't a car. It was a bunker.

The limousine came to a stop in front of the dry cleaner. Two well-dressed men armed with Heckler & Koch MP7 submachine guns loaded with armor piercing bullets, the kind of weapon reserved for Special Forces, stepped out of the car. They radioed back to the driver that the coast was clear—and out stepped the lone passenger from the back.

The passenger wore a double breasted, custom made Italian wool suit, a silk scarf around his neck. His white hair was

231

brushed back, never slicked. He carried a chinchilla fur derby hat, but didn't wear it. On his wrist was a Lange & Söhne Grand Complication watch. In all, he was the picture of elegance and class. The most peculiar thing about the man was his face. It was perfectly normal looking for a man in his fifties, if not unremarkable. But he didn't have a single wrinkle around his eyes. Not a crease on his forehead. Not a line around his mouth. Those who worked for him said it was because he had never once displayed an emotion in his entire life. But maybe that's what made him who he was—

His name was Caliban, the most powerful figure in the solar system.

Caliban strolled toward the entrance to the dry cleaner, his security following close behind but never closer than ten feet. He had made it clear in the past that they were to keep their distance. He needed them, but he didn't like them being within earshot of his affairs.

Lucky was waiting for him outside. He held out his hand to greet him. "Caliban, I'm so glad you came."

Caliban took a look around, unimpressed. "I hope this will be worth my time."

"Discretion, as you can imagine, is key here. That's why we needed this store front. Let's just say the authorities aren't thrilled by what we do here," Lucky explained.

"You's a rich mochafucka ain't you," a voice called out.

Caliban's eyes ticked to the sidewalk, where a homeless man sat on the ground outside of a dilapidated tent that had been patched up with tape, but was barely standing.

Lucky motioned to the security detail. "Get this asshole out of here, will you?"

But Caliban motioned for his security to stay back. He turned to the homeless man. "I am a man of means, yes. Why do you ask?"

"Some people have money. But not everyone can afford that watch," the homeless man said. "I used to fix watches. Fell on some hard times, though. Lost my shop. I always hoped a watch like that would come in. But you don't get many people around here who own a watch like that. Did you know it takes a year to assemble?"

"In fact, I did. That's why I purchased it. I admired the craftsmanship," Caliban replied, then motioned to the man's tent. "What happened to your tent?"

"Some kids from the city came down here. They tore it up. Thought it was funny. They don't know that to people like me, this is my home."

Caliban motioned to his security. "These men will get you into a hotel this evening. You stay as long as you like. I'll take care of the expense."

"Oh, oh my. Mister. I don't know how to thank you."

Caliban nodded. "You thank me by pulling yourself together and opening a new shop. Consider this an opportunity."

He turned and entered the dry cleaner. Lucky was at his side. He stopped and turned to Caliban. "I have to ask: why would you help a random homeless man like that?"

"If you want to bring out the best in someone, you need to invest in them. And that's exactly what I do," Caliban replied, emotionless. He motioned ahead. "Now, shall we?"

Two boys were fighting in the ring. Caliban and Lucky watched from the top of the risers, away from the bettors and the inebriated rich people who had come to bask in the bloodshed.

"These kids, they're hungry. I ain't ever seen anything like them," Lucky said. "They don't just fight to win here. They fight to survive."

Caliban motioned to the boys in the ring. "Where did these boys come from?"

Lucky shrugged. "These two are from the slums of Ganymede. Majority of my boys come from the slums. Some of 'em are criminals out on parole with nowhere else to go. We get some runaways, too."

"And these boys," Caliban asked curiously, "you think they may be of a benefit to my operation?"

"Absolutely. That's the thing about them. They're loyal. Even when they start winning and start earning some coin, they don't go nowhere. They live for the next round. It's like a drug."

Caliban held out an empty hand to his security guard, who without being prompted placed a business card and pen in his palm. Caliban scribbled something on the back, then handed it to Lucky.

"This is the name of someone in my organization. I want you to send him your hungriest fighters. Not the best, the hungriest. He will handle it from here. As you can imagine, I can not be directly associated with your operation."

Lucky nodded. "Of course."

"One more thing," Caliban said. "I have a boy for you. But I don't want him getting any special treatment. Bring him in just like the others."

"Sure thing," Lucky responded. His eyes flared with curiosity. "Who is it?"

"My son," Caliban said, without a trace of guilt. Even the worst, most evil parent would feel a shred of remorse sending their child to a place like the Pits. But not him.

Lucky stared back, astonished. "Why the hell would you send your own son here?"

"Like I said. I invest in people."

"Caliban..." Lucky tried to find the words. "Kids have died here."

Caliban stood and buttoned his suit jacket. "If that's his destiny, then so be it."

He turned and walked away, leaving the other man alone in the risers. Lucky's eyes began to fill with tears. He reached into his shirt and pulled out a rosary he wore around his neck. He kissed the cross, then began to pray.

"Hail Mary, full of grace, the Lord is with thee..."

The White-Haired Boy's foot tapped the floor relentlessly. He sat alone on a bench in the locker room, a row of lockers on either side of him. He could hear the muffled sound of the crowd through the walls. It was Saturday night, the biggest fight of the week. And they were already chanting. "We want blood! We want blood! We want blood!"

And then, from the other side of the lockers, he heard a familiar voice. "Those rich pricks seem like a rowdy bunch tonight."

It was Fearless. He too was sitting on a bench. A row of lockers separated them. The White-Haired Boy couldn't help but smile. "Feels weird to have to fight you."

"Nah," Fearless replied. "It was bound to happen, sooner or later. You had Irish on the ropes. And I still believe... shit, I know you would've beat Sixteen. Would only be matter of time until you sent me to the mat."

The White-Haired Boy chuckled. "Thanks. But I'm not buying it."

"Hey, I've got an idea." Fearless lit up. "What if we just ran?"

"Yeah, right."

"For real, though. I've got plenty of blood money. We could buy a ship. Hang out on New Tijuana for a bit until we figured out where to go."

The White-Haired Boy shook his head. "Yeah, right. You'd blow all your money on Kudo and titties at the Sneaky Lizard before we even got out of town."

Fearless took a deep breath. Then exhaled. "Yeah, you're probably right."

Suddenly, a pair of heavy footsteps began to approach.

Click-clack. Click-clack. Click-clack.

It was as if the White-Haired Boy recognized the footstep's pattern. He knew who it was before they even rounded the corner. He glanced up.

"Dad?"

Caliban stood before him, dressed in his signature suit and scarf, chinchilla derby hat in hand. He didn't smile, nor frown. As was his custom. He was perfectly emotionless.

"Son."

"What are you doing here?" the White-Haired Boy asked.

"Lucky told me there was a big fight tonight," Caliban explained. "So I flew in from Venus."

"You did that... for me?"

"I came to see a fight."

The White-Haired Boy's lips curled to a smile. Even though his father couldn't even bring himself to say he wanted to see his son fight, the fact that he was simply here meant the world to the boy.

"I almost won the other night, you know."

Caliban's eye narrowed. "You almost won?"

The White-Haired Boy grew excited. "Yeah, so, you see, my friend Fearless, that's who I'm fighting tonight, he taught me that I needed to start anticipating my opponent's moves, and so, I'm fighting this Irish kid right, and I'm getting beat pretty bad, but in the third round I realized that his plan was to double jab my ribs then—"

Caliban held up a hand to silence him. Then spoke with an ice cold tone. "What the fuck are you so happy about?"

The White-Haired Boy swallowed. "Well, I um, I'm making progress, so—"

"Progress isn't good enough," Caliban snapped back. "I sent you here to learn how to fight. To win. To learn how to be a man. And you're telling me about progress?"

"I just thought that—"

"Do you know what Lucky told me when I sent you here?" Caliban asked. "He told me that boys have died in this place. He couldn't believe that I would send my own son here. And do you know what I told him?"

The White-Haired Boy didn't want to know the answer. But he knew that his father was going to tell him anyways. He just shook his head.

"I told him that if you died in this place, then that was your destiny. I wouldn't shed a tear. Just like I didn't when your mother took her life." Caliban let his words linger in the air for a moment. And then continued. "You may be all I have left, but I'm willing to lose you too."

And with that, Caliban turned and walked away. The White-Haired Boy sat there for a moment. But he didn't cry. Something was building inside of him. A sensation. It was more than anger. It was a blackness. He had never felt anything like it before. It consumed him.

"Don't listen to him, OK? Remember what I told you. You don't need him. You're an orphan just like the rest of us. We're your family now." It was Fearless. He stood at the end of the row of lockers, having heard the entire thing.

The White-Haired Boy ignored him. He stood up and faced one of the lockers. And then, he began to whale on it. Over and over again. Until the metal began to bend. And his knuckles began to bleed. When he was finished, the locker looked as if it had been smashed with a baseball bat.

The White-Haired Boy dripped with cold sweat. He began to shake. "I told you. He's a monster."

Fearless took him in. "Then prove him wrong."

"I can't..." The White-Haired Boy shook his head. "I can't beat you."

"Sure you can," Fearless said. "I just saw it. That's how you beat me. That's how you beat anyone. You take it from him. You be vicious."

The fight had already gone two brutal rounds. Fearless trapped the White-Haired Boy in the corner of the ring as he delivered jab after jab to his ribs. He could feel them cracking underneath his fists. Both his friend's eyes were almost entirely swollen shut. His bottom lip split open. His ear mangled. He was almost unrecognizable. But as much as he wished the White-Haired

Boy would give up, he refused. He just kept taking the punches. And every once in a while, he would smile. It was as if he was enjoying it. As if he was enduring the beat down to prove a point.

Ding ding ding!

The second round ended. Fearless returned to his corner and sat on a stool. He knew he was going to win. The White-Haired Boy couldn't even sit on his stool. He was slumped over the corner. His body was limp. Fearless worried that he was going to die. And for a moment, he thought maybe he would be better off that way.

Ding!

The third round was beginning. Fearless stood up. But the White-Haired Boy didn't move. He was still hanging over the edge of the ropes.

"Give up... Just give up..." Fearless whispered to himself.

Until, the White-Haired Boy slowly stood straight and wobbled back into the center of the ring. For a moment, Fearless bowed his head in thought. He didn't know if it was better to end this quickly, or to let the White-Haired Boy hang around until the end. At least then it would look like he tried.

Fearless's eye flicked to the crowd. He clocked Caliban in the stands. He was seated with Lucky. When, a bookie approached them. Lucky initially shooed him away, but Caliban stopped him. He reached into his wallet and pulled out a hundred thousand woos. Handed them to the bookie. Fearless was astonished. He couldn't believe what the man was doing. He was betting against his own son.

Ding! Ding! The bell rang twice. It was time to fight.

Fearless reluctantly approached the White-Haired Boy. He squared up with him, knowing that he could end this fight with a single punch. But he decided to do something more elaborate. To end this fight with a bang.

And so, Fearless brought his fists to his chin—then planted his back foot. His front foot lifting and wrapping around his body as he spun, like a serpent coiling around its prey. It was the same knock out kick he had delivered to Nineteen. The one that shattered his jaw. The one, if it connected, might kill the White-Haired Boy.

His foot came around. Ready to deliver the final blow. The White-Haired Boy would never see it coming, even if he could. And as his foot approached the other's face...

It missed. By a split centimeter. His foot so close to the White-Haired Boy's face he could feel the heat coming off his skin. And as Fearless completed the failed roundhouse, his abdomen was now exposed.

And with it, the knife wound. The stitches still intact. It was pink. Not yet healed.

The White-Haired Boy's eyes ticked to the wound. Then he locked eyes with Fearless. For a split second, they held each other's gaze. Then, Fearless gave him a subtle, almost imperceptible nod. An unspoken agreement to strike him in the wound. To end this fight.

The White-Haired Boy balled his fist as tight as he could. Raised it. Then whipped it forward.

And struck the wound as hard as he possibly could.

Fearless yelped in genuine pain. And fell to the ground. He clutched the wound. And tried to stand to his feet. But the pain was too severe.

And then, he collapsed completely.

The fight was over.

The White-Haired Boy had won. He fell to his knees in celebration. Both of his arms raised in the air. The other boys rushed the pit. They surrounded him. Then lifted the White-Haired Boy on their shoulders. For he had defeated the mighty Fearless. And he was the new champion.

But as the White-Haired Boy was whisked away in celebration, Fearless remained on the ground in the fetal position. His eyes flicked across to Caliban in the crowd. He shook hands with Lucky and the other wealthy spectators around him as they shared their congratulations. Until, he turned back toward the pit. And saw Fearless laying there. They locked eyes for a moment.

And then, for the first time, Caliban smiled.

~FIFTEEN~

"Laughing Bull"

A pair of brown eyes slowly blinked open. The sky was a rich pink. Fearless couldn't hear a thing. Just the wind. Softly tickling his ear. He had expected that if he woke, it would be auditory chaos. People screaming as they searched for missing limbs and a fire raging as fuel leaked all over the place. But it was calm. Eerily so. He took a deep breath. Slowly exhaled. As his lips curled to a satisfied smile.

"I'm fucking dead."

When, suddenly a long, foreboding shadow cast over him. It was a man. He was silhouetted by the sun. But Fearless knew who He was. He was sure of it. "God?"

"To some people, maybe." Vicious snickered. His clothes were tattered. His face bruised, battered and bloodied from the crash landing.

"Oh. It's you." Fearless sighed. "I thought I was dead. I was so happy."

Vicious helped Fearless to his feet. About thirty feet away stood what was left of the moon jumper, now an unrecognizable twisted heap of metal and glass. They were on the edge. Not just the edge of town, but seemingly, the world. The atmosphere generators towered over them, spewing vapor thousands of feet into the air in order to make this godforsaken planet a place where human beings could actually live without suffocating.

That was because the most difficult part of terraforming a planet was regulating the atmosphere to make it habitable. Mars, although it was always considered the "closest" planet to Earth in terms of habitability, had a radically different atmosphere. Comprised almost entirely of carbon dioxide, a bit of nitrogen and a splash of argon, Mars's atmosphere was also incredibly thin. And in order to start building the next great metropolis in all of the universe, the terraformers couldn't just transform the atmosphere's composition. They were going to have to create an entirely new atmosphere altogether. And thus, the atmosphere generator was born. A chimney-shaped pipe the size of the Eiffel Tower that spewed a vapor rich with nitrogen, oxygen, and a bit of argon thousands of feet in the air. They called them the stacks. But in order to recreate Earth's atmosphere on Mars, they needed hundreds of them.

The only problem was the sound. A deep, grating hum that if exposed to it for long periods of time would drive any well balanced person off a cerebral cliff. There were reports that a dozen or so workers tasked with building these stacks had inexplicably leaped to their deaths. No one really knew how many. They said the sound didn't reach Tharsis City, but the rumor was that if you laid still in the middle of the night while the world slept and listened closely, you could hear the stacks rattle.

Fearless took in the moon jumper wreckage and cringed. "What about Scotty?"

"He died before we even landed. Remember?"

"For a second I thought he was faking it. I guess not," Fearless replied as he took a look around. "I've never been this close to the stacks."

"Me either," Vicious replied. "Don't these things give you cancer if you stand too close to them?"

Fearless shrugged. "Only one way to find out."

They were miles away from anything. The Tharsis City skyline lingered in the distance, but the buildings were enveloped in a thick haze. A sign that they were farther away than either of them could possibly comprehend—and then some.

"The fuck are we supposed to do now?" Fearless asked.

Vicious motioned to the wreckage. "I was thinking we could use what's left of the ship to make a shelter and the remaining canister of fuel to keep us warm while we try and signal any departing ships that pass by."

Fearless rubbed his eyes. "Yeah, sure, we could do that. If you definitely want to die, that is."

Vicious crossed his arms with a huff. He didn't appreciate Fearless's condescending tone. "And why's that?"

Fearless pointed towards the sky where they could see the faint outline of a ring hovering in Mars orbit. "That's the astral gate way the fuck over there. Which means that's where any passing ships are going. No one is flying out here. Unless, you know, they too steal a ship and force a pilot to fly it who dies mid-flight. Then they will totally fly by us. And also crash."

"Then what do you suggest we do, jackass?"

Fearless grinned. "I'm glad you asked. Look, someone has to perform maintenance on these stacks, right? I mean, not every day, obviously, because we're in the middle of fucking nowhere, but when something breaks down, someone has to come out here and fix it."

Vicious sighed. "Sure."

"Well, then we force someone to come to us. I figure we could use that canister of fuel and some of the metal plane scraps to make a bomb, plant it inside one of the stacks, detonate it, and voila, someone is here to check out what happened and we're our way home."

"Let me get this straight," Vicious said as he scratched his head. "You shat on my idea of making shelter for the night and creating a smoke signal—because you think that building a bomb and *blowing up* a stack is a better one?"

"Pretty much, yeah."

"Do you even know how to build a bomb?"

"Of course I don't. But how hard can it be? A little fuel, a little fire, put it in a bomb-shaped metal thingy, set it off. Badabing, bada boom!" Fearless replied, as he made a child-like explosion noise with his mouth while he used his hands to mimic the bomb's explosive radius.

Vicious didn't reply. He just stood there with his arms crossed. Not uttering even a word.

"I take it that you don't like the bomb idea," Fearless observed after thirty seconds of silence—or as near silence as there ever could be near the stacks.

"No," Vicious replied. "Let's just walk towards the skyline. In any scenario, it sounds like we're going to die. And the longer we wait here, the quicker it will happen. So we might as well take our chances and just walk."

Fearless clapped his hands together. "Good enough for me."

It was even hotter than either of them could have possibly imagined. The incessant hum of the stacks was unrelenting, but the heat the generators produced was somehow worse. The daytime sun on Mars was sweltering to begin with. But this was like being stranded in the desert in a car with a space heater strapped to your chest. Fearless dabbed his forehead with his shirt sleeve, but there wasn't moisture to absorb. He was long past sweating. Vicious wasn't faring much better. The bullet wound in his shoulder had turned black. It was still bleeding, but the blood would dry immediately as soon it dripped out.

Fearless turned to Vicious. "How long you think we've been walking?"

"I don't know. Five, six hours maybe," Vicious replied.

"That's impossible," Fearless said as he motioned to the sun. It was beginning to set over the horizon. The sky slowly beginning to turn from its daytime pink to a dark purplish hue. "The sun's setting. It's almost night."

Vicious took in the horizon ahead. He looked surprised to see the sun falling. He feverishly rubbed his ears. "Maybe it's… been longer than we thought. I don't know. That hum. From the stacks. It's beginning to fuck with my head. To be honest, I'm not sure of anything right now."

"Wait—" Fearless said with urgency. He grabbed Vicious by the arm. And motioned to a shallow crater nearby. "Do you see that?"

Vicious turned toward where he was pointing. The edges seemed to flicker with light. At first bright, then dark. Then bright again. It was a random pattern. Never once repeated. But something new. Over and over again.

"*Fire,*" he whispered.

They turned and immediately headed toward the crater. At first slowly, then their feet quickly picking up the pace. Like children running down the stairs on Christmas morning. Brimming with excitement, but unsure what they would find as they rounded the corner into the living room. Fearless and Vicious reached the edge of the crater. And looked down into it, to find:

A roaring fire. A pot dangling above the flames that bubbled with an intoxicating brew. Beside it, a stack of freshly laundered woven blankets warmed. A few small animal carcasses, skinned and placed on skewers, waited to be cooked. Suddenly, a warm voice called out to them.

"Come, join me."

The voice belonged to an elderly Native American nomad. He wore his hair in long, traditional braids. He wore a blue patterned shawl and an animal fur draped over his neck. He shuffled toward the fire and gave the pot a stir.

Fearless and Vicious traded a glance. *There was no way this could possibly be happening, could it?*

"Do not doubt your reality. Trust in your mind," the nomad said as he waved them down from the crater's ridge. "Now please, join me."

Night had fallen over Mars. Fearless and Vicious sat around the fire with the nomad, the woven blankets wrapped around their shoulders as they feasted on the freshly cooked animal meat. The Martian desert was a terribly cold place to be at night, with temperatures dropping below freezing. But with the nomad and his fire, they were warm. Without him, they surely would have died.

"What is this? Syn-Rabbit? It's delicious," Fearless asked, his mouth full of the meat of unknown origin. He ate ravenously. As if they had been lost in the desert for days. Maybe they had been. At this point, it felt like anything was possible.

"The animal is the Earth. Here for us to consume. It is his role. Just as we have our roles. But his is for us to no longer feel hungry. And for that I am grateful to him," the nomad replied.

Fearless shrugged. "Whatever you say."

The nomad placed a ladle into the pot above the fire and scooped a brown liquid into a couple handmade ceramic bowls. He handed one each to Fearless and Vicious.

Fearless gave it a deep sniff. "This smells... *incredible*. What is this? A bone broth? Or some kind of fermented hooch? God, that smells so good."

"You ask too many questions." The nomad smiled, then turned to Vicious. "You don't ask enough."

Vicious slowly slipped the brown liquid. "How long have you been out here?"

"Many years," the nomad said as he continued to stir the pot. "I don't remember when I arrived. Or how I came. Just that I am here. My purpose is to help wayward travelers find their way."

"Wait, so you live out here, all the time, on the chance that someone might pass?" Vicious asked.

"Not chance. Destiny," the nomad explained. "The people who wander this desert, they are here for a reason."

Vicious chuckled at the absurdity of the nomad's words. "Oh yeah? And for what reason would destiny have me aboard a ship that crashed in the middle of the desert?"

"To have me fix the hole in your shoulder," the man replied, matter-of-fact. "After you speak to your mother, of course."

Vicious's eyes narrowed. "What the hell does that mean?"

"See for yourself." The nomad motioned to the sitting area besides Vicious.

Vicious slowly turned to his left—*only to find his mother sitting beside him.* She was wearing a plain sweater and slacks. Her hair greying. She was simple. And warm. Unlike her husband. The firelight flickered off her face as she smiled at Vicious.

"Hi, hon."

Vicious did a double take. For a moment he thought he might be hallucinating. Or maybe he was dead. Either option would make more sense than his mother materializing out of thin air in the middle of the desert.

"*Mom?*"

"It's been a long time, I know," she said.

Vicious swallowed back the tears. His lip quivered. "This isn't possible. You're…"

"*Dead?*" She shrugged, finishing his sentence. "In one way, yes. But in another, no. Unfortunately, I didn't learn what *this* was until it was all over for me. I wish I had known before I made my choice. I would've stuck around a little longer. For you."

"I miss you so much, Mom," Vicious said, the tears streaming down his face.

"I know you do, honey. You're in a pretty tough spot, aren't you?"

Vicious nodded, ashamed. "Yeah, I am."

"It's not your fault," his mother reassured him. "You take things too far, yes. And you've made mistakes. But who *you* are, deep down, is my fault. I should never have let you go to that place. But your father, he insisted. And I was too weak. I was fighting my own battle I couldn't win. But I should've fought, my son. I should have fought for you. I wish I could make it up to you."

Vicious took in her words. He had waited so long to hear them. But then, something occurred to him. "Maybe you can. Can I ask you a question?"

"Anything, sweetheart."

Vicious took her by the hand. "A man tried to have me killed. He said it was because of who *I* am. Do you know what that means?"

His mother took a deep breath. Then exhaled. "Unfortunately, I can't answer that question. That's between you and your father."

Vicious squeezed her hand tight. "Me and Dad? What does that mean? Mom, please. I need to know. My life depends on it."

She stared into the fire. Her eyes welled up with tears and melancholy. "I wish I had been there for the picture. It was the only time I ever saw him smile. It should have been the four of us. Not three."

"Picture? Of who? You said there were three people?" Vicious frantically asked.

She placed her hand on his cheek. "I love you, sweetie. I wish there was more I could do."

And slowly, she faded away, vanishing into the desert air. Vicious could hardly believe his eyes. Or his mind. He slowly turned back to Fearless and the nomad, who were still sitting around the fire.

"What is this? Syn-Rabbit? It's delicious," Fearless asked with his mouth full of the meat of unknown origin.

Vicious cocked his head sideways. Fearless had already asked that question. And he knew exactly what the nomad would say back to him. He mouthed the words along with him. *"The animal is the Earth. Here for us to consume. It is his role. Just as we have our roles. But his is for us to no longer feel hungry. And for that I am grateful to him."*

Thoroughly spooked, Vicious interrupted them. "Did you guys see that?"

Fearless continued to eat ravenously. "See what?"

"My mom, she's right—" Vicious motioned to the empty seat next to him. "I mean, she was. She was here."

"Your mom was… where?" Fearless asked. His eyes narrowed. He was getting a little concerned about his friend.

Vicious stared at the empty spot where she just sat. "Here. I swear."

Fearless traded a glance with the nomad. "I think you've been out in the sun a little too long today, buddy. Maybe you should try and get some rest. We've got a long way to walk tomorrow."

Vicious slowly nodded. "Yeah, maybe you're right. I'm just going to lay down here. Just for a few minutes."

Vicious slowly laid back. He pulled the woven blanket tight over himself. And glanced up at the sky. And in that moment, shooting stars burned bright across the sky. Vicious softly smiled.

"Hi, Mom…"

And drifted off to sleep.

"Hey. Hey buddy. Wake up. *Hey.* Pal," a voice said.

Vicious's eyes slowly fluttered open. He shielded his eyes as he squinted into the morning desert sun. A man stood above him.

His voice, like his skin, was coarse and dehydrated. Beside him was a storage hovercraft that looked like a shopping cart. It was filled to the brim with scraps of metal and discarded electronics. He was a junkman, a scavenger who roamed the desert in search of discarded trash.

"Where... uh... Where am I?" Vicious asked.

"Your ship crashed," the junkman said as he motioned to the moon jumper. "You're lucky you're alive. I ain't never seen anyone survive a crash like that."

Vicious sat up, frantic. The moon jumper was still smoking and leaking fuel. About thirty yards away, Fearless lay on the ground. Just like he had found him.

"Impossible..." Vicious whispered.

"No, no. I watched your ship crash. Flew right over me. Took me all night to get here. You don't mind if I take a look inside the ship for salvageables, do ya?"

"No, I uh, no. Go ahead," Vicious replied as he scrambled to his feet. He ran over to Fearless, who was beginning to stir awake on the sand. He stood above him, casting a shadow over his face.

"I'm fucking dead," Fearless said with a wry grin.

"No. No," Vicious said, frantic. "That's what you said *yesterday*."

Fearless stared at him sideways. "What do you mean, *yesterday*? We were on the *plane* yesterday. And it *crashed*. But you're alive. Which means I am too, which is a *colossal* bummer."

Vicious tried to remind him, to stoke his memory. "What about the nomad? You remember him, right? He made us food. And tea!"

Fearless stared back at him, concerned about his friend's mental well being. "Do you have *any* idea how insane you sound right now? How much blood have you lost from that fucking bullet hole?"

Vicious placed his hand inside his shirt over the wound. His face twisted in surprise. He quickly pulled back his shirt and exposed his shoulder to reveal the wound had been cleaned and stitched up. He looked to Fearless, eyes wide.

Fearless returned the look, as spooked as his friend. "OK, now how the *fuck* is that possible?"

"I told you, the nomad," Vicious replied, as he shouted for the junkman. "Hey, old man! Can you give us a lift out of here?"

The junkman stuck his head out of what remained of the plane's fuselage. He held a radio in his hand. "Sure. I can give you a ride. But only if I get to keep this radio."

Vicious shrugged, annoyed. "Sure. Whatever."

The junkman grinned. He didn't have any teeth. "Where to?"

Vicious looked to Fearless. Then back to the junkman.

"*East Tharsis.*"

The junkman's pickup sputtered to a stop in front of the old dry cleaner. Fearless and Vicious hopped out of the truck's bed and onto the broken asphalt. They gave the bumper a slap and the junkman drove off in a plume of exhaust fumes.

Fearless took in the dry cleaner. The windows were broken and half boarded up. By the looks of it, it had been years since anyone had been there. To get their shirts pressed, or to watch a fight at the Pits.

"I *hate* East Tharsis," Fearless muttered. "Want to explain to me what the hell we're doing here, again?"

"It's just a feeling I have. I can't explain it more than that.

Come on." Vicious headed towards the dry cleaner's entrance. He motioned for Fearless to follow.

"Oh, great. *A feeling.* Why didn't you say so?" Fearless muttered as he reluctantly followed.

Vicious led the way through the dry cleaner. It was dark inside. The air smelled damp. What remained of the dry cleaning equipment was covered in drop cloths to keep the cobwebs at bay. He approached the vault door and blew the dust off the keypad. He slowly entered the code. *1-2-3-4.*

SHUNK! The vault door unlocked.

"1-2-3-4." Fearless chuckled as he shook his head. "That's Humpty for you."

Vicious slowly pulled the vault door open and flipped a light switch that illuminated the staircase below.

"You ready?" he asked Fearless.

"No," Fearless replied. "But I get the sense that I don't have a choice."

Vicious headed down the stairs with Fearless close behind. They slowly walked the long tunnel. It was covered in graffiti, the work of teenagers that had broken in. And as they reached the end of the tunnel they saw it—*the fighting pits.* They were covered in litter and beer bottles. The risers that surrounded them, the ones where Tharsis's wealthy elite once sat while they chanted for blood, were splintered and broken. It was as if what they had endured as boys was all a bad dream. And what remained was a place where teenagers came to drink beer and empty a can of spray paint.

"This place used to seem *so* big," Fearless said with a hint of deranged nostalgia. "It felt like every fight was the most important fight of your life."

"That's because they were," Vicious replied. "Come on."

Vicious led the way through the dim corridors, past the locker room and the sleeping quarters, until he found what he was looking for—a green door with one of those frosted windows on the top half like a private investigator always had in old movies. On the glass a word was etched in gold letters. **PRIVATE**.

Fearless looked to Vicious. "We came all the way here to sneak into Humpty's office?"

Vicious nodded. And turned the knob. It didn't budge. Locked. He grumbled as he tried to turn it. "*Come on. Come on.*"

Fearless sighed. "Move, will you?"

Vicious stepped back. And Fearless stepped forward. He sat back on his heels, then delivered a powerful kick—and blew the door off its hinges.

They tiptoed as they entered into Humpty's office. Even though they had been gone from this place for years, it still felt like they were doing something wrong. Fearless made his way around Humpty's old steel desk. He opened one of the drawers. A pair of rosary beads sat inside. Fearless held them up. The cross dangled before him.

"I found it," Vicious said from the other side of the office.

Fearless quickly shoved the rosary in his pocket and approached Vicious who was standing before a wall of photos of fighters past. In each of them, Humpty stood with the fighter who had been named the champion that year.

In the center of the wall was a photo of Vicious, his white hair buzzed short. His face swollen and battered. On either side of him was his father, Caliban, and Lucky. They stood in the center of the ring together. Each of them smiling.

"You came here to show me *that* photo?" Fearless queried.

"No," Vicious said as he pulled the photo off the wall and held it to Fearless. "I came here to show you *this*."

Fearless took the photo in, but it wasn't quite tracking. He was lost.

"My father's ring on his pinky," Vicious pointed out. "Recognize it?"

Fearless recoiled in shock at the small, almost insignificant piece of jewelry. "That's impossible. That's a Bloodstone... Which would mean..."

Vicious took a deep breath. A weight simultaneously lifted and crushed his shoulders at the exact same time. However farfetched, it all made too much sense. His father's mysterious business affairs. The money. The clothes. The limousine that would survive a nuclear blast.

Vicious exhaled. And for the first time, uttered the truth about his father.

"Caliban is a Red Dragon Elder."

-SIXTEEN-

"In the End, There Were Two"

The reckoning began on a Tuesday. It was a series of coordinated hits on a scale that the Red Dragon, or any other crime organization for that matter, had not seen in decades. The last big war anyone could remember was during the early days of Tharsis City, when rivals flooded the streets of the solar system's new mega metropolis. Blood wasn't just shed, it had to be. The older guys would tell you it was part of the process, a mafia war everyone could agree on. A way to divide a new frontier into different parcels of territory, street corners, and turf. The Red Dragon ultimately won the war, but gave pieces of their territory on other planets and moons to the other families as a way to keep the bloodshed to a minimum for years to come. That's just how things were done back then. It was old school.

What the Europa Crew did was not. It was a new form of warfare. They didn't want turf. Or territory. Or even someone to stroke their ego. This was about revenge. And maybe that's why they were able to pull off the attacks with relative ease—no one ever saw them coming.

The first hit took place outside of Ana's at four o'clock in the morning. Four Red Dragon foot soldiers stumbled out onto the sidewalk in front of the bar in search of a greasy breakfast to sand down the edges that the tequila had sharpened that night. What they found was an old Cadillac Deville slowly rolling by with the muzzle of an automatic rifle pointed through a custom cut hole in the rear passenger door like the cannon of an old pirate ship. The Europa Crew blew them away right there on the sidewalk, spraying blood across the facade of Ana's like a Pollock. The worst part was, they never even had to roll a window down.

But it wasn't just drive-bys. A car bomb took out a hitman named Cash outside of his luxury high-rise. The blast was so powerful that even the valet who handed off the keys was cut down by a screaming piece of molten shrapnel. The same fate befell another hitman named Zevo. Unfortunately the car bomb also claimed the life of his girlfriend who had walked him to the car for a goodbye kiss, as was her predilection.

Blackeye, the sniper who had unloaded on Fearless and Vicious from the building across from the penthouse the day prior, was, ironically, shot dead through his famed shooting eye. The Europa Crew had gunned down his doorman in the lobby with ease. They took the elevator up to his apartment and knocked on the door. When Blackeye looked through the peep hole, he only saw darkness. He figured it was one of the Red Dragon guys covering the peephole with their finger. It turned out to be the nose of a desert eagle pistol.

A dozen more hits followed throughout the day. Some were more memorable than others. Like the janitor who was thrown from the roof of a high-rise only to land in the middle of a children's birthday party taking place on the courtyard below.

But it wasn't just the Red Dragon rank-and-file who were targeted. The Europa Crew also managed to take out a couple big fish as well. Like Kang, a rising capo who was whispered to be promoted to underboss any day. He was eating sushi at the bar of Lotus, Tharsis City's most exclusive fish joint when a tattooed man in a pristine white chef's coat slit his throat with a butcher's knife. The other patrons didn't even flinch. Not because they were in shock, but because they had waited months for their reservations and weren't about to let a little blood ruin their evening.

In the end, the Europa Crew hunted down and killed twenty-two members of the Red Dragon that day. The targets were not only chosen by their ranking within the organization, but by their skill level so that any future retaliation would be handicapped from the start. At the site of each murder, a three-by-five index card was found nearby. On the front was an intricate drawing of Europa, the mother of King Minos of Crete, riding a bull. On the back was a simple handwritten message.

"Bring us Vicious."

Goldie woke up that morning the way she had every day since the reckoning began—with her finger on the trigger of a sawed-off shotgun. She didn't keep it under the bed, or under the pillow even, she slept with it in her hand, ready to blow away any member of the Europa Crew that made the mistake of coming through her bedroom door. Her Red Dragon comrades had joked about her weapon of choice, but she preferred the way the scattershot would blanket the doorway, the shells erupting with their own particular brand of chaotic mayhem. The sawed-off's inaccuracy would be a blessing in disguise in the dark, she thought. She'd either blow the intruder back the way they came or at the very least clip them and give herself time to figure out her next move. That's what she told herself, at least.

Buzz. Buzz. Buzzzzzzz.

The apartment's dated intercom system crackled to life.

"Package for you down 'ere," a raspy voice announced. Goldie gritted her teeth and shook her head. She walked to the front door where the intercom hung on the wall, her finger still wrapped around the trigger of the sawed-off. Another finger pressed the talk button.

"I didn't order anything. Throw it away," Goldie chomped back.

"It's from your motha. You really want me to throw it in the garbage?"

Goldie took a deep breath and muttered a quiet *goddammit, Mom.* She pressed the button again. "Fine. Leave it on the desk. I'll come down and get it."

Goldie squatted to the floor and pried open a floor vent. She reached her arm inside and felt around for something. Her brow furrowed, not finding what she was looking for, until her eyes lit up. She had found it. Goldie removed her arm. In her palm was a MK2 hand grenade. It was the ultimate insurance policy. If somehow an assailant managed to disarm her, she'd have one trick left up her sleeve. One *very* violent trick. Goldie turned and took a trench coat off the hook next to the door. She placed the grenade in the coat pocket, then slipped her left arm inside. As for the right arm, she draped the coat over her shoulder— covertly disguising the sawed-off at her side and her finger on the trigger.

The old elevator doors shuddered open. The lobby of Goldie's building was sparse. A potted fiddle leaf tree slowly wasted away in the corner next to a yellow velvet couch with questionable stains that the super found on the side of the road. There was a desk for the doorman, but it was never occupied. Mostly because they didn't have a doorman. Goldie's eyes ticked to the brown square box that sat on the surface of the desk. Perhaps her super wasn't on the take from the Europa Crew after all.

Ker-clunk. Ker-clunk. Ker-clunk.

The elevator doors started to shudder to a close—*clank!* Goldie stuck the sawed-off between the doors. She slowly stepped into the lobby, performing a quick sweep of the room. It was empty. She carefully approached the box on the desk. Then poked it with the nose of the sawed-off. Goldie winced, hoping it wouldn't explode. After a moment, the box still hadn't exploded. She shrugged. Perhaps her mom had sent her something after all.

Goldie took the box off the desk and tucked it under her arm. She slowly made her way back to the elevator, while softly singing a ditty by Frank Sinatra to herself. *"Luck be a lady, tonight..."*

She pressed the elevator button. The yellow light flickered. The shaft groaned as the car made its way back to the lobby. *"Luck let a gentleman see..."*

The elevator doors slowly shuddered open once again. Goldie equally slowly stepped forward, drumming the side of her fingertips on the side of the box as she continued to sing. *"Just how nice a dame you can be..."*

A *gloved hand wrapped around her mouth!*

Goldie desperately tried to raise the sawed-off, but the mystery assailant had pinned her arm and the gun to her side.

Which left her with the only option of pulling the trigger and blowing her own foot off. She considered it, momentarily, wondering if she'd bleed out enough to avoid whatever hell awaited her. As for her other arm, it was twisted behind her back, which prevented her from pulling the pin from the grenade and blowing them both to pieces.

And then, they placed a hood over her head.

Everything went black.

Whoosh. The hood was ripped off of Goldie's head. Her eyes rapidly darted around the small, claustrophobic enclosed space that she now found herself in. Suddenly, her gazed turned from one of frantic terror to one of *absolute fury.*

"Are you *fucking* kidding me?!" Goldie seethed.

Sitting across from her were none other than Fearless and Vicious. The three of them were seated inside the back of the catering van. They gave a soft wave—and cringed. *Hard.*

"Look, we realize that you're probably upset," Vicious replied.

"Upset?! *Upset?!*" Goldie snapped back. "*You kidnapped me from my own apartment!*"

"We had no choice. With what's been going on with the Europa Crew we knew that if we showed up on your fire escape again in the middle of the night you'd shoot us dead," Vicious explained.

Goldie scoffed in disbelief. "That's right, I *probably* would have. But you know what you two jerk-offs could have done instead? *Knocked on my fucking door.* This was *completely* irresponsible of you two!"

"You know what's irresponsible?" Fearless chimed in, the grenade in his hand. "Carrying a *fucking grenade* in your pocket!"

Goldie gritted her teeth. "Give me that."

"What? Absolutely not! For all we know you'll pull the pin right now and kill all three of us, you absolute psychopath!" Fearless retorted.

"That's right." Goldie grinned. "I am a fucking psychopath. And so help me god, when I get the opportunity, I am going to shove the grenade so far up your ass that—"

"Enough!" Vicious's voice rattled the van's metallic frame. Fearless and Goldie bowed their heads like a couple of children who had just been scolded. Vicious waited a moment, as silence filled the van. "Thank you. Now, listen. Goldie. I'm sorry."

Fearless shrugged. "Again, she had a grenade, so I don't know what we're apologizing for—"

Thwap! Vicious punched him in the shoulder. Fearless rubbed his arm and glared at him as if to say, *what the hell, man?*

Vicious continued. "The truth is, we need your help. We would've asked, but we couldn't afford for you to say no."

Goldie's eyes narrowed. "Help with *what*?"

"I need to capture Darien Cortez. *Alive.*"

The three friends shared a cigarette as they stood underneath the entrance of the Ellis Montgomery Memorial Bridge. The catering van was parked nearby. It was the middle of the night. The water of the Tharsis River slowly rapped at their feet. It was the only sound that could be heard at this time, besides the occasional car passing above.

"It's impossible," Goldie said as she exhaled a plume of

265

smoke. "Cortez travels in an armored truck. The kind that banks use to move cash. Not to mention, he always travels with at least three armed heavies. So even if you somehow manage to pry him from the armored truck, which you won't, you'd have to kill the heavies, again, which you won't, and then somehow apprehend Cortez alive—did I mention that you won't?"

Vicious stared off into the black water at his feet. "Nothing's impossible."

"Maybe you didn't hear me." Goldie drove the point home. "This isn't happening. And even if we could manage to apprehend Cortez, do you *really* expect the Red Dragon to suddenly welcome you back with open arms? I mean, I heard what you did to Dodd. Granted, he deserved to be tossed off the top floor of a building and splattered on a sidewalk, but *Jesus*, man."

Fearless and Vicious traded a secretive glance. Goldie immediately picked up on it.

"OK—what are you not telling me?"

Vicious took a deep breath. His eyes fell the floor. He locked eyes with Fearless for a moment, then turned back to Goldie.

"My father is a Red Dragon elder."

The cigarette fell from Goldie's mouth and detonated orange ash at their feet. "OK now *that's* impossible."

Vicious shook his head. Then reluctantly continued. "Unfortunately, it's true. I never knew what my father did for a living. He was always very secretive about his business dealings. I knew he had connections within the underworld, but I had assumed he was just playing the game. Paying the players in order to push his deals through. That kind of thing. I joined the Red Dragon in order prove to him that I could make something of myself. To prove to him that I was more than just a rich kid. To prove that I could go into business with him. And then, Dodd tried to have me killed. For what he said was because of who *I* am. I didn't know what it meant. Until a series of events led me to an old photograph pinned up on the wall of a fighting pit in East Tharsis. It was of my father. And he was wearing a bloodstone."

Goldie lit another cigarette. The information had her totally shook. "But if Dodd discovered who your father was, who *you* are, then why would he try to have you killed?"

Vicious shrugged. "I'm still trying to figure that part out. All I know is that he tried to stage it as a business deal gone bad. He wanted me dead, yes, but he wanted to make sure it looked like an accident."

Goldie took this in. Her eyes lit up as she put the pieces together. "So, you want to bring Cortez to your father to prove to him that you above all, after everything you've been through, your loyalty remains with the Red Dragon—and him."

Vicious slowly nodded. "I need you to reach out to Cortez. I'm the one he wants. Tell him he can have me. But we get to set the meeting point. Outside the stacks. Where the desert meets the road."

Goldie shook her head. "He'll never do it."

"Sure he will," Vicious countered. "He knows that I'm on the outs with the Red Dragon. He won't be expecting an ambush."

Goldie chuckled to herself. "Guys, this isn't going to work."

Thwap. Thwap. Thwap.

Goldie and Vicious turned to the sound. Fearless was leaning against the van, softly tossing the grenade in his palm. The explosive's metal husk slapped against his skin.

Thwap.

"Sure it will. You just need a little faith." Fearless grinned. "A big ass bang."

———•———

Thud-thud. Thud-thud. Thud-thud. Windshield wipers wicked rain off the glass of an armored truck as it rumbled down a dark stretch of desert highway. The driver, a heavy set member of Cortez's inner circle with a tattoo of a lightning bolt on his neck, grumbled at the sight. "Unbelievable. Rain's only scheduled once a week on Mars and we're stuck in the fuckin' middle of it."

In the back of the armored truck, Darien sat quietly. His eyes straight ahead. His hands clasped in his lap. He was laser-focused and utterly unflappable. Seated next to him was his right hand, Chucky. He wore a bulletproof vest and an assault rifle draped across his lap. Unlike the others, he only had one tattoo. A single heart under his right eye. He turned to Darien.

"What if it's an ambush?"

Darien chuckled. "Of course it's an ambush. Otherwise, he wouldn't have called us to the middle of the desert. Unfortunately for Vicious, he's outnumbered. He's outgunned. And he's out of his *fucking* mind. The Red Dragon is no longer behind him. At most, he has the pretty boy sidekick with him and the girl who made the call. We, on the other hand, have an army inside of that truck."

Darien motioned to the windshield. The rain had let up slightly, revealing another armored truck rumbling ahead of them. He grinned at the sight. This wasn't going to be David versus Goliath. This was going to be David versus one hundred Goliaths.

Then, Darien called out to the driver. "How much longer?"

The heavy set driver with the lightning bolt tattoo turned around, "Shouldn't be much longer, sir—"

KA-BOOM!

Suddenly, a fiery explosion erupted from the sewers below the highway and sent a manhole cover directly into chassis of the lead armored truck! The hulking vehicle tumbled end-over-end until it came to a rest in a ball of fire, upside down on the side of the highway.

Darien's armored car came to an abrupt stop. Those inside stared at the other truck for a moment, but there was no escape. The members of his organization that had made the trek to the desert were either dead or would soon burn to death.

The heavy set driver popped open the door. Chucky followed suit and turned to Darien, "Stay inside the truck. It's impenetrable. You're safe in here, sir."

The driver and Chucky quickly exited the vehicle with their weapons drawn and quickly closed the doors behind them. Suddenly, the scheduled rain picked up again. Darien craned his neck to see beyond the windshield, but the rainfall was too heavy. All he could do was listen to his men trade fire with Vicious and his ragtag army.

Bullets popped. Muzzles flashed. There were concussive bangs. And screams. Outside the armored truck, it was absolute bedlam. Until it wasn't.

Suddenly, it was quiet. Bar the sound of the windshield wipers.

Thud-thud. Thud-thud. Thud-thud.

It had stopped raining.

The water on the windshield had been replaced with blood.

Darien carefully stepped out of the car, a chrome-plated Desert Eagle clutched in his hand. He slowly took in his desert highway surroundings. A thick smoke billowed from the open manhole. The fire from the upside down armored car continued to rage. And if you listened closely, you could still hear a muffled scream. Darien pointed his Desert Eagle in every direction. And for the first time, he looked desperate.

"Where the fuck are you? You fucking coward! Show yourself!"

Darien looked over at the smoke from the manhole. Something caught his eye. A figure taking shape. The shape of a man *on fire*. A man who had just pulled off the impossible. And as he took a step forward, the figure revealed himself to be—

Vicious.

Darien raised his Desert Eagle. His hand trembling. "You killed my brother! You motherfucker! Why did you kill him?! Tell me why?!"

Vicious raised a confident, quiet hand. "Your brother was a mistake. I am man enough to admit that. But the war is now over. And you have lost, Darien. You could strike me down now, and avenge your brother's death. *Or...*"

Darien's eyes narrowed. The gun still trained on Vicious. "Or—*what?*"

Vicious slowly approached him. "Or, you and I can join forces and take the Red Dragon down once and for all."

Darien slowly lowered his weapon. He considered the offer. "And what's in it for me?"

A grin crept across Vicious's face. "Quite a headache, unfortunately."

Darien's face scrunched in confusion. "*What?*"

CRACK!

Darien dropped to the pavement, knocked out cold. Behind him stood Fearless, his Red Dragon issued nine millimeter in hand. He wiped Darien's blood off the barrel of the gun as he took in his body heaped in the middle of the highway. And shook his head.

"I hate pistol whipping. It feels so… *cliché*," Fearless muttered as he turned to Vicious.

"Get him in the truck," Vicious said as he motioned to Darien's body. "We're going to see my father."

Fearless watched as Vicious turned and disappeared into the smoke billowing from the manhole cover. He scoffed at the order. But part of Fearless knew that Vicious was something different now.

And it was only just beginning.

It had been rumored for years that the Elder Temple of the Red Dragon was hidden on a dark, rocky outpost of the satellite known as Ceres. Getting there was easy. Any person with access to a ship and novice flying skills could land on the desolate asteroid. The problem was getting inside. The temple was buried underneath the rocky surface and only accessible through a single fortified elevator. Inside, the Elders were protected by the most elite faction of the Red Dragon known as the Koban Guard. They served one purpose—to kill anyone, or anything, who tried to even approach the three highest ranking members of the Red Dragon.

Wearing oxygen masks, Fearless and Vicious entered a cave with a single, heavy metal door. Behind it was the elevator shaft. Between them was Darien, still unconscious, his face shoved into an oxygen mask to keep him from suffocating from the asteroid's complete lack of atmosphere. In the distance was Vicious's father's private ship. Ironically, they could finally use it knowing that there wouldn't be someone waiting for them on the other side of the astral gates. The only thing waiting for them was a date with destiny—and he went by the name of Caliban.

"You sure this is gonna work?" Fearless asked.

Vicious didn't answer. There was no elevator button to press. Or intercom to speak into. There was just a single camera looking down upon them. Vicious grabbed Darien by the back of the hair and held him up to the lens. After a moment, the door opened to reveal a small cramped elevator. Fearless and Vicious dragged Darien inside and the elevator began to move.

They both stood in silence as the elevator fell to what felt like hundreds of feet below the surface. Neither of them felt much like talking. This was the end of the road. The end of their absurd, death-defying journey that had felt like it had lasted a year and change. The worst part was, they couldn't really call it death-defying—because it felt like they hadn't defied death just quite yet.

Suddenly, the elevator stopped. And the door slowly opened. Fearless and Vicious stepped inside, with their bounty, Darien, between them. The interior of the temple felt impossibly expansive. A blood-red reflecting pool surrounded them on each side, illuminating the room in its crimson hue. The walls were adorned with centuries-old tapestries and lit by paper-thin lanterns. A towering staircase made of polished stone anchored the room. Fearless and Vicious stood at the foot, unsure of where to proceed.

Fearless and Vicious glanced around the room—and realized they were surrounded by a dozen shirtless, masked men brandishing katanas. These were the Elders' Koban Guard, and both men knew their purpose.

Clap. Clap. Clap. Clap. Clap.

Vicious glanced to the top of the stairs. There stood his father. Caliban. It had been years since they had seen each other. Unsurprisingly, he looked older than Vicious remembered. His skin less vibrant than it once was. His hair thinned. But even at his age, he was still an intimidating force, with deep blue eyes that almost looked black. Even his clapping felt menacing.

"Look at you," Caliban's voice boomed as he slowly descended the stairs. "You've come all this way to bring me this man who has been quite a thorn in the side of this organization."

Caliban reached the bottom. He stood eye-to-eye with Vicious. They felt more like acquaintances than they did father and son.

"What do you want for him?" Caliban asked pointedly.

"Answers. That's what I want," Vicious seethed.

Caliban raised an eyebrow. Then chuckled. "You seem angry, boy."

"And why wouldn't I be? You were going to let Dodd kill me without ever once intervening on my behalf. And he almost succeeded." Vicious gritted his teeth. He wanted to strike Caliban down right there. "What kind of *fucking father* does that make you?"

Caliban began to pace in front of them. "I never wanted to be a father. And I told your mother as much. But she wanted a child. So I granted her that wish. Unfortunately, we had you. For years, you were a disappointment to us all. A whining, sniveling spoiled brat. That's why I sent you to the Pits. For years, we've used the Pits as a recruitment center for the Red Dragon. I knew what kind of *men* come from there. So, I sent you there in hopes that you would learn how to fend for yourself in a world that's colder than you could ever imagine. And then, you surprised us all. Somehow, you beat that unbelievable fighter—the one they called Fearless."

Caliban glanced at Fearless. They locked eyes for a moment. Then Caliban continued to pace.

"And imagine my surprise, years later, when you told me you were joining the Red Dragon. That you had actually been *recruited* by Dodd without my knowledge. Now, I could've intervened and told him who you *really* were but that would have defeated the purpose. If you wanted to be a part of my outfit then you needed to prove yourself like everyone else. So I chose to remain silent and let fate take its course."

Vicious clenched his teeth. There was a significant piece of the puzzle that was missing. That his father had yet to addresses. "Why did Dodd try to have me killed?"

"I believe they call that the *elephant* in the room." Caliban chuckled as he continued to pace. "Many years ago Dodd had a son. His name was Albert. And when he reached the age of twenty, Dodd asked me to allow him to join the organization. I told him that it was a bad idea. That this business is an unforgiving one and that one day Albert may have to sacrifice himself for the greater good of the Red Dragon. And when that time came, he wouldn't be able to protect him. Dodd told me that he wouldn't play favorites and that he would treat his son like any other soldier. Well, a few years later, that day came. One of our assassins took out the wrong target. It just so happened that the man he killed was the son of the head of the Neptune Cartel. And in order to avoid the war, the cartel wanted a head. An important one. So we gave them Albert."

Vicious cocked his head slightly in disbelief. "You gave them Dodd's son?"

"What would you have me do? Dodd knew the risks! This is how the game is played! The Red Dragon was built on loyalty to the Red Dragon and the Red Dragon only!" Caliban shouted, his voice reverberating throughout the room.

Vicious clinched his hands tight. His knuckles turning white. His voice began to shake as he spoke. "You knew all along. You knew what would happen. That one day, Dodd would realize who *I* was and he would have his revenge. That he would kill me because of what *you* did to his son. And still. You did *nothing*."

"That's right, boy. I didn't," Caliban explained with conviction. "I wanted to see if for *once* in your life, you would rise to the occasion. And if you died, so be it. Because if you did, we would have our answer, now wouldn't we?"

Suddenly, Vicious drew his 9mm from his waist and pointed it at his father's head. The Koban Guard quickly swarmed, ready to strike him down. Caliban held up a hand, holding them at bay.

"You're a *monster*," Vicious whispered.

"No, son," Caliban said as he slowly approached him. "I'm simply separating the winners from the losers."

Caliban motioned to one of the Koban Guards for his katana. The guard followed orders and placed it in his hand. With his free hand, Caliban lowered the barrel of Vicious's gun down to his side.

"Finish the job," Caliban whispered as he offered Vicious the katana. Vicious tucked the 9mm back in his waist and took the katana in his hand. He admired it for a moment. How the weight of the handle felt in his hand. How the silver blade was shimmering crimson in blood red light.

And then, in one swift move—Vicious decapitated Darien. His head landed on the ground with a cruel *thud*. Then, Caliban smiled. For the second time. He headed back up the staircase, motioned for Vicious to follow.

"Let's talk, boy. We have a future to discuss."

Vicious and Caliban ascended the staircase together, as father and son. Fearless stood at the bottom of the staircase. His eyes locked on Darien's head. It felt especially violent. Even for Vicious. And for the first time, Fearless worried about the potential for what Vicious could become.

"Fearless," Vicious called to him from the top of the stairs. "My father would like you to join us."

Fearless stood there for a moment. And for a moment, he thought about running—back into the elevator and out into the surface of the asteroid, where there was no air to breathe. He would remove his mask, and collapse onto the cold rock.

And just before he died, he'd roll over and take in the stars one last time.

He'd marvel at how clear they looked.

How he'd never seen them like this.

Fearless exhaled.

Then spoke softly.

"I'll be right there."

TWO YEARS EARLIER

Fearless and Vicious sat in the jail cell. They were still drunk from the night before. Like most mornings these days. Their clothes were covered in blood. But it wasn't their own. They had tuned up those wannabe gangsters outside of the nightclub pretty good. The ones in the black suits with the red trim on the lapel. Neither of them remembered how it started. They just knew how it ended.

Fearless yawned. "You think they serve a decent breakfast? I'm starvin'."

Vicious stared back at him. Dead eyed. His expression dripping with sleep deprivation and sarcasm. "The jail? Oh yeah. Omelet bar. Carving station. It's exceptional."

Fearless raised an eyebrow. Excited. "For real?"

"No, the jail doesn't serve breakfast, you moron," Vicious snapped back. "At this rate we'll be lucky if we get out of here in time for breakfast on Thursday."

Fearless scoffed. "What crawled up your ass?"

Vicious took a deep breath. Then shook his head. "I'm just tired of this, man."

"Tired of what?"

"This." Vicious motioned around the jail cell. "Getting shit-faced, then getting into a fight with some guys we don't know, ending up in jail, then doing it all over again next weekend."

Fearless shrugged. "And what would you have us do instead?"

"I don't know." Vicious contemplated. "But we're destined for more than just this."

An ISSP officer approached and punched an access code into the keypad mounted on the cell door.

SHUNK! *The cell door opened.*

"Frick. Frack. You made bail," the officer relayed.

Fearless side-eyed Vicious. "Who the hell would bail us *out?"*

The mystery donor approached. His hair was slicked back with Vaseline. He wore a gold chain around his neck. He too looked like a wannabe gangster.

Fearless's eyes narrowed. "Who the hell are you?"

"Doesn't matter," the man grumbled. "Those men you tuned up last night? They were my *men."*

"Well, your men fight like shit," Fearless snapped back.

The man's eyes narrowed. He took them in. "Where'd you two learn to fight like that?"

"None of your fuckin' business—"

Vicious quickly stepped between them. Then turned to the man. "Excuse my friend. He's got a hell of a right hook but shit for manners. And look, we appreciate you bailing us out and all, mister. But mind telling me why would you bail out the two guys who beat the piss out of six *of your guys?"*

The man collected himself. Then took a deep breath. "Because I could use a couple guys like you in my outfit."

Vicious raised an eyebrow. "And what outfit is that?"

"The Red Dragon Syndicate."

Fearless chuckled. "Thanks but no thanks. We don't take orders from the mob. And we sure as hell don't wear uniforms."

Vicious concurred. "Yeah, look. We appreciate the offer but that life's not for us."

The man chuckled. And shook his head. "And what is for you, exactly? Because I'll tell you what, fellas. I've been around the block a few times. I've seen lots of guys like you. And at some point, life's gonna catch up with your asses whether you like it or not. Up to you two assholes whether you want to make something of it before you end up in the back of some guy's trunk on your way to a shallow grave."

Fearless grabbed the cell door and pulled it shut. Clink! *He grinned. "Keep your money. We're doing just fine on our own."*

"Youth is wasted on the young." The man shook his head with a chuckle as he dug into his pocket. He pulled out a weathered business card and handed it to Vicious. Then spoke directly to him. And him only.

"Here's my information. You *call me when you're ready to talk." And with that, the man strutted down the hallway and then disappeared.*

Vicious watched him go. Then looked to the business card in his hand. There was a phone number and a single name. There was no telling if it was his first or his last. But it was one that would change the course of their lives forever—

Dodd.

ABOUT THE AUTHOR

Sean Cummings is an American film and television writer. He is currently a member of the writing staff for Netflix's forthcoming television adaptation of *Cowboy Bebop* as well as the staff of Amazon's action-adventure series *Citadel*. Previously, he wrote an episode of the beloved Netflix teen dramedy *Everything Sucks!*. He also writes feature films. Sean resides in Los Angeles, California with his wife, son and their beloved dog, Penny.

For more fantastic fiction, author events,
exclusive excerpts, competitions, limited editions and more

VISIT OUR WEBSITE
titanbooks.com

LIKE US ON FACEBOOK
facebook.com/titanbooks

FOLLOW US ON TWITTER AND INSTAGRAM
@TitanBooks

EMAIL US
readerfeedback@titanemail.com